**She eyed him skeptically. "Clearly you're thinking of someone else. We didn't have our first kiss here."**

Dante's eyes glinted mischievously. "Oh yes, we did. I can't believe you don't remember!"

"Refresh my memory. Please. I can't wait to rub it in your face just how wrong you are."

"All right. We were five, maybe six years old. Our families came out here together for some sort of holiday event. While the adults were listening to Christmas music under the stars, we were having our kiddie party watching *Rudolph the Red-Nosed Reindeer*. When Rudolph fell for Clarice, I was inspired, so I made my move. I kissed you."

Lucy squealed with outrage. "That wasn't a kiss. That was you trying to get some Oreo crumbs off my lips because you were the greediest little kid on the planet."

"What? You know that's not true. That was a genuine, bona fide kiss between two youngsters who had a crush on each other. Denying my version of events is really crushing!"

Lucy let out a hoot of laughter that drew a lot of curious stares from customers. She clapped a hand over her mouth to silence herself. The last thing she wanted was to be at the center of any rumors about Dante. She could just hear the whispers now. Dante reached out and removed her hand from her mouth. Instead of releasing it, he held on to her mittened hand.

Her eyes locked with Dante's and she thought she heard a little sigh slip past his lips. The air was so cold there was fog coming from his breath. In no time flat the atmosphere became charged with electricity. One moment they'd been laughing, and in the very next, something hovered in the air between them that made her want to run in the other direction.

"What can I say? You've always had very kissable lips, Lucy."

# no ordinary Christmas

# BELLE CALHOUNE

**FOREVER**
New York Boston

Forever
Hachette Book Group
1290 Avenue of the Americas, New York, NY 10104
read-forever.com
twitter.com/readforeverpub

First Edition: September 2021

Forever is an imprint of Grand Central Publishing. The Forever name and logo are trademarks of Hachette Book Group, Inc.

The publisher is not responsible for websites (or their content) that are not owned by the publisher.

The Hachette Speakers Bureau provides a wide range of authors for speaking events. To find out more, go to www.hachettespeakersbureau.com or call (866) 376-6591.

ISBN: 978-1-5387-3598-5 (mass market), 978-1-5387-3599-2 (ebook)

Printed in the United States of America

CW

10  9  8  7  6  5  4  3  2  1

To my brother, David Bell. Not a day goes by when I don't think about you and miss you. So thankful you were in my life. And for my sister-in-law, Rebecca, for loving him so well.

# ACKNOWLEDGMENTS

Writing is a solitary endeavor, but in reality, no author is alone when a book is being launched. I am profoundly grateful to my agent, Jessica Alvarez, who is a source of great encouragement and always provides me with a wonderful listening ear. I'm so glad we teamed up. Your wisdom and vision are appreciated.

For my editor Madeleine Colavita, who made the book better by asking the hard questions and pushing me to dig deeper. Thank you for believing in me and in this project. I am so grateful to the entire Grand Central team for all your hard work and dedication.

For my husband, Randy, and my daughters, Sierra and Amber...thank you for being my quarantine buddies in 2020 and for always celebrating my good news and lifting me up. I'm so blessed to have all of you as my cheering section.

And for my friend, author Cate Nolan, thank you so much for letting me ask you a million Maine questions and for sharing my joy about this book.

# no ordinary
# Christmas

# CHAPTER ONE

MISTLETOE, MAINE

Lucy Marshall straightened her glasses and peered out the window of the Free Library of Mistletoe. As head librarian for the past four years, she had gazed at this same view of the town square hundreds of times. But this was the very first occasion she'd been spying on the man who had broken her heart into a million little pieces. Some folks might find her boycotting the parade an act unbefitting of a librarian, but for Lucy, staying inside was her only option. She had her pride after all, and she had no intention of letting bygones be bygones.

At least she had a fantastic view of the unfolding spectacle. And she wasn't freezing her buns off outside. As the sun set, the sky lit up with glorious shades of pink and orange.

The entire town of Mistletoe, Maine, was decked out in tinsel and candy canes and shiny ornaments to herald the arrival of Christmas in four weeks. Six-foot-tall nutcrackers stood at the entrance to the town hall across the way, providing a dose of holiday cheer. Mugs of peppermint hot cocoa were being served around the clock at the Starlight Diner. Every shopwindow in town was decorated in keeping with the holiday season. Normally it was her favorite time of the year, but she wasn't feeling very merry at the moment.

Her past had risen up to greet her like a scene from *A Christmas Carol*. The Ghost of Christmas Past and all that. Bah humbug!

Lucy couldn't remember the last time she had seen such a commotion in her hometown. Hordes of people had gathered in the town square to welcome the hometown hero who'd made good in Hollywood—Dante West. Action-star extraordinaire. One of the highest-paid actors in Tinseltown. Townsfolk held banners and posters bearing Dante's likeness. Flags with his face and form on them were being enthusiastically waved by dozens of kids. One teenaged girl held up a sign asking, WILL YOU MARRY ME, DANTE? Everyone appeared to be giddy with excitement. She was probably the only person in town who wasn't in attendance at the celebration. Even though it made her feel like a four-year-old, she stuck her tongue out at the scene unfolding before her eyes.

A moment later she felt thankful no one was paying any attention to her childish gesture, since it would probably make her look petty. Everyone's interest was focused on the return of the hometown hero. She couldn't really blame them. From where she was standing, Dante looked pretty eye-catching. With his warm brown skin, striking features, and an athletic physique, he was smoking hot, pure and simple. On more than one occasion, Lucy had found herself getting lost in his deep-set, russet-colored eyes. But that was a long time ago. If she was being honest, sometimes it felt as if it had been yesterday.

She rolled her eyes and folded her arms across her chest. For good measure, she let out a ragged sigh. It annoyed her to no end to see so much hoopla directed toward Dante simply because he'd become a superstar in Hollywood. Humph! It wasn't as if he had been awarded a Pulitzer Prize, cured cancer, or run into a burning building to save people. He acted in action movies and dated empty-headed starlets.

Hadn't she just seen him plastered all over one of the scandal-rag tabloids with Missy North, the famous reality star? That in itself spoke volumes. Missy was known for being as deep as a kiddie pool. She happened to be drop-dead gorgeous, Lucy conceded. She imagined most men would jump through hoops to be the special someone in Missy's life.

Even though Dante had been a big celebrity for at least five years now, Lucy still couldn't believe he'd come back to their hometown to film his next movie. It was probably one of those action flicks with a testosterone-laced name like *Maximum Overdrive* or *Total Impact*. Lucy had done her best to tune out all the fanfare surrounding Dante's return, a near-impossible feat in a town that had gone crazy over Mistletoe's golden boy.

Mistletoe wasn't exactly a happening place like Los Angeles. And, to her knowledge, he'd avoided his hometown like the plague ever since leaving for the big lights of Hollywood. He'd only come back briefly for his father's burial. Lucy had gotten a glimpse of him that day at the cemetery. It had been easy to avoid coming face-to-face with him since she'd deliberately remained in the background and skipped the reception.

*Dante West!* Movie star. Mistletoe's favorite son! Her former BFF. The only man she'd ever truly loved. She felt a little pang in her heart as his face flashed before her eyes. Lucy squeezed her eyes shut, reminding herself that she'd buried their relationship firmly in the past. Revisiting it only brought her pain. Seeing the town of Mistletoe celebrate the man who'd ripped her heart to shreds felt like a betrayal. After all, she'd been a loyal resident while he'd made a life for himself far away from the shores of Maine. Celebrity was a hard thing to ignore, Lucy realized, and she shouldn't expect an entire town to harbor resentment against Dante for the way he'd treated her.

She remembered all the mayhem that erupted a few years ago when Dante landed on the cover of *People* magazine's Sexiest Man Alive issue. Every red-blooded woman in the United States had been drooling over him. Sure, he was eye candy, but he didn't have a loyal bone in his body. The way he'd turned his back on his family and his hometown didn't sit well with her.

*And you*, a little voice buzzed in her ear. *Don't forget the way he treated you.*

She shook off the bad thoughts, determined to focus on the things that truly mattered for the duration of Dante's stay in Mistletoe. She'd built a nice life for herself—one she could be proud of. Her job as a librarian fulfilled her. It meant so much to her that she'd spent every waking hour trying to find a way to save it from town cutbacks and a downturn in donations. In addition to loving her career, she also had great friends and family. Sure, her family was a bit all over the place at times, but when push came to shove they stood together as a united front. Which was why it was somewhat surprising to see her parents, Walt and Leslie, along with her little sister, Tess, standing in the throng outside hailing Dante as a conquering town hero. Lucy sputtered at the sight of her close friend Eva Langston bundled up in a pink parka and matching hat.

"Traitors one and all," she whispered. "Trust me, he's not that special."

Problem was, he had been. Once upon a time, Dante had been the sun, moon, and stars in Lucy's life. She knew she was being petty, but it hurt to remember how things had been before he'd hightailed it off to Hollywood without a word of goodbye. At certain times it seemed like she'd dreamed it all. But Lucy knew she hadn't made up all the memories she couldn't seem to shake—sledding down McArthur's Mountain, splitting peanut butter and jelly sandwiches with him in school, or their first kiss on Christmas Eve out at the lake. Or his promise to take her with him to California. That one hurt the most. He'd bailed on Mistletoe and left her in the dust. After only a few years, he'd achieved megastar status in Hollywood. In the end, he'd soared without her in his life. She couldn't ignore how badly it still stung.

Hiding in the library while the town celebrated Dante was an act of self-preservation if nothing else. She didn't want to know if being in his presence still made her weak in the knees. It wouldn't be good for her psyche.

"I knew I'd find you in here."

Lucy turned around at the sound of her sister's honeyed voice. Stella stood there with her hands on her hips, gazing at her younger sister with a sympathetic expression etched on her perfectly rounded face. With her long brown hair, full lips, and mocha-colored skin, Stella was a beautiful woman who turned heads everywhere she went. Somehow she never seemed to be aware of her huge appeal to every male in Mistletoe who had a pulse.

"Hey, Stella. Why aren't you outside with the rest of this town?" Lucy asked.

Stella wrinkled her nose as she walked toward Lucy. "I'm not really into ticker tape parades."

Lucy let out an indelicate snort. "One would think they were giving out gold bars or something, judging by all the commotion."

"I wanted to make sure you were all right." Her sister's eyes radiated compassion. Lucy didn't want pity, not even from her sister. Stella's good heart made moisture well up in her eyes.

Lucy's throat felt as dry as sandpaper. Her older sister knew her better than anyone else in the world. Separated by only a year, the two of them had been as thick as thieves their entire lives. Stella knew more than anyone what Dante's return meant to her. "I-I'm fine. Don't worry about me, sis. I put my big-girl panties on this morning. I've known for weeks this was coming."

Stella patted her back. Ever since they were kids, her older sister had been taking care of everyone in her orbit. She was the most nurturing person Lucy had ever known. No wonder she'd followed her heart and become a second-grade teacher. Lucy wanted to be just like Stella when she finally grew up.

Stella's voice softened. "I know this can't be easy for you, Lucy."

Lucy shook her head. "It's fine," she said in a clipped tone. "I'm all right." The very last thing she wanted was to be an object of sympathy. Been there, done that. And she'd vowed never to go down that road again.

Stella eyed her with visible skepticism. "There you go again, shutting down your feelings. It's okay to admit you're a bit rattled by Dante coming back to town. It's been a long time since you've seen him. The two of you were besties for so many years. Not to mention the period when you were romantically involved. It's bound to sting a bit."

Even though she knew Stella had picked up on her discomfort over the Dante situation, Lucy didn't want to acknowledge it. Perhaps if she could mask her feelings, it wouldn't bother her so much on the inside. Perhaps it wouldn't feel as if her hometown had turned into enemy territory. Maybe the ache inside her would ease up a little bit so she could breathe normally again.

Lucy squared her shoulders and stood up straight. "I'm not upset. And I'm not hiding out in here either. I just think it's silly to close down the library simply because Dante finally decided to come back home." She sniffed. "Everyone here in town is acting as if he's giving out wads of cash or something."

"You have to admit, it is kind of a big deal," Stella said, shifting from one foot to the other. Her sister's expression was sheepish. "He's really famous now. I was just reading an article about him in *Us Weekly*. He's one of the—"

Lucy held up her hands. "I don't want to hear it." She shook her head vigorously back and forth. "I'm already sick and tired of hearing Dante's name."

Stella made a face. "Sis, I hate to be the bearer of bad news, but you're going to have to go live under a rock for the next few weeks if you can't bear it."

"Why should I have to go hide? So what that he's making a big-time movie here? Mistletoe is my hometown. He's the one who left! He's the one who turned his back on everyone." Stella's eyes widened at the sharp sound of her voice. Lucy winced. Her tone sounded strident and biting to her own ears. Normally, that wasn't who she was at her core. She hadn't meant to sound so bitter, but all these feelings were bubbling up inside her, and it was becoming nearly impossible to hide them. Here it was, a few weeks before the most wonderful time of the year, and she was filled with angst and hostility. It wasn't who she wanted to be, especially at Christmastime.

"Maybe it does bother me a little bit," she confessed, lips trembling. Try as she might, she couldn't seem to put a lid on her emotions. "I can't believe I'm letting him get to me after all of these years."

NO ORDINARY CHRISTMAS 9

Stella reached out and wrapped her arms around Lucy, pulling her sister into a tight hug. Lucy nestled against Stella's comforting embrace. "It's understandable. You never really had any closure with him. He was here one day and gone the next. Dante made you a lot of promises he didn't keep. And he never gave you any real answers. Believe me, I know how you feel."

Stella was probably one of the only people in her orbit who could relate to her situation. Lucy hated that her older sister had also been jerked around by someone she loved.

"No, he didn't. After he left town I didn't hear from him for months," Lucy admitted, her lips trembling with emotion. "By the time he finally reached out to me, I didn't want to hear a single thing from him. What could he possibly say at that point anyway?"

Lucy reminded herself to breathe. What was wrong with her? She hadn't allowed herself to vent about Dante for such a long time. She'd worked hard over the past eight and a half years to become a strong, independent woman. Time hadn't stood still, and she was no longer crying herself to sleep over Dante West.

"Why don't we get some ice cream at the diner? That'll make everything better," Stella suggested with a wide grin.

Lucy sniffed back tears and dabbed at her eyes. "That sounds scrumptious. You always know what I need to put a smile on my face. Let me close up the library. We can head out the back entrance so we don't get swallowed up by the crowd."

"Sounds good," Stella said, shooting Lucy an encouraging smile.

As Lucy turned away from Stella, she found herself blinking away more tears. A sharp pang of loss seized her. She pressed a hand against her chest and inhaled a deep breath. *She could do this!* Lucy could hold her head up high and act merry and bright. She could smile and act as if Dante West was nothing more than a memory. It wouldn't be too hard to pretend as if she hadn't missed his friendship. She'd been doing it brilliantly for the last eight and a half years.

They didn't call her Little Miss Sunshine for nothing. Planting a smile on her face, she turned off the main computers and began flicking off the lights. Lucy ushered Stella out of the back door of the library, then let out a surprised sound as cold wet flakes began to fall on her face.

"Ugh. More snow," Stella said with a groan.

"It's fantastic, isn't it?" Lucy asked, ignoring her sister's annoyed expression.

"If you like slipping and sliding all over the roadways," Stella grumbled. "One of these days I'm going to spend the winter in Hawaii."

"Hawaii is beautiful, but Maine is magical," Lucy said as she performed a pirouette.

An unexpected snowfall was the best thing to turn Lucy's mood around. She loved snow almost as much as she adored the Christmas season itself. There was something about the white fluffy stuff that instantly took her back to the joys of childhood. Sledding. Tubing. Skating. Making a snowman in the backyard and drinking steaming mugs of hot cocoa. Growing up here in Mistletoe had been idyllic.

Lucy turned her face toward the heavens and twirled around as fat snowflakes began to drift down from the sky. For the moment, at least, she could rejoice in the simple pleasures of a New England winter and not dwell on Dante's return. There would be plenty of time for that in the hours between darkness and dawn when she tossed and turned in her bed and battled thoughts about the man she had once adored like no other.

* * *

Dante West stood in the town square and looked around him with awe. He was finding it hard to wrap his head around the fact that his hometown was treating him to a full-on celebration. There had even been confetti and streamers. And there was a huge cake with his likeness on it. He felt like a conquering hero. When he'd left Mistletoe eight and a half years ago he'd never imagined this would ever happen.

Growing up he'd always been the mischievous kid who'd been up to his ears in trouble, from skipping school to go crabbing at Blackberry Beach or joyriding in his grandfather's Buick before he had a license. No one back then would ever have predicted his triumphant return. Not even himself. He had to admit it felt really good to be here despite his reservations about coming home.

There were so many ghosts in this town, ones that threatened the peaceful existence he'd built for himself during his years in Los Angeles. But he knew in order to move forward he had to deal with the issues he'd been trying to bury for so many years. He needed closure.

He felt a huge grin overtake his face as he spotted familiar faces in the crowd. Laura Jean Samuels, his elementary school crush. Mrs. Scarborough, his third-grade teacher. She looked exactly the same, except her hair had turned completely white. Matt Delacroix, who'd been a fellow Boy Scout in his troop. From the looks of it, he was a father now. The little boy he cradled in his arms bore an uncanny resemblance to Matt.

Dante felt a pang of regret slice through him. Even though Dante knew he'd never even been close to tying the knot with anyone, he found himself wishing he was that type of guy—one who could have the white picket fence, a house full of kids, and an adoring wife. He'd strayed so far away from those ideals. His life had been focused on his acting career and nothing else for years.

From the moment the limousine had deposited him at the town square, Dante had been scanning the crowd in search of big brown doe eyes and a heart-shaped, tawny-colored face. He felt a stab of disappointment. Lucy was nowhere in sight. After the way things had ended between them, he was foolish to think she'd show up. She didn't owe him a single thing.

From what he'd heard over the years, she was the head librarian at the Free Library of Mistletoe. He looked over at the ornate, colonial-style building, imagining Lucy sitting at a desk inside or digging through the stacks trying to locate a book. It wasn't hard to imagine, although he hated the thought of her stuck in a building all day. Someone like Lucy needed to be out in the world spreading her special brand of sunshine and good cheer.

The town mayor, Wilhelmina "Billie" Finch, held up her hands and motioned for the crowd to settle down. "Good afternoon, everyone. Thanks for coming out today to give one of our own a rousing welcome." She turned toward Dante and flashed him a pearly grin. "Or should I say welcome back? We are truly delighted by your return to Mistletoe and overjoyed that you've decided to pump some money into the local economy by making your next film here. In deep appreciation, we are extending to you a key to the town of Mistletoe in the hopes that you won't be a stranger in the future."

Dante grinned at Mayor Finch and nodded in her direction. "Thank you, Mayor, for welcoming me back with open arms. I can't wait to start filming in my hometown and catch up with friends and family. It's great to be home!"

The mayor patted him approvingly on the shoulder. "We're happy to have you here, Dante. And now, without further ado, I'd like to introduce Mimi West, Dante's mother, so she can present her son with the key to the town of Mistletoe, a place we all know and love."

Dante felt a tightness in his chest at the sight of his mother standing offstage. He'd missed her terribly and seeing her in person caused his emotions to rise to the surface. She'd expressed such joy and pride upon finding out he was being honored in their hometown and that he would be back in Mistletoe to film his next movie. *Having you back will be such a gift to our family.* The words she'd spoken to him a few weeks ago washed over him. Family was important, and he intended to make his a priority.

He would bet his last dollar that his brother wouldn't be in attendance today. Too much water had flowed under that particular bridge. His sisters, Melanie and Abbi, no longer lived in Maine, so he knew it wasn't likely they'd flown home for his hero's welcome. He would have to wait until Christmas to see both of them.

Suddenly, his mother was being ushered onto the make-shift stage. She walked toward him, her shoulders shaking with emotion, tears sliding down her face. Words couldn't express what it meant to him to be in her presence again. He didn't consider himself to be an emotional person, but tears welled up in his eyes at the sight of her. Her long, dark hair had been cut into a pixie style. With her sepia-colored skin and almond-shaped eyes, his mother was an attractive woman who looked years younger than her actual age. It was nice to see her looking so well after losing his father. For better or worse, they had been married for almost thirty years. High school sweethearts. Despite their issues, they'd loved each other deeply.

Dante stepped away from the microphone, not wanting their conversation to be broadcast to the crowd. Once his mother reached him, she threw herself against his chest, all five foot two inches of her. "Dante! Pinch me. I can't believe you're actually here. I've been praying and dreaming about this day for months."

"Mama," he said, choking out the single word. "It's so

good to see you." The last time he'd seen his mother had been at his father's funeral a little over a year ago. Two years ago he'd flown her to Los Angeles for a lengthy visit and they'd been able to spend precious moments together. That had been before his father's leukemia diagnosis and quick decline. Being back in Mistletoe would provide them with quality time to hang out and reconnect.

"My son," she whispered, wrapping her arms around him in a tight embrace that seemed to go on for an eternity.

When they finally separated, Dante reached out and wiped away the tears from his mother's face. "You know I hate to see you cry," he said, trying not to think about all the times he had seen her crying in her bedroom when he was a teenager, courtesy of his father's ill moods and sharp tongue. John West had been a difficult man at times. Loving yet implacable.

"These are happy tears," she said, pressing a kiss against his cheek. The mayor motioned them to come back toward the center of the stage. Once they reached Mayor Finch's side, Mimi stepped up to the microphone. "Here it is, son. The key to the town of Mistletoe." She held the key up high and then pressed it into his palm. The crowd roared with approval. The key felt solid and reassuring in his hand. Despite all his shiny awards and movie contracts, Dante had never felt a sense of validation from his hometown until this moment. His own father hadn't ever wanted to give him accolades or acknowledge his success. The truth was, he'd never really thought it was possible to be honored in Mistletoe, not after the way he'd left.

It humbled him to realize that despite his mistakes, there was a chance at redemption. Truth be told, it was the main reason he had decided to film his next movie here in Mistletoe. He could have finagled deals to shoot his movie anywhere in the world. At this point in his career Dante had major pull in the industry. He was box-office gold, and he'd paid his dues in the business. Although his agent hadn't understood why he wanted to film his movie in "some backwater New England town," Dante had insisted.

It was all part of his personal journey. Mistletoe was a huge chunk of him. He needed to do this. This film was deeply personal for him, and it had been years in the making. More than anything else he'd ever been a part of in the movie industry, this project spoke to his truest self. It would be like drawing back the curtains and revealing himself for all to see.

Coming back home during this most festive time of the year had been a choice, one he hoped would bring him closure, not just with his relationship with Troy and his father's death, but with Lucy, the woman who still owned a large piece of his heart.

# CHAPTER TWO

O nce Lucy and Stella settled themselves into a booth at the Starlight Diner, Lucy began to feel much better. Now she was no longer forced to witness the crowd that had gathered to welcome Dante to town or hear their cries of enthusiasm. That had been pure torture. Thank goodness for the diner and the lure of mocha chip ice cream.

She had to give it to Dean Granger, the owner of the establishment. He really knew how to bling the place out in keeping with the holiday season. Every single booth had a sprig of holly hanging above the table, while there were candy canes and white roses as centerpieces. Christmas music flowed from the jukebox—Nat King Cole's soulful voice sang of chestnuts and open fires. The counter was adorned with tinsel and garlands. All of it made Lucy's soul soar.

The smell of burgers and fries emanating from the diner's kitchen caused Lucy's stomach to grumble noisily.

She hadn't eaten since this morning when she'd grabbed a muffin and some granola. Because she loved her work so much, Lucy had a tendency to lose all sense of time and work straight through her lunch hour. Thanks to Dante's return, Lucy had temporarily lost her appetite. Clearly, it had come back with a vengeance.

"Mmm," Lucy said with a groan. "I think I'm going to order a lot more than ice cream. I have a sudden hankering for a bacon cheeseburger with the works."

"That sounds great," Stella said, practically drooling as she looked over the menu. "Knock yourself out. It's my treat."

"Thanks, Stella." She looked across the table at her sister. "I honestly don't know what I'd do without you. Whenever I'm down you manage to lift me up."

"Thankfully you'll never have to worry about that. We're in this for life," she said, reaching out and extending her pinky to her sister. Lucy linked her own pinky finger with Stella's and grinned. "Till we're old and gray and sitting in our rocking chairs."

Lucy wiggled her eyebrows at Stella. "I don't know about you, but I plan to dye my hair until I'm well into my nineties."

Stella smiled knowingly at Lucy. "I can totally see that."

Within minutes the girls had placed their order with their waitress, Bonnie. Two orders of bacon cheeseburgers and fries with Diet Cokes. Once their food arrived, Stella made Lucy clutch her stomach with laughter as she did spot-on impressions of various townsfolk. Being a schoolteacher provided Stella ample opportunity to study people in the Mistletoe community. By the time their plates were cleared away and their ice creams were brought over to the table, Lucy felt one hundred times better than when they'd walked through the door. The combination of her sweetheart of a sister and mocha chip ice cream served as an elixir for the soul. She was flying high on a sugar rush.

All of a sudden, Stella's eyes bulged and her mouth hung open.

"What's with you?" Lucy asked, taking a huge spoonful of ice cream into her mouth. She groaned and gripped her head. "Brain freeze." She choked the words out as pain hit her forehead like a sledgehammer.

"Lucy, please don't freak out." What was Stella talking about? Hadn't she ever had brain freeze? This was not a freak-out by any stretch of the imagination.

"What do you mean? I can't help it. Didn't you hear me? Brain freeze." She placed her hand on the bridge of her nose and massaged it, praying the agonizing sensation would subside. She'd once heard about placing a penny on your forehead to cure brain freeze, but who had time to reach into their purse to find a penny? It felt as if her face had been submerged in ice cubes.

Stella shook her head. A pinched expression was etched on her face, and her gaze wandered to a point beyond Lucy. She couldn't seem to look away from whatever was behind her.

"What are you looking at?" She felt a prickle at the back of her neck. Lucy glanced over her shoulder. *Whoosh.*

Time seemed to stand still for a moment as she watched Dante standing at the entrance to the diner, surrounded by an entourage, including his mother and Mayor Finch. She quickly turned back around, hoping he wouldn't spot her and Stella. She scrunched down in her seat and reached for her winter hat, jamming it onto her head.

"Please, please, please," she said, repeating the words over and over.

"Stop fidgeting, Lucy. You're just drawing more attention to yourself. You look like you've got red fire ants in your pants."

"What do you want me to do? I feel like I'm about to break out into hives." Lucy began scratching at the side of her face.

Stella gasped. "Oh my stars! He's coming over here!"

"You have got to be kidding me," Lucy hissed. "If you're joking, Stella, it's not very funny, and I will exact revenge. And it will involve spiders. Lots and lots of spiders." Stella had a serious phobia regarding the leggy creatures.

Stella's stunned expression spoke volumes. "I'm not kidding," she said through clenched teeth. "Five. Four. Three. Two. One."

"Hey, Lucy. I thought that was you sitting over here."

Suddenly, Lucy felt goose bumps popping up on her arms. Even though Stella had warned her, the sound of Dante's deep voice caused butterflies to flutter around in her belly.

Lucy swung her gaze up and away from her ice cream sundae. Gawking out of the library window at Dante hadn't fully prepared her for his up-close-and-personal masculine appeal. Her chest tightened. It was no small wonder he was a bona fide movie star. He was Idris Elba and The Rock all morphed into one glorious human being. He was the type of man who could cause a woman to lose her train of thought just by looking in his direction. Being this close to him sent adrenaline racing through her veins.

At approximately six feet tall, his body was rugged and toned. She knew from having seen publicity photos of him that he was ripped to perfection underneath his shirt. With skin the color of burnished wood and soulful brown eyes, Dante was serious eye candy.

She sucked in a deep, fortifying breath and tried to speak past the huge lump in her throat. Embarrassingly, no words managed to come out. Lucy hoped she wasn't drooling at the sight of him. Surely her sister would give her the high sign if she was.

"This was always your favorite booth. Some things never change," he said, the corners of his mouth tilting upward into the same glorious smile that had graced dozens of magazine covers. His smile hit her squarely in her solar plexus.

"Dante. It's been a long time." Somehow she pushed the words out of her mouth without stammering. She deserved a gold star for being somewhat articulate.

"Eight and a half years to be exact," he drawled.

Something about the way he said it made Lucy want to scream. Humph! He sounded mighty proud of it. It had been eight and a half years since he'd fled Mistletoe as if a pack of wild dogs had been chasing him. Eight and a half years since they'd spoken. Eight and a half years since he'd walked away from her and their hometown.

"Congratulations, Dante," she murmured. "You've really done some great things since you left town."

"Thanks for saying so. I've been pretty blessed," he said with a nod. He turned toward her sister. "Stella. You haven't changed a bit."

"I'll take that as a compliment," Stella said, "considering how much things do tend to change with time."

*Ding! Ding!* Her sister was giving Dante a subtle warning about her. Lucy wasn't the same soft touch she'd once been. If Dante pushed her buttons he would soon realize she'd changed in the years since he'd been gone. She was way tougher than the sweet-natured girl who'd rarely challenged him. His movie-star status didn't intimidate her one bit.

Lucy turned her eyes toward her ice cream. It was so creamy and messy and gooey.

"Lucy. Don't," her sister said in a pleading voice. Her brown eyes were filled with caution.

How was it possible that Stella could read her mind? After a lifetime of togetherness and sharing bedrooms and secrets as kids, Stella knew where all the skeletons were buried. She knew Lucy like the back of her hand. The good, the bad, and the ugly. At the moment Lucy was struggling with the ugly.

All Lucy could see was Dante's too-handsome-for-his-own-good face. And that annoying smirk!

*Really?* What exactly did he have to smirk about? He'd come back to town as if he hadn't snuck out of it like a thief in the night. Pompous idiot!

Lucy imagined how good it would feel to dump her ice cream sundae all over Dante's head. She would probably have to stand on the booth to do it, but it would be so gratifying. It would definitely give her a feeling of accomplishment. Perhaps then she wouldn't have this tight little ball knotted up inside her chest at the very thought of him.

She felt a smile tugging at the corners of her mouth as she imagined the ice cream trickling down his face and chest. It would be a huge mess. For once he wouldn't be so smug and perfect. Maybe then he would realize what a jerk he'd been to her.

"Lucy. You're the town librarian. You have a reputation to uphold." Stella's voice cautioned her to be sensible. She now had two angels sitting on her shoulders—one good and one very bad.

Dante looked back and forth at the two sisters and frowned.

"Am I missing something?" he asked, scratching his jaw. "An inside joke?"

Lucy's fingers were itching to do something naughty. It was such a strong impulse. Normally she was very restrained. Calm, cool, and collected at all times. Over the years she'd perfected the art of pretending as if she didn't have a care in the world. It allowed her to nurse her hurts on the inside and not become an object of pity. She'd mastered the art of holding her head up high.

There had always been something about Dante that made her want to walk on the wild side. He'd been the devil sitting on her shoulder and tempting her to veer off course.

Before she could give in to temptation, she stood up abruptly from the table, grabbing her coat and purse in the process. The only way to resist was to get as far away from Dante as her legs would take her. Escape was her sole option.

"I-I have to go," she blurted out, dragging her gaze away from Dante. "I'll call you later, Stella." Before she changed her mind, she darted toward the exit and pushed the door wide open. Once she got outside, Lucy took a deep, cleansing breath of fresh wintry air. Snow was falling all around her. For a moment she closed her eyes and lifted her face up toward the sky. This type of weather always gave her a feeling of serenity. *Breathe*, she reminded herself.

"Wait, Luce!" She heard Dante's voice calling after her, using the old nickname he'd uttered a million times in the past. Lucy didn't stop walking. Why should she? It had taken him all this time to even remember she existed. Not once had he tried to explain things in person. Nothing he could possibly say to her mattered in the slightest bit.

Suddenly, Lucy felt herself slipping and sliding in her boots. Strong arms gripped her, preventing her from wiping out on the snow and sludge. "I've got you," Dante said, holding her up by her arms. Lucy waited until she had both feet solidly on the ground before pushing him squarely in the chest, managing to make him stumble. Dante's quick reflexes saved him from falling over.

Dante narrowed his gaze as he stared at her. "That wasn't very friendly of you, especially considering I just stopped you from landing on your butt."

For a moment she felt badly about shoving him, but it had been better than bombarding him with ice cream. If he only knew how close he'd been to getting up close and personal with an ice cream sundae.

He folded his arms across his chest and regarded her. "So back there in the diner I had the strangest feeling you were thinking bad thoughts about me. Am I right?"

Lucy avoided eye contact with Dante. Now that the moment had passed, it seemed really childish. What was it about this man that brought out the teenaged version of herself? "I might have had a passing thought about dumping my ice cream on top of your head," she confessed, looking down at the ground rather than gazing into his intense brown eyes. "But I thought better of it." Thank goodness for smart older sisters and cooler heads prevailing.

"Something tells me you've been waiting a long time to do something like that."

"You have no idea," she said, lifting her gaze to meet his. Seeing Dante brought back all the hurt and sleepless nights, the tears and recriminations. To this day he had no idea how badly he'd wounded her. She wasn't sure he even cared.

"Okay, maybe I had that one coming," Dante admitted, making a face. "Maybe I have a lot of things coming."

"Maybe?" She let out a frustrated sound and turned away from him. They had planned to leave Mistletoe together and he'd left without her. In her eyes he was no hero.

"Lucy, wait! Please. Talk to me." His voice trailed after her.

Lucy stopped in her tracks. She felt Dante's gentle touch

on her arm. He turned her around so they were facing each other. She shrugged off his touch, knowing she was defenseless against him. Lucy didn't like the churning in her stomach or how it made her feel to hear the rich timbre of his voice as he said her name. And he was standing way too close to her for comfort.

Being in Dante's orbit was dangerous to her equilibrium. He was like a fiery comet blazing across the sky. It was hard not to be mesmerized by him. And before she knew it, Lucy would be scorched by his flame.

"Don't, Dante. It's all water under the bridge." His deep-set brown eyes were intense as they gazed into her own.

"Is it? Because it doesn't feel like it. We never had closure. Not really."

"Whose fault is that?" she asked, throwing her hands in the air.

He made a frustrated sound. "It's mine, Lucy. All mine. I was the one who left, who ran away without telling you goodbye face-to-face."

"Yes, Dante. It was all you! I can't believe the first words out of your mouth to me weren't an apology. Back there in the diner you acted as if we parted on good terms."

"If you remember, I tried to apologize to you back then, but you refused to take my calls or see me." He massaged the bridge of his nose. "You're right. I should have pulled you aside and apologized. I owe you that."

"What bothers me the most is you blowing into town as this megastar who's done no wrong. And the whole town is ready to fall at your feet."

"I don't view it that way. I'm making a film here and they're grateful for the boost to the local economy."

"I just hope you keep your promises to the town," she said, jutting her chin out.

Dante made a frustrated sound. "What are you angrier about, Lucy? Not getting an apology or the fact that I achieved superstar status?"

Lucy's mouth hardened. Nothing had changed between them. Dante still didn't get it. He was still the same selfish, entitled jerk who had broken her heart all those years ago. He had no idea how devastated she'd been after his abandonment or the way in which it had wrecked her self-esteem. Perhaps he had just been toying with her the whole time. Maybe she really hadn't meant anything to him. That knowledge hurt her more than it should. After *eight and a half years*, Dante should be nothing more than a faded memory. A footnote in her life story.

"I see you haven't changed," she said through gritted teeth. "Someone should have told you to check your ego once you hit the town limits."

She turned on her heel and stormed away from him, muttering under her breath the entire way. This time Dante didn't call after her, nor did she expect him to. He had shown her his true colors when he'd bailed on her and Mistletoe. Not one single thing had changed, except that he was now a movie star, one who seemed to hold the entire town in the palm of his hand. From the looks of it, she was the only one who didn't think Dante West walked on water.

* * *

Dante watched Lucy as she stormed away from him. She was making her way gingerly, as if she was worried about slipping again. He wanted to run after her, but he realized there would be no point in doing so. He would probably just make things worse. She was so angry at him he could practically see steam coming from her ears. So much for coming back to Mistletoe and making things right with Lucy.

Why did he always put his foot in his mouth with her? Old habits died hard, he supposed. During his years in Hollywood, Dante had learned the fine art of being charming. It had helped him immensely in the business of becoming a movie star. But something about Lucy made him revert back to the lanky teenaged boy who'd allowed nerves to take over in social situations.

Dante muttered angrily to himself. He should have told her why he'd left town all those years ago. But in order to do so Dante would have to tell her about his fractured relationship with his father. Growing up in the West household had taught him to keep family matters inside the West home. He didn't like to talk about their falling out or the regrets he had about not coming back to see his dad before he'd passed away. Lucy had grown up in an idyllic household, so he'd never imagined she could relate to his situation.

But he should have told Lucy the truth back then. She hadn't been like anyone else he'd ever known. She'd been his best friend and his girlfriend all rolled into one. They had made plans to leave Mistletoe together, yet he'd blindsided

Lucy by packing up all his belongings and abruptly leaving town after a huge blowup with his father. The fight had almost gotten physical, which had emotionally gutted him. He hadn't wanted to stick around and run the risk of another volatile argument between them. All he'd left by way of an explanation for Lucy had been a brief note and a promise to stay in touch. He'd been a coward not to tell her the news face-to-face, but at the time he'd felt as if he might implode if he didn't leave.

Dante hadn't lived up to any of the things he'd written to her in his goodbye letter. No wonder she thought so poorly of him.

Dante shook his head at the grim reality of what had transpired after he'd left town and arrived in Hollywood. It had taken every ounce of his focus just to keep his head above water in Los Angeles. Even though he'd planned on keeping in touch with Lucy, it had gotten harder and harder to fulfill that promise with each and every passing day. He'd been broke and jobless, sharing a studio apartment with four other wannabe actors. Things had quickly spiraled out of control when one of his roommates had stolen the rent money and used it on drugs, leading to their eviction. As a result, he'd been homeless and sleeping in his car. He hadn't even been able to afford a cell phone. When he had finally reached out to her months later, she'd told him off and refused to answer any more of his calls. And it had completely destroyed him.

Losing Lucy had been like allowing a little bit of magic to leave his life. He wasn't sure he'd ever recovered from it. If he tried to tell Lucy about his clashes with his father and his fear that he might give up on his dreams if he'd stayed, she would probably laugh in his face. After all these years, he wouldn't blame her. It was way too late to smooth things over.

Dante headed back into the diner. All eyes were on him as he entered the establishment. He wondered if everyone inside had noticed him running after Lucy. From what he remembered, this town had big eyes and ears. He forced himself to smile as he walked over toward Mayor Finch, his mother, and the rest of the party, who had been seated at a large table during his absence.

Dante hated how much he cared about what people thought of him. He knew it had everything to do with his profession and the harsh glare of the media spotlight. He always had to stay alert and on his toes. It was a shame he had to feel this way even in his hometown.

"Dante! We were wondering what was taking you so long," his mother said, patting the seat beside her.

"I was just catching up with an old friend," he said as he sat down next to her. Images of Lucy flashed before his eyes. She had grown into a very beautiful woman. She'd always been really pretty, but she was an absolute stunner now. Her jet-black hair hung about her shoulders in loose waves. Her skin was the color of almonds. Lucy's heart-shaped face showcased amazing cheekbones. Although she hadn't smiled at him, Dante knew firsthand how dazzling it could be when she laughed or grinned. Her smile had always knocked him off his feet.

"If I remember correctly, you and Lucy Marshall were a lot more than friends," Mimi said in a teasing voice. His mother's comment drew smiles and nods from the other people at the table. Small towns like Mistletoe had long memories, he realized. He felt a sudden stab of discomfort at the thought of Lucy being the object of the town's pity all those years ago when he'd left her in the lurch. His actions back then were born out of desperation and ambition, but Lucy and his family had suffered because of them. Shame threatened to swallow him up whole at the idea of wounding so many people he cared about.

Even though he was struggling with his emotions, Dante put on a smile. "Lucy has always been amazing." It was the truth. She'd always been extraordinary, which was why he'd never been able to forget her or the precious moments they had shared. He felt the heat of his mother's gaze, but Dante didn't look at her. He was too afraid of her seeing straight through him.

The ding of the bell heralded the arrival of more diners. Dante swung his gaze up and froze at the familiar frame entering the diner. *Troy.* He hadn't seen or spoken to his brother since their father's funeral. Dante knew he'd hurt his family by staying in town only long enough to see his father buried, but he'd been overwhelmed with guilt about not being present during his dad's illness. He'd beat a fast path out of Mistletoe so he didn't have to face up to his actions.

Wasn't that the very same thing he'd done when he'd left his hometown the first time? Running away seemed to be his signature move. Suddenly, his throat felt tight and he struggled to keep it together. He'd been in town for less than twenty-four hours and he was already falling apart at the seams. For so long he'd been ignoring the broken pieces of his life, but being back was dredging it all up again. He'd made so many mistakes with Troy. Could he ever bridge the chasm between them?

When the man turned in his direction, Dante realized he'd been mistaken. It wasn't Troy at all. Although they shared the same physique and complexion, their faces really didn't favor each other. His mother reached out and tightly squeezed his hand. Her eyes radiated motherly love and compassion. She seemed to know exactly what he'd been thinking.

Dante didn't know what was wrong with him. Normally, he prided himself on being stoic and keeping his emotions at bay. Coming back to Mistletoe was a game changer. Suddenly his feelings were resting right on the surface.

Dante let out a deep sigh. He hadn't just come back to town in order to film a movie and get closure with Lucy. When he'd left Mistletoe, Dante had unknowingly fractured his relationships with his family members. And judging by the fact that his siblings hadn't shown up today at the celebration in his honor, things were a far cry from being fixed.

His reasons for coming home were way more personal than making a film in his hometown and receiving a hero's welcome. He was back in town to make things right with the people he'd once wronged and to fulfill a promise he'd made to himself after nearly losing his life.

# CHAPTER THREE

Lucy was having a fabulous dream. She was dressed to the nines in a long, flowing red evening gown and a man in a tuxedo was twirling her around the dance floor. There was a crowd of people clapping and cheering them on. As the tempo increased she found herself being spun around at a frenetic pace. She felt breathless as she looked into a pair of deep brown eyes flecked with gold.

"Lucy!" The singsong voice blaring in her ear served as the ultimate wake-up call. It also meant her beautiful dream had been cut short. It was a shame, considering she usually dreamed about missing library books or being caught out in public wearing only her underwear.

She opened one eye, then quickly shut it once she saw her little sister standing next to her bed. All she wanted was a few extra hours of sleep and another glimpse of the darkly handsome man from her dream. Clearly she was asking for way too much.

This, she realized for the umpteenth time, was the problem with living right next door to her family. When she'd bought the newly renovated farmhouse it had seemed like such a brilliant idea. She'd been filled with a heartwarming feeling as soon as she'd seen the finished product. The place had been transformed in a matter of months from an abandoned wreck into a cozy house that was the perfect blend of modern and classic. Lucy had made an offer on the spot.

At times like this, when her ten-year-old sister was staring at her as if Lucy were an exhibit at the science museum, she wished she'd bought the fixer-upper on the other side of town. In a moment of sheer madness, she'd forgotten about the benefits of privacy.

"Tess, I'm sleeping in this morning," she said with a groan. "We've talked about this before. Boundaries!" She needed to sleep off last night's encounter with Dante. She felt conflicted about her behavior. On one hand she truly believed Dante deserved her salty attitude, while another part of her wished she'd kept her cool as Stella had advised.

Lucy felt a jab in her chest. She squealed. "Ouch!"

"Aren't you going to be late for work?" her sister asked.

"It's Saturday and I'm not working today. I do have a hair appointment and some errands to run though," she explained. "How did you get in here anyway?" she asked, hoping she hadn't left the door unlocked. Mistletoe was a low crime community, but you could never be too careful. After binge-watching *Forensic Files*, she wasn't taking any chances.

"I made a copy of your spare key when I was dog sitting Astro for you."

Her beagle, Astro, who'd been lying at the base of her bed, raised his head and let out a little noise at the mention of his name. Even he seemed outraged by Tess and her lack of boundaries.

Lucy groaned. "Tess! You can't do something like that without asking." She didn't bother to remind her little sister about boundaries again. It would fall on deaf ears. Tess was the type of kid who wielded her status as the baby of the family like a sharp sword. She poked first and asked questions later.

After a few moments of silence, Lucy closed her eyes. Maybe Tess would get the hint and beat it. Was it too much to ask to be able to sleep in on Saturday morning?

"I need to ask you something." Her sister's voice penetrated the quiet. Lucy peeked her head out from under her pink-and-white-rose-adorned comforter. It was one of the only items in her house she'd truly splurged on after discovering it at a local vintage store. Although the price tag had made her gasp, Lucy hadn't been able to leave the store without purchasing it.

Tess was still standing next to her bed looking as adorable as ever with her wide brown eyes and curly mane of hair. Lucy knew she should just accept that she wasn't going to get any more shut-eye.

"It better be important," she said, frowning.

Tess was biting her lip. "Is it true you used to date Dante West?"

"Wh-who told you that?" she asked, sputtering. Surely no one in town even remembered their high school romance. But then again, people in small towns never forget a thing.

Her sister shrugged. "I just heard it through the grapevine. One of Mama's friends." She rolled her eyes dramatically. "You know how they love to gossip."

Lucy let out an indelicate snort. Despite her tender age, Tess was quite proficient at spreading stories around Mistletoe. At this rate, Lucy realized, she'd be a pro by her teen years.

"We did briefly date in high school," she acknowledged, unwilling to tell her kid sister about their extensive history as best friends leading up to their romance.

Tess was shifting around from one foot to the other. "Do you think you could ask him for a favor?"

Lucy thought her eyes might bulge out of her head. "A favor? What are you talking about, Tess? I haven't seen him in almost nine years! I'm hardly in a position to ask him for anything. He'd probably laugh in my face if I asked him for a can of soda." Especially after her snarky behavior last night. Dante might run in the opposite direction if he saw her coming. The realization that he might not want anything to do with her caused a sharp twist in her stomach. It was strange feeling this way since she'd convinced herself she didn't want to see his gorgeous face ever again.

"I might have told the kids in my class I could get him to come in for our guest-of-the-week program," Tess said in a muffled voice. Her head was down and she was looking at the floor. She refused to meet Lucy's gaze.

"You did what? Seriously, Tess. Why would you do that? You don't even know the man."

"But you do," Tess said in her most angelic voice, swinging her gaze up to meet Lucy's.

When had her baby sister perfected this hangdog look? And her tone was a perfect blend of sweetness and innocence. It was downright scary.

All of a sudden, the sound of a barking dog rang out from outside. As a result, Astro let out a low growl and began making yipping noises. He ran toward the window and got up on his hind legs as he peered out of it. She had to admit it was pretty adorable, considering Astro had nothing to back up his bark. He was in the lightweight category of guard dogs. All growl and no grit.

"Is that Rufus outside? What is he barking at?" Lucy asked, sitting up in bed. Rufus belonged to her parents. Their whole family knew Rufus barked at only two things— strangers and cats. She sincerely hoped it was the chubby orange tabby from down the road. Lucy wasn't big on uninvited guests, especially when she was supposed to be catching some extra sleep or vegging out in her pj's to *Stranger Things* on Netflix.

Tess walked over to the window and peered through the blinds. She let out an excited squeal. "Oh my gosh! It's him!"

"Him who?" Lucy asked. Dread churned her stomach into tiny knots.

Tess turned back toward her with widened eyes full of excitement. "It's your famous ex-boyfriend! He was in the driveway, but now he's heading toward your front door."

No way! Dante wouldn't come over, not after the way they'd argued last night. Her body's immediate response was to freeze up, right before pure adrenaline began pulsing through her veins.

"Tess! If this is a joke..." she said in a warning tone. She wouldn't put it past Tess to pull her leg about Dante. That's how her little sister rolled. In the not-so-distant past Tess had made her parents believe that a reindeer was grazing in their backyard. In fact, it had been a dog munching on their bushes.

"I'm not kidding. Just you wait. The doorbell is going to ring any moment now. Five. Four. Three. Two. One." Just then the doorbell rang.

"Oh no! Seriously?" Lucy asked in a whisper.

"Why are you whispering? He can't hear you from outside." Tess was now giggling as if Lucy was the lamest person she'd ever seen in her life.

Why would Dante seek her out the morning after their awkward run-in?

Astro *woof*ed and ran toward the door before Lucy could grab hold of him. Tess raced after him, her footsteps echoing down the hall on the hardwood floors.

"Tess! Tess! Do not answer the door. I am not entertaining a guest in my pajamas," she instructed in a raised voice. Especially not a drop-dead gorgeous ex. "Tess! Do you hear me?"

Seconds later she heard the sound of the door being opened, followed by her sister's chirpy voice welcoming Dante inside. Lucy moaned and slapped her palm to her forehead. This wasn't happening! Her idyllic Saturday morning sleep-in had been interrupted by her nosy little sister and a famous celebrity she used to date.

Lucy jumped out of bed and tiptoed down the hall. She could hear the chatter of voices down below—Dante's husky tone mixed with her sister's childlike one. What colossal nerve! Who exactly did Tess think she was answering Lucy's door and inviting Dante to come inside? And why was he here in the first place? Last night hadn't exactly been warm and fuzzy between them. Was he a glutton for punishment?

"Lucy! You have a very important guest straight out of Hollywood!" Tess's voice reminded her of nails on a chalkboard. Why in the world was her sister torturing her like this? She'd made it perfectly clear not to answer the door and that she didn't want to see Dante. But now he was already inside her house and Tess was schmoozing with him. No doubt she was buttering him up so she could ask him to be her special guest at school.

*Reminder to self: Make Tess pay dearly for this.*

It would serve Tess right if she changed the locks to her house. Problem was, Lucy would never do such a thing to her baby sister. Just the thought of Tess's cherubic face staring at a door that wouldn't open caused a pang in her heart.

"One moment," Lucy answered in a strangled voice. There was no graceful way out of this now that she'd been put on the spot. She would have to go downstairs and come face-to-face with Dante when she'd literally just hobbled out of bed. Her hair was a wild mess and she hadn't even brushed her teeth yet or washed her face.

Suddenly, she snapped out of it. Hiding up in her bedroom was pointless and totally juvenile. It was time to put her big-girl panties on. *Never let 'em see you sweat*, she reminded herself. She wouldn't give Dante the satisfaction of seeing he'd rattled her by showing up at her home. It was time to channel her inner Beyoncé.

She darted into the bathroom adjoining her bedroom. She took a quick glimpse in the mirror and groaned. Her hair looked like a rat's nest while her skin had seen better days. She'd been so emotionally exhausted last night she hadn't taken the time to wash off her makeup or moisturize. Lucy quickly pulled her hair up and twisted it into a topknot. She reached for her cleanser and washed her face, then put on a thin layer of blush-colored lip stain. She reached for her primer, foundation, and bronzer, carefully applying each product to her face. She threw off her Rudolph the Red-Nosed Reindeer pajamas and replaced them with a pair of slim-fitting jeans and her favorite oatmeal-colored sweater. Lucy released her hair from the elastic and ran a brush through it until it was loose and wavy.

She looked at herself critically in the mirror. Considering she'd just gotten out of bed, she looked pretty presentable. Or at least half-decent. Why did she care anyway? She wasn't trying to impress Dante. Ha! She couldn't even think it with a straight face.

Lucy grabbed her glasses from her bedside table and put

them on, even though she really didn't need to use them very often. She had a pretty weak prescription. Wearing glasses always made her feel stronger. They were a shield she hid behind. Over the years she hadn't been able to let go of the crutch. At the moment she needed the support.

She followed the sound of voices, which led her to her bright and airy kitchen. With its all-white decor and sparkling-new appliances, it had been one of the major selling points.

In the clear light of day, Dante looked scrumptious in a white Celtic cable sweater with a pair of black cords. She almost stopped in her tracks at the sight of him sitting at her kitchen table across from Tess. Judging by his socks, she assumed he'd taken his shoes off at the door.

His tawny-colored skin and strong jawline lent him a distinctive look. He smiled at her, showcasing a set of un-forgettable dimples. Back in the day those little indentations had made her knees go weak. At the moment they were making butterflies swirl around in her stomach.

"Morning," he said, lifting a mug to his perfectly shaped lips and taking a swig of tea. Tess had laid out Lucy's tea set, complete with sweeteners and milk, along with several boxes of various tea flavors. She'd even put out a plate of blueberry scones. It was clear they were having a grand old time, guessing by the huge smile etched on her sister's face. She was in ten-year-old heaven.

It wasn't difficult to see why Hollywood had snapped him up and made Dante West one of the biggest box-office draws in recent memory. He radiated pure charisma.

"Good morning, Dante," she said, shocking herself by making her voice sound unbothered. "What brings you over here?" After last night's tension, Lucy was determined not to lose her cool. She wasn't proud of her emotions boiling over. This was her opportunity to showcase a more polished version of herself.

"I'm sorry for interrupting your morning, but I have something to run by you." He swung his gaze toward Tess who was leaning forward in her chair and listening to his every word.

"Don't mind me," Tess said with a smirk. "I'm just here for the scones." She took a big bite of her scone and began making contented noises as if she was a connoisseur of baked goods. Lucy rolled her eyes. At some point she really did have to pull her sister aside and have a serious discussion about manners, as well as acting her age.

Dante drummed his fingers on the table. "I have a proposition for you," he said, his eyes glinting as he locked gazes with Lucy.

The word *proposition* brought to mind all manner of things Lucy didn't want to think about. Moonlit kisses. Making out in the back row of the Regal movie theater. Skinny-dipping at Spinnaker Lake. She didn't want to take this walk down memory lane even though moments from the past were crashing over her in unrelenting waves. It was so much easier to pretend as if she didn't miss Dante being a huge part of her life. It felt so much better to dislike him than to yearn for everything she'd lost.

She swallowed past the huge lump in her throat. "What is it?"

"I want to film some scenes for the movie at your library."

Lucy couldn't have been more shocked if he'd told her he was moving back to Maine and leaving Hollywood in his rearview mirror. She felt her eyes widening. Words eluded her. Never in a million years could she imagine her library being used as the setting for an adrenaline-producing action film. Was he completely out of his mind? An image of her precious books being blown to smithereens flashed before her eyes. She couldn't allow such mayhem to take place there. Not on her watch.

Dante was calmly staring at her with single-minded focus, clearly waiting for her reply.

Stalling for time, Lucy cleared her throat. "I-I don't think that's a good idea, Dante. The library isn't built for high-action scenes with explosives and fights." She winced. "We have rare books there. It's way too risky for our inventory." She scrunched up her nose. "The townsfolk wouldn't approve."

"Well, if it makes any difference in your decision, it's not an action movie, Luce," he explained, sending shivers down her spine by using his old nickname for her. "It's a love story. There's not a single explosion in the whole film."

A love story? She let out a squeak. Since when did Dante make anything other than action flicks? His characters had survived so many explosions, fans had started calling him Inferno. "A love story?" she asked, surprise ringing out in her voice.

Dante nodded. "Yes. You look shocked. Is it so hard to believe?"

"I thought you only made action films." She wasn't going to admit it to Dante, but she'd seen just about every movie he'd ever made. There wasn't a romance film among them! Not that she couldn't imagine him romancing a beautiful actress on and off set. Over the years she'd seen enough snippets about him to know he wasn't exactly shy when it came to the ladies.

"I'm the writer, producer, and director of this film," he explained. "It's probably the most important movie I'll ever make because it's a departure for me. I'm laying it all on the line with this one." There was a strained quality to his voice, one she easily recognized. He was nervous. Clearly this film was a high-stakes endeavor for him and his production company.

"Makes sense," Tess said with a nod. "Serious films could get you major cred in the industry. You might even get a Golden Globe, an Oscar, or a Palme d'Or."

Lucy frowned at Tess. A Palme d'Or! What ten-year-old even knew about the Cannes Film Festival or the awards they bestowed? Tess needed to stay out of grown folks' business and focus on being a kid. She ought to divert her sister's attention away from this conversation as soon as possible before she asked to be an extra on set. Tess wouldn't hesitate to insert herself into the unfolding situation.

"Tess. Astro is sniffing at the back door. Could you take him out for me, please?" she asked, knowing she wouldn't refuse or make a fuss. Her sister loved Astro as much as Lucy did. Maybe more.

Tess groaned as she got up and headed toward the back

door. Lucy watched as she planted her feet in Lucy's boots, then grabbed one of her coats from the coat rack. Lucy stifled a giggle at the sight of her shuffling around in the snow in boots and a winter jacket that were several sizes too big. She felt a squeeze in her heart. At moments like this, the love she had for her baby sister felt as if it might swallow her up whole. Although she could be a huge pain in the butt, her wide-open heart and innocence were endearing.

When Tess drifted out of sight Lucy swung her gaze back to Dante. It was a strange feeling to be staring into his soulful eyes after all this time. No matter what else changed about a person over the years, their eyes always stayed the same.

"The terms of the agreement would be generous, Lucy. I'm prepared to make this a very lucrative partnership for the library."

The number that rolled off Dante's lips caused her to gasp. The library was in dire need of financial support in order to offset the town's budget crisis. When tourism had dipped in Mistletoe there had been a ripple effect on local businesses and civic entities. As a result, donations to the library had shriveled up. Money had been stretched really thin for the past few years. She'd done as much as she could to keep things going in a positive direction, but the lack of funding hampered even the best of intentions. This type of money would be nothing short of a miracle. Her head began to spin at all the possibilities.

A donation of this amount would allow Lucy to implement badly needed programs for the community, as well as supplement the library's inventory, add library hours, and invite local authors in for workshops and programs. She could actually purchase the latest bestsellers from the *New York Times* list. They could even host bingo nights and write-ins for aspiring authors. It would be a game changer for the Free Library of Mistletoe. And a dream come true for Lucy.

Her mind began to whirl with the pros and cons.

### *Pros:*

1. She'd receive a big fat ginormous check for the struggling library.
2. Loads of media attention would be focused on the library.
3. The library would be immortalized on film. Pretty cool!
4. She would fulfill her goal of saving the library.

### *Cons:*

1. She would have to see Dante on a regular basis or at least on filming days.
2. The day-to-day operations of the library might be compromised.

Lucy didn't have to rack her brain to figure out what her answer should be. Given what was at stake, it was a no-brainer. If someone had told her last night she would be agreeing to Dante's proposal she would have called them all sorts of crazy. But in the cold light of day she had to face facts. The library's financial situation was precarious, and this infusion of cash could help turn things around. Allowing her personal feelings to get in the way would be selfish.

. She sucked in a deep breath. "Yes, I think we can work something out that's beneficial to both of us. I'll have to run it by the board of directors, but I can't imagine they'll have a problem with it, as long as we set certain ground rules."

Dante rubbed his hands together. "That's wonderful news. I'm glad I took a chance and came over here. I wasn't so sure I should ask after last night."

The look Dante sent her was probing, as if he was interested in rehashing what went down between them outside the diner. She had no intention of opening up that can of worms at the moment. Tess was bound to come back inside shortly, and Lucy didn't need an audience to witness the discord between them. It was best to not even respond.

"You were really angry at me, and believe it or not, I get it," he said, his voice sounding way more tender than she wanted to acknowledge. All she truly desired was to keep thinking of him as the big bad bogeyman from her past. That way she would be wearing an impenetrable suit of armor whenever he was around.

She folded her arms across her chest. "I'm not going to apologize for anything I said, but I could have been a tad more civil," she conceded. She was trying so hard to be the bigger person, as Stella had suggested. Considering their tangled past, someone should give her a medal. Maybe the town of Mistletoe should throw her a parade.

"Well, I promise you, I'm a lot better at following the rules these days."

"I imagine so," she responded, her lips twitching despite her desire to remain reserved. "There really wasn't anywhere to go but up."

Dante chuckled. His eyes danced with mischief. There were little dimples at the corners of his mouth. He still resembled the boy who'd been her best friend and partner in crime. In a matter of seconds, all the years melted away. Dante had always been the mastermind and she'd gone along with his schemes rather reluctantly. It had been hard to resist his charm and soulful brown eyes. He'd had her wrapped around his little finger.

For a moment their gazes locked and held. Something intense pulsed in the air between them. It felt electric. It seemed as if all the oxygen had been sucked from the room. Lucy reached out to hold on to the edge of the kitchen table. She suddenly felt light-headed, as if a slight wind might blow her over. Dante appeared a bit startled too, as if he'd been knocked a bit off-kilter. Lucy could see it in his eyes. Perhaps she wasn't the only one who felt a bit out of her depth.

The back door suddenly swung open, immediately diffusing the situation. Tess appeared in the doorway alongside Astro, her cheeks reddened from the cold. Her expression couldn't hide her natural curiosity.

"I'm back," she announced with a cheeky grin and a

wave of her hands. "What did I miss? Did you guys reach an agreement?"

Lucy nodded. Since her sister was part bloodhound, Tess would find out soon enough anyway. "We did," she said, casting a quick glance in Dante's direction.

"Your sister has agreed to let me film parts of my movie at the library, so I guess I'll be seeing you around, Tess," Dante answered, a grin lighting up his face.

Tess immediately began jumping up and down as she shed her boots and jacket. "Oh, this is so exciting. Wait till I tell the kids at school." She walked over to Dante and high-fived him. Lucy felt her heart lurch. It hadn't taken Dante long to pull Tess into his web. The ten-year-old already seemed enamored of him and they'd just met. It was understandable, Lucy thought. She knew firsthand how Dante could get under a person's skin and stay there.

"I should get going," he said, his gaze shifting back to Lucy. "Tess mentioned you have an appointment this afternoon."

Lucy gasped, then glanced at the kitchen clock. She was scheduled to get a wash and set in forty-five minutes at Rita's Beauty Shop and she still needed to do a few things before she headed out the door. She'd almost completely forgotten about her appointment while discussing the film with Dante. "Yeah. I have to get going so I'm not late," she explained. Dante's presence in her kitchen had driven all thoughts about her hair appointment out of her mind. He'd been in town for only a few days and yet he was already serving as a major distraction to her orderly world.

With a wave of his hand, Dante turned to leave the kitchen.

"Wait! There's one more thing. As part of this deal, I'd like you to agree to be Tess's guest of the week at her school." Lucy felt a smile tugging at her lips as she watched Tess's face light up. "It's really important to her."

Dante looked over at Tess and winked. "It would be my pleasure. Just tell me when and where. I'll be there." Sincerity rang out in his voice. "Thanks again, Lucy. You won't regret saying yes." Just then a little jolt ran through her body. For a moment Lucy felt as if she was in the presence of the old Dante, the one who'd once been imprinted on her heart. The playful, vibrant side of him had been on display this morning, particularly in his interactions with Tess. The rich sound of his laughter touched a part of her that had been lying dormant ever since his departure. This was the man she'd fallen in love with and cherished with every ounce of her soul. This was the man a part of her still ached for in the quiet hours between darkness and dawn.

As Dante turned and walked out of the room, a sigh slipped past her lips. Why was it so difficult not to get sucked back into his world? A few moments in his presence and she was as pliable as a piece of clay. A cloud of doubt had settled over her in the last few minutes. Was she really doing the right thing? Had she agreed to Dante's request too quickly? Would she be able to handle it without getting swept away by his charm and good looks? Did she have the strength to keep things on a professional level?

Suddenly, Tess appeared in front of her, beaming up at

her with a childlike smile. For the moment, all was right in her little sister's world. "Lucy, I love you." She wrapped her arms around Lucy so tightly she felt almost breathless. Lucy lowered her head to press a kiss against her sister's temple. Tess smelled of cinnamon and freshly fallen snow. Lucy wished she could capture this moment for all time so she could remind Tess of it when she got older. Moments like this were so fleeting and fragile. In a heartbeat Tess would be a teenager wanting to hang out with her girlfriends and whatever boy she was crushing on.

"I love you too, Tess," she said. "Just remember there's not a single thing I wouldn't do for you. Now or ever."

"Same here," Tess said in a muffled voice. "I'll always have your back."

Her heart felt full, almost to the point of overflowing. Tess was going to get her wish and the library would benefit tremendously from this arrangement with Dante's production company. It was a winning proposition for everyone, even if it made her feel as if her life had been turned upside down.

There was no way of sugarcoating it. She would have to deal with Dante on a regular basis now. It was unrealistic to imagine she could hide away in the library whenever he came around with his film crew. As head librarian, she was duty bound to be a professional. She needed to act as a protector of the library, to make certain nothing precious was destroyed in the filmmaking process. That would mean seeing her ex-boyfriend up close and personal on occasion. Her palms moistened at the prospect.

Lucy inhaled a deep, steadying breath. She just had to suck it up and deal. Part of being an adult meant putting one's own feelings aside and making decisions for the greater good. The well-being of the library hung in the balance, and she knew that to save it from financial ruin she had to put her needs last. Lucy was good at doing that. She'd been doing it for years, ever since Dante had shattered all the plans they'd made to share a life together. Ever since he had fled their hometown and disappeared from Lucy's life his betrayal had been resting on the surface of her heart.

Although she'd worked hard to make her life orderly and predictable, Dante's return had already blown things wide open.

# CHAPTER FOUR

Stepping out into the frosty December air served as a reminder that Dante wasn't in California anymore. The sweet scent of vanilla still clung to his nostrils. That particular aroma had always hovered around Lucy like a soft cloud and this morning was no exception.

As Dante drove away from Lucy's house, a feeling of triumph rose up inside of him. Lucy probably still despised him, but she was on board with his plan for the movie. Based on Lucy's initial reaction to his presence in town, he'd figured she would be a lot more resistant to the idea of him filming at her place of business. He should have known better. Lucy would do anything for her beloved library, and a few months ago he'd learned from his mother that it had recently suffered from serious cutbacks. Although he'd obtained tentative permission months ago from Mayor Finch, he didn't want Lucy to feel as if she was being run over by a semitruck. He wanted her to be fully on board with his project, which was why he'd shown up at her door this morning dangling a carrot. If she'd said no, Dante would have backed off.

Seeing Lucy in her cozy little house that was situated right across the way from her childhood home had tugged at him. How many times had they climbed the maple tree in her backyard or chased after salamanders in the nearby woods? He'd been a fixture at the Marshalls' home when he was a kid. Their doors had always been open to him and he'd considered them as his second family.

He could barely contain his excitement. Making this movie right here in Mistletoe was the result of him stepping out on a limb of faith and pushing past his action-star image. For so long he'd wanted to take a chance and do something different from his usual high-octane, adrenaline rush–producing films. It wasn't as if he was looking to win an Oscar or anything, but he yearned to show off some of his directing skills so he could be taken seriously in the industry. Although he was grateful for his success in action films, there were only so many times he could make the same movie. He was tired of blowing up buildings and chasing bad guys. He wanted to do something that showcased his broad range of talent.

And this film would be special. Not only because he was going back to his roots and filming in his hometown, but because he'd written the script as a love letter of sorts to Lucy and the town of Mistletoe. In making this movie, he was going to be wearing his heart on his sleeve about the woman who'd stolen his heart back when he was a teenager.

It wasn't a comfortable position for him to be in, but he'd made a promise to himself to live his life differently after the accident.

He'd spent so many years becoming a well-known actor that he'd deprived himself of personal connections. Sure, he had friends and important contacts in the movie industry, but he didn't have anyone who knew him inside and out. Dante didn't have love in his life. And there weren't people in his orbit who would deeply mourn him if he passed away.

He winced as the memories of his accident crashed over him. He'd been in Peru filming a movie when a stunt had gone wrong. His injuries had been severe, and he'd been in the intensive care unit for ten days. Thankfully, his PR team had been able to keep the news out of the press, who had only reported that he'd been involved in an accident on set. To this day, even Dante's mother wasn't aware that her son had been perilously close to death. Dante hadn't possessed the courage to tell her after all she'd been through with his father's illness.

Determined to shake off the grim thoughts, Dante focused on the festive shops lining Main Street. Christmas decorations were on full display in storefront windows and lampposts. A huge Christmas tree decorated the town green. Soon the town would hold the tree-decorating ceremony, complete with a live band, Santa Claus, and dancing elves. Dante grinned at the coffee shop sitting at the corner of Main and Grand. It reminded him of his favorite java spot in Los Angeles with a New England twist. A hunter-green and brown sign announced that the Coffee Bean was open for business. After parking his rental car and placing some change in the meter, Dante made a beeline for the shop. He hadn't had time earlier for his morning cup of Joe and his body was craving its daily pick-me-up.

On his way inside, Dante was the object of numerous stares and whispers from customers. He was used to the attention since it tended to follow him wherever he went. He waved in the direction of a group of ladies who'd been in his graduating class. If he wasn't mistaken, one was Gillian Robinson, his seventh-grade crush. Strangely enough, she still looked the same with her shoulder-length auburn hair, full eyebrows, and big brown eyes. Back in the day he would have done anything to win Gillian's heart. She hadn't been impressed by his scrawny body and squeaky voice. A year later he'd grown six inches and gained twenty-five pounds of pure muscle. Then he'd discovered football right before entering high school. But by the time Gillian finally noticed him, Dante had moved on. His life had been focused on football, family, friends, and Lucy. At the time it had been all he'd wanted and needed.

Dante stood in line behind a few other customers gazing at the menu board until it was his turn to be waited on by the barista, who let out a little squeal when she spotted him.

"I think I'll try the special...the hot chai," Dante said, pretending as if he hadn't heard her making a fuss out of him. It always ended up being a slightly awkward experience for him.

"Hot chai coming right up. I'm Willa, by the way. It's on the house, Mr. West." The young woman giggled and sent him a flirty look filled with adoration. Dante had no intention of flirting back. Willa looked as if she might still be in high school.

"Are you sure? I don't want to get you in any trouble." People were always giving him free stuff wherever he went. Although it was nice, it usually made him feel uncomfortable. He hadn't really done anything to deserve such special treatment other than becoming a highly paid and well-known actor. Refusing never went over well, so he'd learned to accept with a smile and gratitude. The last thing he wanted was for people in his hometown to think he was using his celebrity status to get freebies. On the flip side, Dante didn't want to appear ungrateful. It was all a delicate high-wire act.

"It's my pleasure," she said in a chirpy voice. "We're all so happy to see you back in Mistletoe, Inferno."

Inferno was the nickname he'd been given by a Hollywood director after starring in one of his movies. His agent had loved the moniker and used it to promote Dante's action-star image. The public had eaten it up and the name had stuck.

"Well, you've made me feel right at home, Willa," he said, reaching for his cup of chai and grinning at her. "Thanks again." He did a double take when he spotted his face on the side of the cup along with the words *It's Going to Be a Dante West Christmas*.

"Breaking hearts all over town. I see you're up to your old tricks again."

The familiar voice washed over him like a refreshing

rain. Dante would know it anywhere. As soon as he turned around, Dante chuckled at the sight of his old friend, Nick Keegan. His lighthearted nature always made Dante smile. Thanks to Nick, his high school years had been full of laughter and pranks. Nick was the type of person everyone gravitated toward because of his kind demeanor and jovial personality.

"Hey there, superstar. Long time no see." The man standing before him had always turned heads with his russet-colored skin and winning smile. He was the type of person who had a knack for putting everyone in his presence at ease. Back in the day, he'd been voted most popular boy in their class. Dante, on the other hand, had gotten most likely to get arrested on prom night. Ouch! That still rankled.

"Nick! I was hoping to run into you." Dante leaned in for a quick hug. Nick and his brother Luke had been two of Dante's closest friends in high school. Troy had also been part of their friend group. For years they'd played football together with Dante playing quarterback and Nick being tight end. Their friendship had continued well after Dante's departure from Mistletoe. To this day, Nick was one of his dearest friends, despite the miles that stretched out between them. With his rugged frame and a height of six foot three, Nick had been an all-star athlete. His plans to enter the NFL draft had been sidelined by a serious injury. His future adrift, Nick had devoted himself to another passion—search and rescue. It was yet another thing he was great at doing.

"Do you have time to sit down?" Nick asked, tightly gripping his cup of Joe.

"Sure. I've actually got some time on my hands," he said, feeling fortunate he'd walked into the Coffee Bean this morning. Back in California he never had much time to unwind with friends because of his hectic filming schedule. Even though he was going to be busy filming here in town, he'd carved out time to simply experience the wonders of Mistletoe.

"Cool logo," Nick drawled as he smirked and pointed toward Dante's face on his coffee cup. "I want to be you when I grow up."

Dante shook his head. "Trust me, your life with Miles is way cooler."

Nick led the way to a table by the window. Dante unfolded himself into a chair and took a moment to enjoy the wintry view as he took a sip of his drink. It rarely snowed in California and he missed the fluffy white stuff. There was never that scent of impending snow hovering in the air. Across the street sat the Lobster Shack, a favorite seafood restaurant with a devoted following. Kyle Williams, the owner, had come up with an award-winning menu. Dante couldn't think of the last time he'd eaten a Maine lobster drizzled in melted butter or gone crabbing at Blackberry Beach. The marina glimmered in the distance, the ocean full of ice chunks and fishing boats. There had been that time back in sixth grade when he, Nick, and Troy had snuck on board one of the fishing boats and enjoyed the adventure of a lifetime. There'd been hell to pay when they were discovered, but it had been well worth it. He hadn't realized how much of this town had been imprinted on his heart and soul. It was indelible, like a permanent tattoo.

"I'm sorry we missed you at the parade the other night," Nick said, his voice tinged with regret. "We'd just gotten back from New Hampshire. It's important for Miles to connect with his grandparents." He made a face. "We don't see them too often."

"No worries, although I'm still waiting for you to come to California with my godson. I want to take him hiking in the canyons and to my favorite hibachi place on Sunset."

"I've been meaning to take you up on your offer," Nick said with a grimace, "but things have been a bit rough lately."

That was putting it mildly. Nick's wife, Kara, had been killed in a horrific car accident a few years ago. Their love story had been a beautiful one, and it had been a devastating blow to Nick and Miles to lose their center. Clearly, things hadn't improved much. It was unimaginable that Miles had lost his mother at six years old.

"No need to apologize. I know how tough things have been since you lost Kara."

Nick winced. "It's been two years, but it still seems as if we're stuck in this strange limbo. Unable to move forward and terrified of sliding backwards."

"She was a huge part of your life, Nick. It's going to take some time to heal. You two were the real deal."

A wistful expression crept over Nick's face. "We had it all, didn't we? I couldn't have asked for a better woman. I just wish we could have grown old together."

Dante nodded, knowing there were no words he could say to fully capture what Nick had lost. A thick lump gathered in his throat. He'd missed so much of their love story being so far away from Maine. It wasn't the only thing he hadn't been able to witness up close and personal. When his dad's illness had taken a turn for the worse, he simply hadn't been around. It was hard to process that he would never get a do-over. Those precious moments had slipped through his fingers. That's why he had to make the most of the time he had in Mistletoe. An opportunity like this might never come his way again. He wasn't going to leave with a host of regrets.

"Speaking of the real deal, have you seen Lucy since you've been back?" Nick asked, curiosity in his tone.

"Yes, we've talked," he admitted with a nod. "Needless to say she wasn't too thrilled to see me. I almost got frostbite when we came face-to-face."

Nick burst out laughing. Even though Lucy's initial reaction to seeing him had hurt, Dante joined in on the laughter. It felt like old times sitting here with his childhood friend and shooting the breeze.

"For a while there the two of you were hot and heavy." Nick wiggled his eyebrows. "I thought you guys were going to go the distance. I've never seen a couple so into each other."

Dante made a face. "Things were great until I left town and lost her trust. Can't say I blame her for holding a grudge."

"That was pretty cold, Dante. She was really wrecked after you took off. I'm not going to lie. I was mad at you as well. I couldn't believe you didn't even tell me you were leaving until months after you landed in California." He leaned across the table. "You know there were some serious rumors flying around about your whereabouts and why you took off. There was a lot of gossip about you and Lucy."

Dante felt as if he might have to pick his jaw up from off the floor. "Do I even want to know what they were saying?" Like most small towns, Mistletoe had its fair share of townsfolk who enjoyed flapping their jaws. Sadly, truth and fiction were often blended in the tales. From what he remembered, it had gotten way out of hand at times. He hated knowing he'd placed Lucy's name on the lips of town chatterboxes. No wonder she couldn't stand the sight of him. Even as a teenager, Lucy had been very responsible and mindful of her reputation. And in one fell swoop he'd placed her in a terrible position.

Nick shook his head. "After all these years it doesn't matter. It's best not to dredge it up. You've really done well for yourself, Dante. This town is incredibly proud of you. Between you and Luke, you're town heroes." He raised his cup in a gesture of cheers.

Luke Keegan, Nick's brother, was a Navy SEAL who was currently serving in Afghanistan. As far as heroes went, Luke ran circles around him. He'd received the Medal of Honor, one of the military's highest distinctions. Dante knew he wasn't in Luke's league, but he appreciated Nick's vote of confidence.

"That means a lot to me, although your brother is the real hero. Who would ever have thought I'd be welcomed back to Mistletoe with a ticker tape parade?" He let out a throaty laugh. "I guess they forgot about all the trouble I used to get into."

"Lucy believed in you more than anyone else. She was always hyping you up and telling anyone who would listen how you were going to become a household name one day."

"Before or after I left?" he asked. He thought he already knew the answer, but his curiosity got the better of him. When it came to Lucy he didn't have much sense.

"Before," Nick said, acknowledging what Dante had suspected. "When I asked her where you'd gone after you took off, she told me never to mention you again. And I didn't. Not even once." Nick's comments made the hairs on the back of his neck tingle. It gave him a glimpse into Lucy's reaction to his departure. It wasn't pretty.

Dante drained the last of his drink. Would he ever stop feeling guilty about leaving Lucy, his family, and his friends in the lurch? At the time he'd acted from a place of sheer panic and a desire to get away from Mistletoe as fast as he possibly could. He wasn't sure he could ever fully explain his departure in a way anyone could understand. Staying would have meant giving up his dream of becoming an actor. But also tensions with his father had escalated to a boiling point. When they'd gotten in each other's faces and Dante had fisted his hands at his sides, he'd been terrified of his own anger. It had felt as if they were on the brink of a physical altercation. He had to leave before he did something he would regret.

"I wish I'd handled things differently," he conceded. "Part of being back here gives me a shot at fixing things."

Nick's eyes widened. "With Lucy?"

"Not just with Lucy." He sighed. "I need to repair things with my family. Troy, in particular." Dante hadn't had a civil word with his brother for years. Troy had iced him out at his father's funeral. They hadn't spoken since.

Nick let out a low whistle. "I was wondering what was up between the two of you. I assume things are still frosty?"

"Chillier than a Maine winter," Dante quipped. "Troy's a lot like my dad. They don't bend easily."

"Troy's a lot like your dad?" Nick asked, letting out a hearty chuckle. "That's hilarious."

"What? You think the old man and I were alike?" Dante asked, feeling stunned by the comparison. John West had been strong-willed and inflexible. He and Dante had butted heads throughout his childhood and adolescence. Dante couldn't remember a time when his dad had been proud of him. That knowledge still served as a swift kick in the gut.

"Two peas in a pod. It was one of the reasons you clashed so much. Neither one of you ever wanted to give an inch to the other." Nick picked up his coffee and polished off the contents.

"When did you get so smart?" Dante asked, mulling over his friend's comment. Never in a million years had he ever thought he and his pops were similar. The truth was he probably hadn't wanted to see what had always been right under his nose. Dante had spent years resenting his father's failure to see his potential, but perhaps there had been a lot more going on than he'd been willing to acknowledge.

He'd known that Pops loved him, but they'd had trouble resolving their issues with each other.

Nick grinned. "I was always at the top of the class. While you were being chased by all the girls, I was hitting the books."

Dante scoffed. "You didn't have your nose in a book all the time. I seem to remember you being the mastermind of some of our wildest schemes. Remember the prank with the principal's car?"

Nick raised a finger to his lips. "Shh. Don't ever tell Miles that his dad was a rebel without a cause. I want him to believe I always walked a straight and narrow path. That way I'll have a chance of keeping him in line. I am not looking forward to the rebellious years."

"Whatever you say. He won't hear a thing from me." Dante chuckled as high school memories came into sharp focus. Those halcyon days had been filled with pure magic. Friday night lights at the football field and gazing up at the moon from Hawk's Hill. He wished he'd appreciated it more at the time rather than looking off into the horizon for something better. Growing up in Mistletoe had given him a rock-steady foundation, as well as a loving family and a host of friends. And Lucy. He couldn't have asked for more. If he could go back in time, Dante would hold on to things a little tighter and cherish the precious moments that were now nothing more than dust in the wind.

When Dante and Nick parted ways a few minutes later, he sat in his car for a few moments contemplating his next move. After his meeting this evening with the film crew,

Dante would have some breathing room for a few days. He didn't have to head back to the set until Tuesday morning, so the rest of his weekend was free, except for a few hours of running through the script and making any necessary adjustments. He let out a ragged sigh and leaned over so his head was slumped on the steering wheel.

He'd been ducking this moment ever since coming back to Mistletoe. Dante knew he couldn't avoid it any longer. It was time to seek out his younger brother and squash the beef that had been causing tension ever since he'd skipped town. It was ridiculous to be filming in their small home-town and not be on speaking terms with Troy. Back when they were kids, Troy had been his best friend and closest ally. They had been inseparable—from the sandbox to Boy Scouts to the football field. Everything had blown up once his father had been diagnosed with leukemia. Nothing had been the same between them since. Dante feared it never would be.

* * *

"You agreed to what?" Stella was gaping at her with eyes that threatened to pop out of her head.

For the hundredth time since she'd agreed to allow Dante to film at the library, Lucy wondered if she'd made the wrong decision. The expression on her sister's face increased her worry tenfold. Between the two of them, Stella had always been the sensible sister while Lucy had been a bit more rash in her decision-making. Was she being foolish to think she could deal with Dante's proximity while he filmed at the library? Had she agreed to his proposition too quickly?

"Okay, just hear me out," Lucy said, holding up her hands. "I had two choices. My first choice would have been to tell him to kick rocks. The second choice was to say yes and get a big fat check for the library." She let out a frustrated sound. "I could never forgive myself if I didn't jump at the chance to help out with the library's deficit. And let's face it, if I'd said no he could have gone way over my head for a yes. How could I explain turning down an opportunity to put some money in the library's coffers? You know how bad the situation has been."

Stella knitted her brows. "But you'll have to see him all the time. The library isn't big enough for you to avoid him. Need I remind you that you had a mini meltdown about him being back in town just yesterday?"

Lucy frowned at her sister's usage of the phrase *mini meltdown*. She wouldn't exactly describe it that way. In her opinion, it had been a breakthrough, not a breakdown.

"I know, but it's a small price to pay so my library can flourish." Lucy put on her best fake smile. "He also promised to show up for Tess as her special guest at school."

Stella groaned. "And deeper and deeper you go into the rabbit hole."

"What's that supposed to mean?" Lucy asked in a huffy voice.

"You're getting tied up in him all over again. He's back in town for less than forty-eight hours and you're already making nice with him." Stella *tsk*ed.

Lucy drew herself up to her full height of five foot four inches. "Making nice? Did you actually say those words out loud to me?"

"That's what it sounds like to me," Stella answered in a quiet voice. She folded her arms across her chest and began to tap her foot on the hardwood floor.

"I was not making nice with Dante. I was trying to make the best out of a crappy situation. There's absolutely nothing I can do about the fact that he's back in Mistletoe. The mayor literally handed him the key to the town. He's got a Mistletoe fan club the size of Texas." She paused to catch her breath. It felt like steam was coming out of her ears. She couldn't admit it to Stella, but it still hurt that Dante had accomplished so much greatness after cutting her loose. It made her feel like such a fool for believing he'd been just as much in love with her as she'd been with him. With Dante's return to Mistletoe so many buried emotions were rising to the surface. Lucy wasn't sure how long she could hold it together without erupting.

*Take it easy*, she reminded herself. Dante was going to be in town only for the holidays. Before she knew it, he'd blow back out of town just like a snowstorm. And her beloved library would financially benefit from Dante's production. *Namaste.* Deep breaths.

"I'm worried about you." Stella's eyes began to mist over. "I saw what Dante did to you last time around. I don't ever want to see that defeated look in your eyes again."

Lucy hugged Stella. She loved how her big sister still looked out for her even though she was a grown woman.

Stella's heart was as wide and constant as the deepest ocean. Even though she would continue to cry on her sister's shoulder, she needed to face this situation with Dante on her own. "It's time I got my degree in adulting, Stella. The hard part is already over." She shrugged. "Seeing him for the first time felt like a thunderbolt. After all these years I suppose I built him up in my mind and idealized our relationship. I don't love him anymore. Those feelings died a long time ago." Stella didn't need to know that the sight of Dante caused Lucy's tummy to do somersaults. It certainly wasn't love, she reassured herself. He was a gorgeous man who made women melt by simply being in his presence. That's why they paid him the big bucks in Hollywood.

Stella eyed her with suspicion. "You were pretty hyped up yesterday about a man who you don't care about."

"Okay, that's fair. I may have been a little salty, but I needed to get all that out of my system. You said it yourself. I didn't get any closure with Dante. And then he comes sweeping back into Mistletoe as this larger-than-life figure, applauded by the entire town. Can't a girl feel some kind of way about it?"

Stella narrowed her gaze as she studied Lucy. "You're right. It's okay that you vented," she said. "You're allowed to feel any way you want to about Dante. Who am I to judge?"

Lucy heard the emotion in her voice. She reached out and squeezed Stella's hand. Although she didn't bring it up in conversation much, Lucy knew her sister was still dealing with her own heartbreak, which she'd handled in a much more low-key manner than Lucy. While it had always been Lucy's style to wear her emotions on her sleeve, her older sister had been calm and cool on the surface. Stella had gone inward, never allowing anyone to see her pain and humiliation after being dumped by her fiancé.

Lucy rubbed her hands together. "All I want is a ginormous amount of money to make magic happen with the library." She clapped her hands together. "Show me the money. With these funds from Dante's production company, things are really going to improve at the library. We may even be able to add some more hours for the patrons on Saturday." Lucy could feel a big smile tugging at the corners of her mouth. Excitement was building up inside of her at the prospect of being able to help fix some of the issues at the library instead of standing around wringing her hands about it.

The library was way more important than her angry feelings toward Dante.

Stella's voice softened. "I know how much the library means to you, so it sounds like you did what you had to do. I'm sure Dante knew he was dangling an irresistible carrot in front of your eyes."

Lucy knew Stella was right. He, more than almost anyone else, knew what the library meant to her. Back when they were young and in love and besties, it had been one of their hangout places. Lucy had worked at the library stocking shelves and she'd fallen in love with the place and with Dante. Her chest tightened painfully as the memories assailed her senses.

Why, after all this time, did they still cut so deep? Why hadn't she completely moved on with someone else? She wasn't one of those women who believed everyone had to be booed up all the time, but surely she should have had at least one significant relationship since Dante.

*Because you loved him.* Truly. Madly. Deeply. It hadn't just been puppy love. For Lucy, it had been more authentic than anything she'd ever known in her young life. Dante had been her everything. Until he wasn't. It had taken her years to mend her broken heart and push him to the back of her mind. It hadn't been easy, but she'd done it.

But now he was back in Mistletoe. And Stella's cautionary words were worrying her a little bit. Dante had an abundance of charm and their history together showed she was vulnerable to him. Who wouldn't fall for the guy? He was even more appealing now as a famous movie star with the world at his fingertips.

It was so easy for someone like Dante to waltz back into town and lay claim to everything he wanted. She'd wanted things too. Back when they'd dreamed of a future together Lucy had planned to travel the world once Dante landed some acting jobs in California. They'd talked about Lucy attending school at UCLA while Dante went on auditions. Somewhere along the way, Lucy had stopped dreaming. And it was all Dante's fault. He'd made her believe in the futility of her aspirations. He'd convinced her that her hopes weren't important the day he'd left her behind.

This time around she was going to make sure to grab ahold of the things she desired as well. Once and for all she was going to excise Dante from the deepest regions of her heart. And unlike the last time he'd raced out of town, Lucy wouldn't be crushed by his departure when he headed back to Hollywood.

# CHAPTER FIVE

D ante pulled up in front of West Hardware Store and parked his rented SUV two doors down. When he stepped out of his vehicle he stood back and surveyed the exterior of the store. It had changed a lot since the days when his dad ran the place. A fresh coat of paint, along with a brand-new brass-and-black sign plus new trim had revitalized the store. It no longer resembled something from a bygone era. Dante grinned at the sight of the fully lit Christmas tree shimmering from the front window. It had been a holiday ritual for his family to come to the store and help set up the Christmas display.

He felt a pang at the notion that he hadn't been around to help Troy with the holiday setup. If he was being honest with himself, it had been almost a decade since he'd helped out with the family business. It was probably one of the many reasons his brother couldn't stand the sight of him. Dante was the one who'd run away from Mistletoe.

Dante took a deep breath before he pushed open the door and entered the hardware store. A rush of nostalgia swept over him as he inhaled the familiar scent of wood and dust. A picture of his dad leapt out at him from behind the counter. With his dark good looks, chiseled features, and the dimple in his chin, John West had been a handsome guy.

He felt a squeeze in the middle of his chest as he gazed at the photo. He'd give anything for his dad to walk through the doors of the shop and greet him with a hearty slap on the back.

"I'll be right with you," a voice called out from the back room. Not wanting to stand on ceremony, Dante headed in the direction of his brother's voice.

For a moment he stood at a discreet distance and studied Troy. With only a year separating them, the two brothers had often been mistaken for twins. At six feet tall, Dante was an inch or two taller with a more rugged physique. Troy was broader, with the shoulders of a linebacker.

"Hey," Dante said, speaking from across the room. "How's it going?"

Troy swung his gaze up at the sound of his voice. His jaw clenched at the sight of him. He grunted out a greeting that Dante couldn't quite make out. At least he'd gotten a response, Dante reasoned. Troy had been radio silent ever since the funeral, with Dante's attempts to reach out going unanswered.

"What brings you by?" Troy asked. "I thought you'd be somewhere signing autographs or something."

Dante gritted his teeth. So it was going to be like that,

was it? Troy was like a dog with a bone. He just couldn't let it go. "I thought it was time we settled things between us," Dante said, walking toward Troy until they were only mere inches apart from each other.

"I've got work to do," his brother said in a clipped tone. "Some of us have to pay the bills."

Dante sucked his teeth. "Don't start that with me. It's getting really old. I know what work is."

Troy rolled his eyes. "Sure. I've seen the pictures of you in the tabloids sunbathing all over the globe with Victoria's Secret models. Such a chore."

He clenched his fists at his side. Troy loved to diminish Dante's career and the hard work that had earned him a spot among Hollywood's highest-paid actors. His little brother acted as if Dante hadn't worked extremely hard to earn his success. It royally pissed him off. He'd suspected for a long time now that Troy was jealous, but it didn't justify him acting like an idiot. Suddenly, all his plans to repair things with Troy went up in smoke. He wasn't the one being nasty and sarcastic. As usual, Troy was throwing grenades in his direction.

He could fight fire with fire. If Troy wanted to go below the belt, he could go lower. This back and forth was what they'd done throughout their childhood. The familiar rhythms of their sibling dynamics were hard to resist.

He shrugged. "What can I say? I get to do what I love. You should try it sometime," Dante drawled. "It takes courage to follow your dreams. But I guess you wouldn't know about that, would you?"

*Bam!* Drop the mic. It was the crux of Troy's issues with him. He resented Dante for daring to reach for the brass ring. Back in the day his brother had wanted to pursue a career as a writer, but he'd left it by the wayside in order to run the family store.

Troy glared at him. Steam was practically coming out of his ears.

"Look at you," Troy sneered. "Coming back to town like a rooster, crowing about your success. You haven't changed one bit. Still the same old showboat."

"And you're still stewing because you didn't get to live the life you imagined. It's not my fault that I made a success of myself."

Troy jutted his chin in the direction of a newspaper.

"Take a copy on your way out. I know you love good press." The look in Troy's eyes hinted he had something up his sleeve.

Dante glanced at the paper. The *Mistletoe Gazette*. Even from this vantage point he could read the headline. "*Dante West. Hero or Heartbreaker?*" Dante read on. "*Mistletoe's hometown hero has left a swath of broken hearts in his wake in Hollywood. Should the women in town run for cover?*" The words felt like sawdust in Dante's mouth. Who would have written such trash? He wasn't a man who went around trampling on hearts, and he certainly didn't consider himself a hero. In his eyes, men like Luke Keegan who fought battles for America's freedoms were heroic. He loved being an actor, but he wasn't saving people from burning buildings or risking his life on foreign shores.

The headline rattled him. Mistletoe was the last place on earth Dante would have expected to print scandalous headlines like this one. He grabbed the newspaper from the table. Troy's name was at the top as the writer of the article. Dante's jaw dropped. Had Troy really written a hit piece on him? His own brother?

"This is garbage and you know it. When are you going to get over yourself and this resentment you're harboring toward me? We're family!"

Troy let out a brittle laugh. "Family? What a joke. We haven't been that in a long time."

Anger flared inside him. "Retract this crap or you'll be hearing from my attorney." Dante seethed. He'd had enough of this nonsense with the tabloids back in Los Angeles. He hadn't expected to be raked over the coals in Mistletoe.

Troy stuck his chin out. "Hit me with your best shot. Go ahead and sue me."

Dante walked over to Troy, crumpling up the newspaper as he advanced in his direction. He threw it down in front of him. Troy closed the distance between them so they were standing almost chest to chest. Dante's hands bunched into fists at his side as anger surged inside of him. Troy was pushing it. And he was messing with the wrong one. Clearly he'd forgotten how many times Dante had kicked his butt when they were younger.

A loud whistle cut through all the noise roiling around in Dante's head. "All right, boys. Enough! You're acting like five-year-olds." Lucy was standing in the doorway with a frown knitting her brows together. She moved in their direction, placing her body in the middle of them with her palms facing outward to push them away from each other.

"Lucy, I can handle this. You don't need to get involved," Dante said. She was the last person he wanted as a referee between him and his knucklehead of a brother.

"Dante. Why don't you come outside with me and get some fresh air?" Lucy suggested as she placed her hands on his chest and backed him up a few steps. "I'll come back later for my order, Troy."

"Good riddance, big brother," Troy muttered. "Don't let the door hit you on the way out."

Lucy grabbed ahold of Dante's sleeve and led him to the door. Once he was outside, a cold, biting wind whipped against his face. It was just what he needed at the moment. He let out a strangled sound of frustration.

"Are you okay? What brought that on?" Lucy asked. He turned around to face her. Her big brown eyes radiated concern. It cut through his annoyance with Troy to know that on some level Lucy still cared about him. He didn't want to examine why it meant so much to him.

"I'm fine," he said. "Some things never change. He's trying to trash me in an article he wrote for the town newspaper. I should have known better than to come over here."

Lucy's eyes widened. "You two really know how to push each other's buttons."

He frowned. "I forgot how annoying he can be," he said. "I swung by to see if we could squash things. He was hostile from the moment I said hello."

Lucy shook her head. "It's such a shame. Back in the day you two were joined at the hip."

"That was a long time ago. I don't know why I even bothered trying to make things right between us."

Lucy shrugged. "Maybe because he's your brother. And you love him."

"Not today I don't." Both of them knew it wasn't true, but he was still aggravated and on edge from the confrontation. Lucy was right on the money regarding his past closeness with Troy. Once they had been practically inseparable. Like Dante, his brother had been a member of the football team. Troy had always been much better than him. There had even been talk of Troy heading to the pros after college, but he'd dropped out of school and ruined his prospects. That, along with his snuffed-out writing dreams, had left him bitter.

The division between them bugged Dante, but he was helpless to change things for the better. Maybe he needed to face facts. Some things weren't fixable.

Lucy held out her arms and began moving them wildly around. She starting dancing as if she was attending a Zumba class. "You need to shake it off," she urged him.

Dante cocked his head to the side and studied her. She resembled a flamingo doing a wild dance. The women he knew back in California would never do such a thing in public. Most of them were too concerned about their image to cut loose. "That's what I've always liked about you, Luce. You really don't care about making a fool of yourself," he said with a low chuckle.

"Thanks a lot," she grumbled, making a face at him. "Some gratitude I get for trying to ease the tension."

He placed his hands over his heart. "I'm very grateful to you. I needed that laugh."

A slight smile hovered around her lips. "Okay, good deed done for the day. I'm heading back inside to pick up my order."

Dante wasn't quite ready for Lucy to walk away from him, even though she looked mighty good from the back. She had curves in all the right places. The years had been good to her. She'd filled out quite nicely. She'd always been stunning, but now she was downright spectacular. Lucy had blossomed like a radiant chrysanthemum. He wished he'd been around to see her transformation.

"Lucy!" he called out. "Are you busy?"

She turned around and eyed him with a great deal of suspicion. "That depends. Why are you asking?"

"I'm heading out to the Christmas tree farm on Butternut Ridge. I want to scope it out for a last-minute filming location." He shifted from one foot to the other. Lucy's steady gaze was making him nervous. "I added a scene to the script and I'm thinking that Sawyer's would make for an amazing visual. Pine and balsam trees as far as the eye can see. A perfect snapshot of Maine."

Lucy didn't say a word. She simply gaped at him. Seconds ticked by without her saying anything. What was he thinking? Lucy didn't want to hang out with him. Just because she'd been worried about the showdown between him and Troy didn't mean she'd forgiven or forgotten.

He was seriously wondering if he'd overstepped by even asking her.

"So, are you going to keep me hanging?" he asked, fully expecting her to turn him down.

The beginnings of a smile curved her lips upward. "You had me at Christmas tree farm."

# CHAPTER SIX

Lucy had no idea how she'd ended up driving with Dante to Sawyer's Christmas tree farm. If anyone had told her a few days ago that she would be seated in his passenger seat as he drove them to one of her favorite destinations in all of Mistletoe, she would have laughed herself silly. But here she was, swaying to the rhythm of Mariah Carey's "All I Want for Christmas Is You" and belting out the words to the song. Dante was tapping his fingers on the steering wheel and humming to the beat. She had to stop herself from sneaking glances at him. After all this time it was odd to be in such close proximity to him. It made her feel a little bit breathless. But there was no way she could have turned down a visit to Sawyer's. Not in a million years.

She was a sucker for the holidays and Christmas trees and anything remotely festive. Her family had been getting their trees at Sawyer's for as long as she could remember. For Lucy it was a magical place where holiday dreams came true. Listening to Christmas music on the radio was a bonus. Unless he had amnesia, Dante knew all of these things about her.

It wasn't as if she really wanted to spend time with him. But it wasn't something she could avoid either, since he was starting filming in a few days at the library. Mayor Finch had already called to impress on Lucy the importance of ensuring everything ran smoothly. The town of Mistletoe would benefit tremendously by being affiliated with Dante West. It was clear to Lucy that she was being asked to roll out the red carpet for Dante and his crew.

The idea of spending time with him still wasn't totally comfortable to her, so perhaps it was a good thing that they got reacquainted so it wasn't awkward. Stepping in between Dante and Troy at the hardware store had been an impulsive act. She hadn't wanted the two of them to come to blows, and from where she'd been standing it had looked pretty volatile.

Dante turned the volume on the radio down. He pointed at his ears. "Sorry, but I'm trying to save my hearing till I'm at least forty."

"Oops. Sorry about that. I can't resist the holiday music," she confessed. "It's such a short window of time if you really think about it. They start playing the songs in November and by December twenty-sixth they've moved on to something else."

"You're not trying to avoid talking to me, are you? Turning up the volume that high is pretty much a conversation killer."

"I can't think of a single reason why I would do something like that," she replied in a syrupy-sweet voice. Surely Dante didn't have the impression that they were back to being besties. What were they supposed to talk about? The strange turn of events that had them together scouting out a possible film location?

"So, tell me about your life. Something not related to your work at the library," Dante said.

Lucy fidgeted in her seat. This was why she should have turned Dante's invitation down flat. He was quizzing her. Why would he want to prod and poke into her business? Compared to his exciting life, hers was a virtual snoozefest.

"Well, after I finish my day at the library I head over the town line to Bourne. There's a club there called the Limelight. That's when I turn into my alter ego, Lucinda." She couldn't keep a straight face and began cracking up.

"Come on. I'm serious," he said, his lips twitching. "Update me on what you've been doing for the last eight and a half years or so."

Lucy glanced over at him. Even in profile he was disgustingly handsome. He had a strong jaw, great eyebrows, and a classic nose. Why did men always seem to get better with age? Even the ones who'd battled cystic acne and worn Coke-bottle glasses tended to glow up.

"I went to college at Bowdoin. Then I got my master's in library science. I came back to work at the library and now I'm head librarian." She shrugged. "It's not rip-roaringly exciting, but I'm happy with it."

"That's great, Luce. You always dreamed of being head librarian."

*I had other dreams too*, she wanted to say. Instead she bit her lip and kept quiet. What would be the point in reminding him of something they both already knew? If he'd wanted the life they'd once planned out, he wouldn't have left her high and dry.

"Now you," she said. Lucy already knew Dante's Hollywood story, but she was desperate to fill up the silence. The quiet made her remember. Every word. Every touch. Lucy was a pro at stuffing down the memories. She couldn't allow Dante's return to turn things upside down. As it was, she could barely focus with him sitting mere inches away. A woodsy scent clung to him, appealing to her senses and distracting her from everything else but him.

"Work occupies most of my time. I've been trying to make a name for myself in the acting world, so there hasn't really been time for anything else. At last count I've been in more than twenty-five films." He sent a quick glance in her direction. "I hope that doesn't sound like I'm bragging, but I'm pretty proud of it."

"As you should be," she said. And she meant it. What he'd achieved was nothing short of miraculous. It wasn't every day that a small-town boy from Maine catapulted himself into a household name. It was even rarer for a Black actor to make a big splash in the competitive world of Hollywood. He was like a comet blazing in the sky.

"So, are you single?" Dante asked. She could hear the curiosity in his voice.

"At the moment, yes," she said. She didn't bother telling him that she'd had a shocking lack of romance in her life since his departure. "What about you? I seem to recall reading about you in one of my favorite magazines. You're quite the ladies' man."

Dante scowled. Clearly, she'd hit a nerve. "Don't believe what you read in the scandal rags. Most of it is garbage."

Lucy wasn't brave enough to ask about a certain reality star he'd been photographed with on numerous occasions. She didn't want to run the risk of Dante thinking she still held a torch for him or that she followed every move he made. Because she didn't. Not even a little bit.

"I have to admit, it's a little strange being back home," he said.

"Strange how?" She smirked at him. "It must be nice to have everyone fangirling over you. I could rescue the library from financial ruin, a raging fire, and a flood, yet they still wouldn't throw a parade for me. Or give me a key to the town."

"You've always been beloved in this town. Me, on the other hand..." he said with a shake of his head. "I don't think this town knew what to make of me. It's wonderful to be here, but I feel like I've missed so much." A tremor was visible along his jaw. "I had coffee with Nick this morning. It still bothers me that I was out of the country filming when Kara died."

Lucy heard the regret in his voice. There was no doubt in her mind that he'd truly cared about Kara. She knew he was Miles's godfather, so it was obvious his friendship with Nick had been tight over the years.

She let out a huff of air. "That was a rough one on all of us. It happened so fast. One minute she was dropping off Miles at school and the next she was gone in a horrific accident." A feeling of deep loss swept over Lucy. They'd all grown up together in Mistletoe. Kara had been a sweet and vivacious person. She and Nick had dated all through high school. Unlike her and Dante, they'd gone the distance by getting married and having a family. A drunk driver had stolen their happily ever after from them, and nothing had been the same since. Kara hadn't even made it to her thirtieth birthday. The world had lost a bright light and Nick had lost his true north, the one who'd always kept him on track. Miles had been robbed of a loving mother. None of it had been fair.

Dante stopped at a bear crossing sign. She could feel the heat of his gaze on her. When she turned toward him, she felt her heart stop. Moisture pooled in his eyes.

"I didn't mean to bring up something so traumatic. I've just been trying to figure out a way to help Nick and Miles. Clearly, I'm still struggling to find out how I can do it in a meaningful way."

His words tugged at her heartstrings. It was evident how much he cared about the Keegan family. In the aftermath of Kara's death, the town had rallied around the family. Nick's brother, Luke, had even managed to come back from the Middle East to support them.

On pure instinct, she reached out and touched Dante's hand. "I think having you here is the best medicine of all."

Touching his skin hadn't been the best idea. Right away

she felt as if an electric current were running between them. Her fingertips were practically scorched. Lucy quickly pulled her hand back. Dante shot her a quizzical look. She wondered if he'd felt it too.

Thankfully, they'd just arrived at their destination and Dante was forced to focus on driving into the gated entrance. A large green-and-red sign decorated with holly welcomed them to Sawyer's Christmas tree farm. Lucy let out a little yelp of excitement and clapped her hands together. Suddenly, she was transported back to childhood when it was just her, Stella, and their parents. Tess hadn't even been a twinkle in her parents' eyes at that point. Coming to Sawyer's had been a yearly ritual filled with fun, frivolity, and the magic of the holidays. Picking out the perfect tree to place in front of their living room window had been a blast. Things had been so much simpler then. She still adored Christmas, but she no longer looked at it through a childlike lens.

"We're here," Dante announced, dragging her away from thoughts of Christmases past. Once he found a spot in the lot, they both exited the vehicle and surveyed the wonder of the famous landmark. Lucy watched as Dante closed his eyes and spread his arms wide. "Aaah," he said, sounding as if he'd arrived at the top of a Himalayan mountain after a demanding trek. "Someone needs to bottle the smell of a Maine Christmas tree farm. They'd make millions." He winked. "And it would be good for the soul too."

She wasn't about to disagree with him. There was something so calming about this scent. It could probably lull babies to sleep and make the worst curmudgeon weep with happiness. It was an elixir.

As they walked toward the rows of trees, several people stopped and gawked at Dante. He was good-natured about it, grinning and saying hello but not stopping to confirm his identity. A few folks rudely snapped pictures on their phones. Dante didn't appear to be overly bothered by it, which was very generous of him. Lucy couldn't imagine how difficult it would be to live any kind of normal life with his type of fame.

"Is it always like this?" she asked in a low voice. Lucy wasn't used to people gawking at her with such fascination. It was kind of creepy as far as she was concerned.

"This is nothing," he said with a laugh. "I've had paparazzi go through my trash and get so close to me I could tell you what they ate for breakfast."

Lucy made a face. "Well, that's just gross."

"My sentiments exactly," he said, chuckling.

She liked the sound of his laugh. It was deep and hearty, bringing to mind the younger version of him that she'd fallen madly in love with when she was a teenager. This, she thought, was the Dante she'd spent countless hours with all over Mistletoe.

"Dante. You've got to be kidding me!" A voice rang out behind them.

When they turned around, Lou Sawyer, the owner of the tree farm, was standing there with a stupefied expression.

"Lou!" Dante called out, his face lit up with delight. The two men exchanged a heartfelt bear hug. Lou was a beloved member of the Mistletoe community. With his salt-and-pepper hair, twinkling blue eyes, and perpetual grin, Lou radiated good vibes. Both she and Dante had known Lou ever since they were toddlers. In many ways, he represented the joy of the holidays. His Christmas tree farm had played a role in the lives of most of the folks who lived in Mistletoe. It was a holiday staple in these parts.

"Hey, Lucy. I can't believe this guy surprised me like this," Lou said, jerking his chin in Dante's direction. "The single best teenaged employee I ever had. I didn't expect you to come all the way out here. I imagined you'd send one of your crew members to check the place out."

Dante looked around him and spread out his arms. "And miss all of this? No way, Lou. My memories of this place are ingrained in me. It's the most serene and beautiful place in all of New England."

Lucy didn't know if she'd ever seen Lou smile so wide. She wasn't sure if he would ever recover if Dante didn't select his tree farm as a site for his movie. She couldn't say she blamed him. Being chosen by Dante would give Lou's business a lucrative payday and a great deal of free publicity. It might even make Sawyer's Christmas tree farm famous outside of this region of Maine.

"That's what I like to hear," Lou said. "I'll get out of your hair so the two of you can look around in peace. Let me know if you have any questions. And don't forget to grab some hot cocoa and marshmallows." With a wave of his hand, Lou headed over to some customers who were eyeballing a gorgeous Fraser fir.

"I think he might cry if you don't pick this place," Lucy said in a low voice. "He seems really stoked about it." The thought of Lou being disappointed made Lucy's heart ache.

Dante quirked his mouth. "It has to feel right for the movie," Dante said. "This particular scene is a pivotal one in the film. It's when both of the main characters come to a huge realization."

He began walking back and forth between rows of trees with Lucy trailing behind him. He stopped in his tracks and looked around. "It's just like I remembered it. My favorite part of being here was always the sleigh rides and hot chocolate."

"Mine too," she said as she took a walk down memory lane alongside him. "Remember the bonfires where we toasted marshmallows after we picked our special tree? And how we would all huddle under blankets on the sleigh rides? Those are some of my fondest Christmas memories."

"Those were the days," he murmured. "Wait. I'm going to correct myself. We had our first kiss here. That had to be the best moment I've ever spent here."

First kiss? She knew the exact location of her first official kiss with Dante, and it certainly hadn't been at Sawyer's Christmas tree farm.

She eyed him skeptically. "Clearly you're thinking of someone else. Maybe Gillian Robinson. Or Fran Simmons. We didn't have our first kiss here."

Dante's eyes glinted mischievously. "Oh yes, we did. I can't believe you don't remember!"

"Refresh my memory. Please. I can't wait to rub it in your face just how wrong you are."

"All right. We were five, maybe six years old. Our families came out here together for some sort of holiday event."

"Twinkle Under the Stars," Lucy said. She remembered the event vividly, even though she'd been in first grade. All the decorations for the holiday extravaganza had been stars. Silver, gold, red, and green. It had been a little girl's dream. And there had been trees shimmering with glittery stars. Lucy had been in six-year-old heaven.

"See. You remember," Dante said, nodding. "While the adults were listening to Christmas music under the stars, we were having our kiddie party watching *Rudolph the Red-Nosed Reindeer*. When Rudolph fell for Clarice, I was inspired, so I made my move. I kissed you."

Lucy squealed with outrage. "That wasn't a kiss. That was you trying to get some Oreo crumbs off my lips because you were the greediest little kid on the planet."

"What? You know that's not true. That was a genuine, bona fide kiss between two youngsters who had a crush on each other. Denying my version of events is really crushing!"

Lucy let out a hoot of laughter that drew a lot of curious stares from customers. She clapped a hand over her mouth to silence herself. The last thing she wanted was to be at the center of any rumors about Dante. She could just hear the whispers now. Dante reached out and removed her hand from her mouth. Instead of releasing it, he held on to her mittened hand.

Her eyes locked with Dante's and she thought she heard a little sigh slip past his lips. The air was so cold there was fog coming from his breath. In no time flat the atmosphere became charged with electricity. One moment they'd been laughing, and in the very next, something hovered in the air between them that made her want to run in the other direction.

"What can I say? You've always had very kissable lips, Lucy." Dante's words caused tremors to reverberate through her body—from head to toe. He moved closer to her so that only a few inches separated them. His nearness was making her legs feel wobbly. She looked up to meet his gaze as something hummed and pulsed all around them. He radiated pure heat.

Crazy as it seemed, she had the distinct impression that Dante was thinking about kissing her. He was getting closer and closer to her while his eyes were focused intently on her mouth. And suddenly she was imagining what it would be like to lock lips with him after all this time. What it might feel like to have Dante move his lips over hers. Instinctively, she took a step backward. He was way too close for comfort. For a moment there she'd been mesmerized by his seductive brown eyes and laidback charm. She knew all too well how easy it would be to fall right over the edge and into his arms.

"I-I really have to get going," she said in a trembling voice. "I wasn't expecting to even come out here today. I've got a lot of errands to run in town." She clenched her hands at her sides. She sounded like a nervous schoolgirl instead of a polished and professional head librarian. Without uttering another word, Lucy quickly turned on her heel and headed in the opposite direction.

"Lucy!" Dante called after her. "You're going the wrong way!"

After realizing she was heading away from the lot, Lucy reversed course and walked back toward Dante, who had the good manners not to smirk at her as she walked past him. His brows were knitted together in a look of utter confusion. She really didn't know what she would have done if he'd laughed at her. Her emotions were on the verge of overflowing. She was frustrated and confused and mad at herself. If he'd planted one on her, Lucy wasn't sure she wouldn't have kissed him back. And that made her upset with herself and Dante. His ability to draw her toward him like a magnet was maddening. Honestly, she'd had about enough of him for one day. She'd been foolish to accompany him on this outing and now she regretted it. Sure, there had been lighthearted moments between them where she'd truly believed that they could move beyond their tangled past, but there had been other times when the awareness between them had threatened to rage out of control.

She didn't want to forget how awful he'd been to her because it would mean she'd forgiven him. And she didn't! She hadn't! Lucy didn't want to get sucked in by him because she didn't have a good defense against his massive appeal. It annoyed her to no end that she'd gotten a slight thrill out of the prospect of locking lips with her famous ex.

What was wrong with her? A kiss wouldn't erase the past. As they walked past the gift shop, Lou popped out.

"Hey! Where are you going?" Lou called out to them. "You two didn't even have your hot cocoa. What's the big rush?"

Dante sent Lou a thumbs-up and shouted back, "Next time, Lou. I want to use your tree farm in the film. I'll give you a call later with all the details."

Lou let out a celebratory shout. "You won't regret this, Dante!"

Dante called out, "I know I won't."

Lucy turned away and increased her stride. It felt imperative that she create some distance between her and Dante, if only for a few minutes. She could hear the sound of shoes crunching in the snow behind her. By the time she reached the car, he'd caught up with her.

"Wait up, Luce. Where's the fire at?" he asked, a bit out of breath. Humph! For an action star, Dante sure needed to work on his cardio fitness. He should be walking circles around her.

"I just need to get out of here," she explained, avoiding all eye contact as she jumped in the passenger side of the vehicle once he'd unlocked it.

She could feel Dante's eyes on her as he got situated in the driver's seat. He wasn't saying anything, but she knew he was wondering what was up with her. At the moment she didn't really care whether he viewed her as moody or fickle or a downright lunatic. Although she usually loved visiting Sawyer's tree farm, Lucy was full of regret about joining Dante on this little excursion. She'd let her guard down with him, and as a result, Lucy had placed herself too close to the fire.

Dante had almost kissed her. And the truth was, a part of her had wanted him to do it more than she'd ever wanted anything in her life.

# CHAPTER SEVEN

W ho said you can't go home again?" Dante asked as he pulled into the driveway of 22 Silver Bell Lane.

Things had been running way too smoothly for him ever since he'd arrived in town. He should have known better than to expect his run of good luck to continue for long. One of his principal actors had come down with a bad case of the flu, making it impossible for him to be in the film. Dante had been forced to hire a last-minute replacement based solely on a recommendation from a fellow actor. The replacement actor was flying into Maine tomorrow morning so he could meet up with the rest of the cast for rehearsal. Things had to go flawlessly or they ran the risk of coming up against delays, which ultimately meant costs would run over budget.

To make matters worse, last night a boiler problem at the Knightsbridge Inn had left Dante and his crew without accommodations. The entire place had been in disarray with no heat or hot water. He'd spent the morning making arrangements for his cast and crew to stay at various Airbnbs throughout town for a few days until the issues were fixed. Because Mistletoe was so small, the inn was the only establishment of its kind in the area. Because he had been able to secure lodging only for the cast and crew, Dante was relocating to his mother's place. She'd been ecstatic when he'd called her earlier to ask if he could stay at her house.

*Come on over*, she'd said. *I never understood why you weren't staying here in the first place. There's plenty of room.*

He wasn't sure if his mother was playing an innocent act. She knew that her two sons were at odds with each other. With Troy still living at the house, Dante hadn't wanted to rock the boat by staying under the same roof as him. But now, fate hadn't given him much choice. Bunking at his childhood home was the only thing that made sense given the scarcity of housing in Mistletoe. He would be so busy filming and trying to keep the cast focused that he wouldn't even be here much. It would simply be a place to crash at night.

Dante smiled as he stood on the wraparound porch of his mother's house and looked up at his childhood home. The two-story white colonial held so many childhood memories. It had been a place filled with joy. The West family had been a large and boisterous clan, known throughout town for being athletic and energetic.

His mother swung open the door before he'd even knocked. Her arms were wide open.

"Dante! Welcome home," Mimi said, wrapping her arms around his waist and letting out a squeal of excitement. For the life of him, he didn't understand how a petite woman like his mother could practically squeeze the breath out of him.

"Okay, Mama. You're going to have to let me go so I can come inside. It's tough to breathe when you're hugging the life out of me."

His mother released him, and Dante stepped over the threshold into the house. Once he was inside, Mimi wagged a finger in his direction. "That'll teach you to stay away from home for so long. I've missed you like nobody's business."

He bent down and placed a loving kiss on her temple. "Well, you've got me till after Christmas, Mama. That should make you happy."

"You have no idea. I can't think of the last time we spent the holidays together." She clapped her hands together. "I can't wait to bring you to my bridge group and my book club. They've been dying to meet my famous son."

Dante wanted to groan. Mimi West was a very humble woman, but when it came to her oldest son she enjoyed showing him off to her buddies. More times than not, her cronies wanted to play matchmaker between him and their daughters. It was always painfully awkward for Dante since he never wanted to insult his mother's friends or make it seem as if he was a Hollywood snob.

"I'm going to be busy filming, but I'll see what I can do."

She beamed at him. "Come to the kitchen so you can

taste some of my blueberry-lemon bars. I just made them and they're delicious." She grabbed his hand and led him into her homey kitchen that served as the center of the house. An excellent cook and baker, Mimi had won the yearly Mistletoe bakeoff on several occasions with her vast array of desserts. The blueberry-lemon bars were Dante's personal favorite.

"You don't have to tell me twice," Dante said as he sat down at the kitchen table and helped himself to the treat.

His mother sat down across from him and shook her head. "I'm so proud of you for choosing Mistletoe as a shooting location. A town like this could really benefit from extra income."

Her belief in him made his chest tighten with emotion. They'd always had a close relationship and she'd had his back in good times and bad. His mother had never shamed him for leaving his hometown to make a career for himself in Los Angeles. If there was a president of the Dante West fan club, it would be Mimi West.

"I made a lot of mistakes on my way out of Mistletoe. This is a great opportunity to try and do some good here."

She tweaked his cheek. "I believe in you. We all make mistakes. It's what we do next that matters most."

Her poignant words hit him squarely in his heart. "You know you're my best girl, right? You've set the bar really high, and I'm not sure I'll ever find a woman who has your wide-open heart."

His mother winked at him. "She's out there, son. You just have to make sure to keep your eyes and your heart open."

The sound of the front door opening drew their attention to the fact that it was no longer just the two of them. Loud footsteps rang out in the hallway. Within seconds Troy was standing in the doorway to the kitchen. He walked straight past Dante without a word of acknowledgment and placed a kiss on their mother's cheek before heading to the fridge. Dante wondered if this might be the time to settle things outside the way they'd done back in the day. It was high time his little brother manned up and dealt with his bitterness. Dante might just have to shove his fist in his brother's face to make him see things clearly.

"Troy. Don't you dare walk past your brother without speaking! You know I didn't raise you like that." Mimi's tone was filled with a bristling anger her sons both recognized. A softie at heart, Mimi wasn't the type of mother who tolerated rudeness or disrespect. She wasn't afraid to call her kids out even though they were all grown adults.

Troy pulled out a container of apple juice from the fridge and turned around to face Dante. "Hey," Troy mumbled. The greeting was far from friendly. He'd made a point to speak to Dante in the most minimal way possible.

"Hey," Dante said in response. A thick tension hung in the air like a dense fog.

"What are those bags for?" Troy asked, his eyes focusing on Dante's luggage like laser beams.

"Dante's going to be staying here," Mimi said in a no-nonsense tone that brooked no argument. She seemed to be waiting for Troy to make some sort of comment or voice his disapproval. Instead he simply stood there with a shuttered expression.

She looked back and forth between them, her beautiful face marred by a deep scowl. "I don't know what's going on between the two of you, but I suggest you fix what's broken. It's time to put these petty issues to rest. It's what your father would want for his sons." Her voice broke as her slight shoulders shook and tears slid down her cheeks.

At the same time, both Dante and Troy strode to her side to comfort her. Dante drew her into his arms and she buried her face in his chest as Troy patted her back in a soothing manner. Dante felt like an ass. He and Troy were breaking their mother's heart with their fractured relationship. She'd already lost her husband and was still getting used to life without him. It would be a long time before she was past the mourning stage, if ever. Losing the love of her life would stick with her for the remainder of her days. They all needed to be sensitive to that fact and do their best to help in any way possible.

"Please don't cry," Dante begged her. "We'll straighten things out."

"Or die trying," Troy said. His lips twitched with merriment. The familiar saying made Dante chuckle. It was an inside joke between the two of them going all the way back to their middle school years. Clearly, Troy hadn't forgotten the good times or the rapport they'd once shared. Somehow it had gotten buried under the weight of their conflict. Perhaps, now that he was back in town, they could wade through the mess together. For the first time in a long time, he felt a small glimmer of hope about getting back to a place where they'd finished each other's sentences.

His mother raised her head. "See! It's not that difficult to get along, is it?"

Dante and Troy locked eyes. He wasn't getting a warm and fuzzy feeling from his little brother, which meant Troy wasn't going to make it easy for him to broker peace between them. But he'd seen a chink in his brother's armor just now, and he planned to keep hammering away at it until he broke through. His mother wanted peace between her boys, and Dante wanted to make her happy while he still could. His time in Mistletoe was limited. Before he knew it, he would have to fly back to California to film additional scenes for the film and work on postproduction. He had a bucket list of things he needed to set right before he headed back to his regular life. Lucy's face flashed before his eyes. Yesterday he'd gotten a glimpse of the Lucy he'd fallen head over heels for all those years ago.

She'd let down her defenses and shown him the sweet, tender side he'd always adored. She'd gone into protective mode when he and Troy had gotten in each other's faces. It took him back to when she'd been his number one defender against anyone who messed with him. Despite her unassuming façade, she'd always been a firecracker with a wicked sense of humor. Dante had gotten a glimpse of that as well during their outing.

Things had been going well until he'd made the stupid comment about her oh-so-kissable lips. He'd been speaking the absolute truth, but it had been way too soon to say something so intimate. Her response had been to get as far away from Dante as she possibly could. Right before his eyes he'd seen her revert back to the standoffish version of Lucy, the one who'd wanted nothing to do with him.

Lucy still hadn't forgiven him for leaving her behind, and he was starting to wonder if she ever would.

\* \* \*

Lucy stood back and surveyed the main area of the library. All morning she'd been busy decorating the place with Christmas bling. The smell of pine cones drifted through the air along with peppermint from the diffuser she had placed at the circulation desk. There was nothing in this world quite like the holiday season to kick her spirits into high gear. She didn't understand those who went all *bah humbug* and griped about it. What wasn't there to like? Sparkling lights and peppermint hot cocoa. Santa Claus and gaily wrapped presents. Elf on the shelf and heartwarming holiday movies. It was a little slice of *ho ho ho* heaven.

"Do you think it looks Christmasy enough?" she asked as she took a few steps back and surveyed all the decorations with a critical eye.

Lucy had been able to create a festive atmosphere on a shoestring budget. A gorgeous tree—donated by Sawyer's Christmas tree farm—sat in front of the large bay window. She'd decorated the tree in the style of the Victorian era, which gave the tree an elegant appearance. She'd strategically placed red poinsettias all over the library, providing the space with pops of color. At the entrance to the library Lucy had constructed a Christmas tree composed of books. It was whimsical and unique. Garlands decorated with berries and pine cones hung by the staircase. Just for fun she'd set up a little area where patrons could get a Polaroid picture taken of them standing next to the tree and holding up a library book of their choice.

Denny Clark, her coworker who ran the children's program, let out a hearty chuckle. "Is that a serious question, Lucy? You have more Christmas decorations than the Christmas Village shop down on Main Street."

Lucy grinned. It had been her goal to make the place look festive. Mission accomplished! "You know me so well. That's exactly what I wanted to hear."

"Anything for you," Denny said as he hustled over to the story-time area so he could lead toddlers in a reading project. For the hundredth time Lucy wondered if Denny had the hots for her. Stella swore up and down that Denny was madly in love with her, but the very idea of it was ludicrous. He was much younger than her and she'd never thought of him as anything other than a friend and staff member. But she had to wonder about his feelings at moments like this one when his eyes lingered a little too long and held a hint of something deeper than friendship.

Lucy shook off her suspicions about Denny and dug into the huge pile of library books that needed sorting and stacking. Although there were other staffers who could take care of these chores, Lucy enjoyed performing these tasks. It reminded her of her teen years when she'd known without a shadow of a doubt that she would one day become a librarian.

Although Lucy loved working at the Free Library of Mistletoe, the one downside was that she was indoors all day. The library did have lots of windows, but she still yearned to be outside in the fresh air, especially since today signaled the day voting began for the title of most festive holiday decorations. Mistletoe would be bursting at the seams with Christmas cheer as businesses vied for the coveted title bestowed by the townsfolk. At lunchtime, she decided to seize the moment and take a long, brisk walk through town. She very rarely took her full hour for lunch, but today she was going to use every minute of her break. Her staff was very capable of holding down the fort in her absence. She pulled on her navy-blue wool coat and a white knit hat, then replaced her heels for a sturdy pair of winter boots. After stuffing her wallet in her pocket and putting mittens on, she was all set to head into the great outdoors for a while.

Despite the winter chill hovering in Mistletoe this time of year, Lucy loved Maine weather. The wind whipping across her face made her feel energized and vital. She called out and waved to all the townsfolk she crossed paths with as she walked from the library, down Main Street and toward the town green. She couldn't imagine not living in a place where she could interact with friendly, warm faces each and every day. Lucy still longed to travel the world and see all the places she dreamed about, but Mistletoe was the only place she wanted to call home.

Lucy strolled past the downtown shops at a leisurely

pace, pausing to enjoy the artfully decorated windows. Everything looked merry and bright. It gave her warm fuzzies seeing all the wreaths and tinsel. As she crossed the street to make her way to the town green, Lucy noticed a small number of people gathered by the gazebo. As she walked closer, she spotted one of the baristas from her favorite coffee shop. Willa Jeffries was a recent high school graduate who was obsessed with all things related to pop culture. Lucy wouldn't be surprised if she was president of the Dante West fan club.

"Hey, Willa. What's going on?" Lucy asked.

"Hi, Lucy. It's so exciting! They're filming some scenes for Dante West's new movie! I'm going to ask if I can be an extra."

Of course. She knew that Dante was filming all over town, but she hadn't heard any talk of filming taking place on the town green. With the majestic Christmas tree standing tall and proud next to the gazebo, the location was a no-brainer. It was nice to know that Dante still knew all the best places in Mistletoe. He hadn't forgotten its charm. The entire town would come together in one week's time to deck the tree with ornaments and lights. It was one of Lucy's favorite Mistletoe traditions. Because she enjoyed the town's holiday festivities so much, she'd made a point to get more involved this year. Lucy had volunteered to be in charge of Santa's Village, the area where kids in town lined up to meet Santa Claus. Other than the lighting of the tree ceremony, Lucy thought the meet and greet with Santa was the most heartwarming event.

Lucy swung her gaze around the area. Surprisingly, not too many people were gathered, no doubt because of work schedules and school being in session. Lucy had a feeling that most weren't aware of it. If they had been, she was sure the town green would have been swarmed with high school kids wanting to catch a glimpse of Inferno.

Lucy was able to easily get a spot near the front where she could enjoy the action. She caught a glimpse of Dante standing on the sidelines intently watching the scene unfold. On several occasions he yelled cut and went over to speak with the actors. Even from a distance Lucy could tell he was a perfectionist when it came to his work. He appeared to be coaching the actors so they could get the scene right.

As she continued to watch, the male actor lifted the actress up by the waist so she could place an ornament on the Christmas tree. Lucy sucked in a deep breath as she caught a glimpse of the actress's face. She was Lucy's doppelganger. It was jarring just seeing her own face reflected back at her. She looked more like her than either Stella or Tess. Lucy was beginning to feel a strong sense of déjà vu. It washed over her in such intense waves that she felt dizzy. Was she going crazy? Her heart started thundering in her chest and her palms were sweaty. Was this what she thought it was?

She was in such a daze that she wasn't even aware the scene had ended until she heard Dante's voicing calling out to her. She slowly walked toward him, past the cordoned-off area, as her head buzzed with questions.

"Hey there," he said, flashing her a million-dollar smile.

"I'm so glad you came down to watch. I would have invited you, but I assumed you were working."

"I'm on my lunch break," she said. Her head was still spinning.

"So, what did you think? First impressions?" he asked. Lucy could tell he was nervous awaiting her verdict. He still had the same tell. A tremor in his jaw was pulsing like crazy. It was a little bit endearing to see him on pins and needles waiting for her opinion.

"From what I saw it looked romantic and very intense. Definitely a movie I'd be interested in watching."

"Yes! That's what I was going for," Dante said, letting out a sigh that sounded a lot like relief to Lucy's ears. The creases around his eyes softened once she'd given him her thoughts, and he no longer appeared so tightly wound.

She bit her lip. "I might sound certifiable, but is this film about us? I know that might sound self-absorbed, but the ornament, the massive tree on the town green, the way he hoisted her up. We did that, Dante. And your lead. She looks like me. We could be sisters."

Dante didn't respond for a second, which made her wonder if he was questioning her sanity. Heat flamed her cheeks. Why hadn't she just kept her mouth shut? Just as she was about to apologize for sounding so self-indulgent, he nodded. "I'm sorry. I should have said something sooner. You're not imagining things. It's our story."

* * *

Dante winced at the look on Lucy's face. Not only was she stunned, but she looked a bit pissed off, judging by the frown on her face. Her brows were furrowed, which was a sure sign she wasn't pleased. His stomach tensed up at the realization that his grand gesture had backfired. There had been so many times when he'd written her a letter telling her about the film, but each and every time he'd crumpled it up and thrown it in the trash. He'd taken the easy way out instead of dealing with it head-on. And now she was standing here in front of him utterly flabbergasted by the revelation.

"Why?" she asked. "I don't get it."

Why? What could he say that wouldn't sound shocking or insincere? Lucy had no idea that he'd thought about her almost every day for the last eight and a half years. How could he put his feelings into words without sounding ridiculous? She'd written him off years ago, but he'd never gotten over her. Not by a long shot.

All he could do was tell her the truth. "Because it was the most important romantic relationship of my life. Nothing since has even come close, Lucy."

Lucy didn't say anything, but her eyes began to blink fast and furiously. It was a sure sign she was struggling to process his explanation.

"I didn't just come back to make this movie. I came back to try and mend things with the people I care about. You're one of those people. On some level this movie explores the realest part of my life here in Mistletoe."

She vigorously shook her head, her dark strands swirling

around her shoulders. "You can't undo the past. It's not as if you can push a button and fix everything."

Anger surged up inside of him, threatening to swallow him up whole. Couldn't Lucy see that he was trying? He truly wanted to make things right, or at least put his best foot forward. He'd written the script for the movie as a love letter to their youthful relationship. It had been a painful process to relive those moments and face the fact that he'd singlehandedly ruined something beautiful and genuine. It wasn't fair for Lucy to be so dismissive.

He counted to ten and took a few calming breaths. He had a hard time with being misunderstood. It had been the crux of his issues with his dad. Troy as well. It was wrong of Lucy to paint him as this cavalier person who didn't have regret or remorse. It couldn't be further from the truth.

"Don't you think I know that? It's not about erasing the past. It's about acknowledging my mistakes and trying to bridge the gap," Dante said.

"Why? Why do you even care? You have everything in this world a man could ever want. Why is this so important to you?" she asked in a raised voice. Her arms were folded across her chest and she was breathing heavily.

It was a loaded question, and he wasn't sure if Lucy was ready to hear his truths. But he was in too deep now to back out. He moved closer to her, feeling the need for intimacy in this moment. Needing to make Lucy understand where he was coming from.

"Don't you get it, Lucy? When I left Mistletoe I was only focused on making a big splash and getting famous. I was running toward something, but I was also trying to get away from all the fights I was having with my dad. I wasn't thinking about all the bridges I was burning or how lost I would be without you or my family or my friends. It's taken me almost nine years to get to this place where I have the courage to confront the past. That can't be a bad thing."

She shrugged. "I honestly don't know what to think. It feels like a publicity stunt. There's been a lot of hoopla surrounding your return to Mistletoe. And now your film is about our relationship. All of this is happening at the same time as you're trying to branch out with your directorial debut. I can't help but wonder."

Lucy's words served as a dagger to his heart. She sounded so cynical. He knew his actions had been messed up, but he was a new man. Back then he'd allowed fear and desperation to cloud his judgment. He'd been so eager to pursue an acting career that he'd set fire to his life on the way out of Mistletoe. The decision to write the script and film the movie in his hometown had brought up a lot of issues from his past. And rather than run away from them, which he'd always done, Dante had decided to face it. It hurt like crazy that Lucy was questioning his sincerity.

"Are you serious?" he asked. "You really think this is all for show?"

Instead of answering, Lucy kept quiet and looked down at her boots. Her nonresponse spoke volumes. She didn't want to acknowledge that he'd come back to town with the best of intentions. All she saw was a fake.

"I guess you really don't know me at all. Maybe you

never did," he said, shaking his head with disbelief over her baseless accusations. She had no idea how wrong she was, and she didn't seem to care either. He turned away from her and began walking back toward the set, his strides full of anger and purpose. All this time he'd held Lucy in such high esteem. Perhaps the years had changed her in immeasurable ways he was just beginning to realize.

Maybe he didn't know Lucy Marshall at all anymore. And that realization hurt more than anything had in a very long time.

# CHAPTER EIGHT

Y ou really need to get a tree, Lucy, and then put lots of presents under it with my name on them." Tess grinned from ear to ear at the idea of a mountain of gifts awaiting her on Christmas morning.

"You're a stinker," Lucy said, playfully pulling on her sister's pigtail. "Didn't anyone ever tell you Christmas is about giving, not just receiving?"

Tess sighed dramatically. "I know that. And I'm almost done with all my Christmas gifts. They're all one of a kind and homemade. You really do have to pick out your tree soon because all the good ones are going to be taken by the time you get around to it." Tess stood in Lucy's living room with her hands on her hips, surveying the area by her large bay window.

"I know. I've been meaning to do it, but I've been super busy lately," Lucy explained.

"Weren't you at Sawyer's the other day?" Tess asked,

looking up at Lucy with nothing but sugar and spice sparkling in her eyes.

"How did you know that?" she asked. It never ceased to amaze her how quickly gossip spread around Mistletoe. It was a sad shame that her little sister had been eavesdropping so hard that she'd heard about Lucy's visit to the Christmas tree farm.

Tess shrugged. "What can I say? I've got my ear to the ground."

"So, what are they saying?" Lucy asked. She hated gossip, but if her name was at the center of it, she wanted to know exactly what was being whispered.

"Oh, this and that," Tess said, trying to play it cool.

"Do you want chocolate ice cream tonight or not? If so, you better give up the details." Lucy wasn't above bribing Tess for information, especially since she'd allowed her sister to have a sleepover tonight. On a school night, no less. She wasn't quite sure how Tess did it, but she always managed to wrap Lucy firmly around her little finger. Her parents were no better. Sometimes she thought Tess ruled the roost over at her parents' house, but maybe it was a result of her being so much younger than herself and Stella. Tess had been Walt and Leslie's late-in-life baby—a total and utter surprise, according to her parents. At times she wasn't sure they'd ever recovered from the shock.

"Weeeeell," Tess said, drawing out the word in dramatic fashion, "they were mainly dishing about how Dante West can charm the birds from the trees. Somebody said you were a blue jay and that you were bound to get your heart broken all over again."

A blue jay! Someone had actually compared her to a bird! Lucy felt heat stain her cheeks. It was embarrassing to be gossiped about by the citizens of Mistletoe. Especially in such an unflattering light. They seemed to think she was going to repeat the mistakes of the past.

"Lucy, did Dante break your heart once?" Tess asked. Her brown eyes looked troubled, and Lucy hated that her sister was worried about her feelings.

Lucy opened her mouth to deny it but thought better of it. What was the point in lying to her sister? It was her job to teach Tess life lessons, and she had learned so much from having her heart smashed into little pieces by Dante.

"Yes, he did," Lucy admitted. "We were young and in high school. We'd grown up together and he was my best friend before we fell for each other." She felt a smile stretching across her face. No matter how things had ended between them, Lucy had to admit their love story had been amazing.

They'd grown up together in Mistletoe, becoming closer and closer with every passing year. Dante was the popular football player while Lucy had been the sweet girl with her nose always stuck in a book. When he'd kissed her one Christmas Eve when they were sixteen, Lucy remembered asking him what had taken him so long. From that point forward, they'd been inseparable. High school sweethearts who'd dreamed of taking the world by storm and making a life together. Not for a single second had Lucy believed they wouldn't go the distance and live out all their dreams. So when Dante had left town without her, it had truly felt as if the bottom fell out of her world.

"So what happened? Why did he break up with you?" Tess leaned forward and gazed at Lucy with wide eyes, hanging on to Lucy's every word with bated breath. She couldn't backtrack now. Only the truth would suffice, even though she had no idea how to break it all down for a ten-year-old.

"That's a good question," Lucy said. She let out a deeply held breath. Tess had stars in her eyes when it came to Dante, and Lucy had no desire to trash him. At the same time, she wasn't going to sugarcoat it. "You see, Tess, Dante really wanted to pursue a career in acting. He wanted it so badly that he left everything in Mistletoe so he could pursue those dreams. That's not a bad thing, but the way he left was kind of lousy because he didn't say goodbye. And he stayed gone for a really long time." Just putting it into words caused a groundswell of emotion to grab ahold of her. It had been such a shock to wake up to a world without Dante in it. It was now painfully obvious that she'd never really recovered from it. She'd done her best to stuff it all down, but it had always been resting on the surface.

Tess bit her lip and furrowed her brow. "It's great that he became famous, but it sounds like he had to give up a lot to get it," Tess said. "Most of all, you."

Out of the mouths of babes. Her baby sister wasn't blind to the fact that it had been a trade-off. Fame and fortune versus Mistletoe and the people who loved him. But judging by what Dante had told her yesterday, he deeply regretted the way he'd blown out of town and he yearned to make things right. She hadn't given him any credit for wanting to make amends, even though he seemed genuine. Her lingering anger toward him regarding the past had clouded her judgment.

"All right, Tess, I think it's time for a bubble bath and pj's. You have to get up for school in the morning," Lucy said as she looked at her watch. "If you play your cards right I'll make you some blueberry waffles in the morning."

Tess let out a squeal of delight. "Oooh! My favorite breakfast of all time. I'm going to come down and say good night after I put my pj's on, okay?"

"Of course," Lucy said as Tess gave her a hug. "I want my good-night kiss."

Lucy watched Tess scamper upstairs and out of sight. She loved her little sister's optimism and fighting spirit. Had she ever been so fearless? So free? When she was Tess's age she'd chased salamanders in the woods, built forts out of scraps, and dreamed of faraway places and epic adventures. Although she loved her life, Lucy had to admit there were experiences that had slipped through her fingers. Travel. Furthering her education. Love. All those things were still on her bucket list. Every now and again she fantasized about stepping outside of her comfort zone and pursuing those dreams, but the timing never seemed right.

No matter how hard she tried, she couldn't get Dante out of her mind. She hadn't been very nice to him at the town green, and it filled her with regret. Was hurt a legitimate excuse to cause pain to someone else? Lucy had seen the agony in Dante's eyes when she'd questioned his reasons for coming back home. Lucy had always tried to be a good person, but in that moment, she hadn't succeeded. She'd allowed bitterness to take over. That wasn't who she was or who she wanted to be.

It had been a shock realizing that his film was about the two of them. And she still didn't know how to handle his bombshell news that she was the most significant relationship in his life. Hearing it come out of his mouth had been earth-shattering. She hadn't had the proper time to fully digest it. Instead, she'd done everything in her power to push him away even though she knew he'd been showing her his vulnerability.

It still blew her mind that Dante had written a script about their love story and that he was now filming it in their hometown. Although she hadn't reacted well to the news in the moment, she'd come to the realization that it was pretty awesome. And it had to mean something that Dante had chosen to follow this path back to Mistletoe and his past.

She just wasn't sure exactly what.

* * *

*Flowers!* Dante thought with a snort. He was a world-famous celebrity with access to anything under the sun, yet he was standing at Lucy's doorstep clutching a bouquet of roses, lilies, carnations, and tulips. He'd gone back and forth about whether he should even try to apologize, but being in the wrong didn't sit right with him. He cared way too much about Lucy to let this moment pass them by. Even though she'd said some hurtful things to him, he needed to be the bigger person. He'd been the one to set everything in motion eight and a half years ago, and nothing had been the same between them ever since.

Dante wanted to tell her that he was sorry for not being up-front about the movie he was filming. He really should have told her the very first night they'd come face-to-face, but her reaction to seeing him had made him think twice. Lucy had been so full of anger toward him that he'd chickened out. Clearly, it hadn't been the smartest of moves, judging by Lucy's reaction when he finally did tell her the news.

She hadn't been impressed. Not even a little bit. He seemed to have taken several backward steps in their relationship, and he needed to make things right.

When it came to Lucy, he struggled with basic common sense. He wouldn't admit it to a single soul, but she made him nervous in a way no other woman ever had. It was an edge-of-your-seat, heart-pounding sensation that caused pure adrenaline to race through his veins whenever she was nearby. Even thinking about her resulted in his pulse racing.

He stared at the holiday wreath decorated with tiny red-and-green ribbons dotted with lobsters. Dante chuckled at the whimsical decoration. Only in Maine would you find lobsters on a Christmas wreath. Most of the houses in town were already lit up with Christmas lights, although Lucy's lights hadn't yet been strung up. Before he could knock, the front door swung open. Lucy was standing there in a dark pair of formfitting jeans and a thick ruby-colored cable sweater. Her dark tresses were swept up in a high ponytail with tendrils cascading to her shoulders. He tried not to let his gaze linger on her curves. Frankly, her body defied logic with her small waist, rounded hips, and generous backside.

"Dante! What are you doing here?" she asked, clearly startled by his appearance at her home.

He held out the bouquet. "These are for you. I need to apologize for blindsiding you about the movie. That was wrong of me. I need to own that."

She tentatively took the flowers. "These are gorgeous. Come inside. It's freezing out there."

Dante quickly crossed the threshold before she changed her mind. Being inside Lucy's cozy and inviting house felt good. She'd created a warm and homey vibe. The smell of peppermint hovered in the air and a soft glow emanated from the living room.

"I should have told you the truth from the very beginning," he said.

"You should have," she agreed with a nod.

"That's all I wanted to say." Dante didn't want to belabor the point with Lucy or run the risk of annoying her any further. Sometimes an apology was enough.

"I'm sorry too," Lucy said, shocking him with her admission. "I shouldn't have doubted you. I have a hard time separating Dante 2.0 from the ex-boyfriend who hurt me like nobody's business. It wasn't right of me to doubt your sincerity."

He nodded. "It didn't feel good to hear, but I understand where you were coming from," Dante said. "You have no reason to trust me. All I can say is that my reasons for coming back are genuine." He met Lucy's gaze. "Whether you think I'm grandstanding or not, you've always been special to me."

Lucy's lips trembled, and her brown eyes turned a rich merlot color. "If that's true, why did you take off like that? Why couldn't you say goodbye to me and explain everything to my face? That would have made all the difference. As it was, I felt like you threw me away on your way out of town."

He wanted to reach out and take Lucy in his arms to comfort her, but he knew that he needed to finally explain himself. He owed her nothing less, especially since she was still wondering what had happened and why. Maybe he could give her a sense of closure by telling her. Maybe he could free both of them. Perhaps then he wouldn't feel so racked with guilt.

"I left because I was terrified that if I stayed a day longer, I'd never leave at all. Each and every day things were getting more strained between my dad and me. He didn't believe in my dreams and he made it abundantly clear to me that he thought I would fall on my face. He wanted me to stay and run the hardware store with him. We had a pretty intense argument, and it almost got physical. After that, the thought of staying terrified me."

Once the words came out of his mouth, Dante felt as if he could finally breathe around Lucy. She was standing mere inches away from him, her gaze on the bouquet. She was fiddling with the petals rather than looking at him. When she raised her head, there was no mistaking the moisture pooling in her eyes. She placed the bouquet down on the hall table and focused on him.

"I understand being afraid. I've been there. But what about me? We had plans to go to California together. You just left, Dante. One day you were here, dreaming right alongside me. Then the very next you were gone. That note you left didn't give me a single answer. And it took you months to finally reach out to me by phone."

The emotion in her voice threatened to bring him to his knees. He'd done her wrong on so many levels. "And by that time you didn't want anything to do with me," Dante said, old hurts rising to the surface. "If I remember correctly, you pretty much told me to crawl into a hole and die before you hung up." Just remembering that devastating phone call caused him to wince. It had been a huge blow. All his fantasies about him and Lucy had crashed and burned that day. And he'd realized that he alone was responsible.

She threw her hands in the air. "After what you did, do you blame me?" The question hung in the air between them like a grenade ready to explode.

Dante looked down and idly fumbled with his fingers. Did he blame her? Of course he didn't. In leaving Lucy behind, Dante had made the biggest blunder of his life. It had been born out of fear and pride. He hadn't been able to fix it months later when he'd gotten on his feet and won his first role. Dante wasn't sure he'd ever healed from losing Lucy. Part of his relentless drive to achieve superstardom had been a result of their breakup. He'd taken all his tortured feelings and stuffed them down in a dark hole while he clawed his way to the top of the movie industry.

How was Lucy to know how shattered he'd been by the end of their relationship? He'd never been able to tell her. Maybe he should have tried harder. Although it was almost nine years too late, he needed to get it off his chest.

"I know what it did to you, Lucy. But it did things to me too. I know it was my fault, but you weren't the only one who was broken. I was lost without you. I tried my best to hold it together, but everything fell apart. My money dried up really fast and I couldn't call home for help. Not after the way I left. I couldn't even afford a cell phone."

Lucy clasped his hand in hers. She squeezed it gently, then quickly let go. She seemed to be at war with herself over how to act toward him.

"You should have reached out to your family. They would have helped you. No matter what went down before you left, they would have been there for you."

He shuddered. His own pride had stopped him from getting help from his family. He'd regretted it ever since. "It got bad," he admitted. "I was too ashamed to tell anyone, but I slept in my car for months."

Lucy let out a shocked sound. Her beautiful brown skin blanched before his eyes. "Dante! I-I can't believe things got so awful for you."

He rocked back on his feet. "It's one of the reasons I don't take anything for granted in my life. I've been at rock bottom scratching just to survive," he said. "So, you see, I'm glad you weren't with me, because I wouldn't have been able to shield you from the bad things. I would have just brought you down."

"Is that why you didn't contact me? Because of the shame?" she asked. "And your cell phone?"

"Yes. In the beginning, absolutely nothing worked out as I'd planned. I had zero to offer you in California, and by the time I did, you didn't want to hear anything I had to say. Believe me, I don't blame you. I let pride get in the way of us and it burned me."

Lucy's eyes welled up and he knew she was about to cry. He hadn't told her any of these things to make her sad or to draw tears. His confession was long overdue. Part of being back in Mistletoe was taking stock of things. If he truly was going to repair relationships with the people he'd left behind, he needed to peel back the layers. He needed to be guided by the truth.

He wanted so badly to reach out and touch her. To give her comfort. "Hey now. Please don't cry. Because if you do, it's going to make me feel way worse than I already do."

"I'm not going to cry," she said, ducking her head. "I think that I might have something in my eye."

He placed his hand under her chin and lifted it up so that their gazes locked and held. Dante leaned closer and examined her eyes. "I don't see anything but the most gorgeous pair of brown eyes I've ever seen." Lucy's skin blushed prettily at the compliment. At this moment she looked more beautiful than ever. Dante knew it might not be the time or the place, but all he could think about was kissing Lucy senseless.

* * *

It felt as if she might be going crazy. Suddenly, she was Alice in Wonderland tumbling headfirst down the rabbit hole. Dante's soulful brown eyes had the power to pull her under. Something strong pulsed in the air between them as she struggled to process this rapid atmospheric shift. Lucy felt a rush of adrenaline flow through her entire body. With one step, Dante swallowed up the slight distance between them until they were only inches apart. When he reached out and touched her skin, a jolt went through her body. He began to lightly stroke her jaw with his thumb. Lucy looked up at him, feeling as thunderstruck as the very first time she'd known he was going to kiss her. She was far from being sixteen years old, but the butterflies fluttering around in her belly made her feel like a teenager again.

"Lucy." Dante murmured her name right before his head dipped down and he placed his lips over hers. His mouth was warm and inviting. For a moment she simply breathed him in, reveling in his spicy, woodsy scent. As his lips began moving against hers, Lucy kissed him back with equal intensity. The kiss started off leisurely, like a slow-burning fire. Within seconds it intensified, turning into pure molten lava. Lucy parted her lips, allowing Dante's tongue to slide inside.

How had she managed to forget the taste of Dante's lips or the way his kisses made her go weak in the knees? It wasn't as if she hadn't been kissed in the past eight and a half years, but this was way more than locking lips. This felt like surrendering to something bigger than the both of them combined. It was pure heat and electricity. They didn't call him Inferno for nothing.

She felt his hands around her waist right before he pulled her against him so that they were melded together. Lucy could feel his heart thumping in his chest. Her own heart was beating just as wildly. She reached up and wrapped her arms around his neck, drawing him closer. Kissing Dante was way better than she remembered. She was floating, soaring, flying into orbit.

As the kiss ended and they moved away from each other, Lucy wanted to pull him back toward her and continue kissing the life out of him. She looked up at him, marveling at how the years had only intensified his dark good looks. She wasn't sure if he was aware of his magnetic pull, but he had it in spades.

She felt a tad guilty about hooking up with Dante while her baby sister was upstairs taking a bath. At ten years old, Tess was old enough to get herself ready for bed, but she wouldn't put it past her to hear Dante's voice and make a grand appearance. That's the last thing Lucy needed or wanted.

"I really should check on Tess. It's past her bedtime."

"Go take care of your sister. Good night, Lucy," Dante said. He leaned down and pressed a kiss on her temple, his lips like a gentle breeze as they touched her skin.

"Night, Dante," she said in a low voice as he stepped out into the wintry night. She watched for a few minutes as he strode down the walkway and stepped into his vehicle. He zoomed off with his taillights blazing crimson.

Lucy shut the door behind Dante and placed her back against the wood as she pressed her eyes closed and let out a huff of air. She needed a few minutes to recover from the intensity of what had just occurred. In a million years she never would have imagined the turn this night had taken. Hearing about Dante's initial experience in California had been shocking and emotional. Her heart ached for all he'd been through. He'd always been so proud, so it must have been devastating to undergo such a hardship all by himself. All this time Lucy had been imagining Dante leaving Mistletoe and instantly living the high life in Hollywood. It hadn't been true. None of it. Not by a long shot.

When she finally opened her eyes, Tess was standing a few feet away from her, decked out in her fuzzy reindeer pajamas and matching slippers. Her eyes looked like saucers in her little face. Her brown cheeks were flushed. *Uh-oh!* Lucy knew that expression. She'd seen it countless times. Had she been spying on them as they kissed?

"H-how long have you been standing there?" Lucy asked, flabbergasted by the thought of Tess watching her make out with Dante.

"Only for a few minutes," Tess said, wiggling her eyebrows. She rubbed her hands together. "I came down just in time to see the good stuff."

Lucy sputtered. "Tess! Why didn't you just go back upstairs...or cough or something?" Perhaps it was time to give Tess a crash course in etiquette.

"It was so romantic, Lucy. Are you back together? Are

you and Dante West falling in love all over again?" Tess crossed her fingers in prayer-like fashion.

Lucy let out a groan and slapped her hand against her forehead. "Please don't start any rumors. We are not getting back together. It was just a moment in time when we got caught up in the past. And you are not to tell a single living soul about this."

Tess began giggling. "So it's okay for me to tell dead people?" Her shoulders shook with laughter. She covered her mouth with her hand and continued to chuckle.

"Don't tell anyone, dead or alive," Lucy said through gritted teeth. "Under any circumstances." The last thing she wanted to deal with were rumors floating around town about the local librarian and the Hollywood action star. The residents of Mistletoe would eat it up and go back for seconds. And well after Dante had skedaddled out of town, Lucy would have to deal with the fallout. Thanks, but no thanks.

"Sheesh! I promise not to say anything," Tess said with a slight eye roll.

"Thank you," Lucy said, knowing that her baby sister might slip up and spill the beans despite her promise. Being a popular and talkative little girl was a bad combination when it came to town gossip. Lucy hoped Tess would keep her word.

"What is it? You're staring at me," Lucy said, wiping at her mouth in case her lipstick had gotten smeared during her kissing session with Dante.

"Nothing's wrong. I'm just in awe! I really want to be you when I grow up. If I was a grown-up lady and a movie star kissed me, I wouldn't care who knew about it." Tess winked at her. "Matter of fact, I might even tell a few people."

"It's complicated," Lucy said, holding back a chuckle. Way more tangled than a ten-year-old could even begin to understand. It was actually nice that Tess still had an innocent outlook. The thought of someone breaking her heart one day was terrifying.

"It may not be any of my business," Tess said, "but I think Dante likes you. A lot. I can't say I blame him either. You're a babe, Lucy."

Against her will, Lucy felt a smile tugging at her lips. Tess's big heart and endearing personality made her the most loving girl in all of Maine. As much as she'd been an unplanned event in her parents' lives, Lucy couldn't imagine a world without her sister in it. She had changed all of them for the better.

"Let me go tuck you in to bed, little lady. Remember... blueberry waffles await you in the morning," Lucy said as Tess reached out and slipped her hand in Lucy's. As they mounted the stairs, Lucy called out to Google to turn off her living room lights. She couldn't help but notice that the space in front of her living room window was bare. It would look so much better with a festive balsam tree gracing the area. Normally her tree would have been up by this point in the holiday season. For weeks she'd gotten sidetracked with the news of Dante's return, so much so that finding a tree had gone by the wayside.

Tess was right. It was high time she purchased a Christmas tree and spread some holiday cheer around her home.

# CHAPTER NINE

Dante woke up at the crack of dawn as light swept through his window. The glow from the rising sun was a much better way to say hello to the morning than a blaring alarm clock. He had to admit that sleeping in his childhood home was doing wonders for his REM sleep. He couldn't think of the last time he'd slept so soundly. There was something magical about being under this roof again, which is why he'd decided to stay on despite the boiler issues being fixed at the Knightsbridge Inn. Nothing compared to home.

After quickly showering and putting on his clothes, Dante ventured downstairs. The smell of bacon and eggs wafted in the air, causing his stomach to groan in appreciation. It was going to be a long day of filming, and his mother's cooking would be the perfect thing to sustain him throughout the morning. As he stepped into the kitchen, he stopped short. It wasn't his mother who was cooking up a storm. Troy stood at the stove whistling as he whipped up breakfast.

Just as Dante was about to head out of Dodge, Troy turned around and jerked his head in the direction of the kitchen table.

"Sit down. There's no harm in us sharing a meal." His mouth quirked. "I'm sure we can make it through sausage and eggs without killing each other."

Dante grabbed a glass from the cabinet and sat down at the butcher block table. He poured himself some orange juice and watched as Troy finished making breakfast. His brother cooked with such elegance and grace that it made Dante think of some of the famous chefs he was acquainted with back in Los Angeles and all over the world. A few seconds later Troy was placing a plate down in front of him with a heaping amount of food—eggs, sausage, bacon, and grits. Troy sat across from him with an identical plate of food. Instead of juice, he had a mug of steaming coffee by his plate.

For a few minutes they ate in companionable silence. It didn't feel as strained as Dante would have imagined it might. Was this a sign that things were thawing between them? He wasn't sure. Troy was nothing if not unpredictable. When their father was sick, it had been Troy who'd cooked for him in order to give Mama a break. Although Dante had stepped in to pay all the medical bills, Troy had been the good son, the one who'd physically been there for their father. Dante couldn't help but feel as if his being in California while Troy held down the fort in Maine was at the heart of their conflict.

"So, I heard from Lou that you're using the tree farm as

a shooting location. He's over-the-moon excited about it," Troy said as he took a bite of the grits.

"Yeah," Dante said. "It's a special place. It would be perfect for the scene I'll be shooting."

"So what made you want to direct? Did you get tired of those blockbuster paychecks?" Troy asked. The look on his face was a mixture of skepticism and humor. Dante honestly wasn't sure if his brother knew how badly remarks like this one got under his skin. Each and every time it felt like he was pricking at him with a sharp object. When Troy said it, Dante got the impression his brother didn't think he was worth the big money.

For some reason, Troy particularly loved to make comments about Dante's bank balance. Truthfully, it had gotten old a long time ago. Dante sensed an underlying resentment about their differing incomes, but he wasn't going to apologize for being successful. He'd earned every penny the old-fashioned way—by working harder than anybody else and making smart investments with his money.

"Yeah, that's it," Dante snapped. "Those ginormous paydays can be a real pain in the butt." Troy let out a begrudging laugh. It was nice to hear him chuckle since those moments were rare between them. Back in the day there had been nothing but brotherly love between them, and Dante ached to get back to that place in time. He couldn't expect it to happen overnight.

"I actually wrote the script for this film, so it's a labor of love, so to speak. It's my baby from start to finish. I'm writing, producing, and directing," Dante said as pride swelled in his chest. Creatively speaking, this was the most important work of his career.

Troy nodded as he continued to eat. "Sounds like you're branching out in a new direction. That's good. You don't want to be stuck in one lane."

Dante nearly fell out of his chair. He'd expected some more snide comments or even a joke or two, but Troy sounded almost supportive. Maybe hell really had frozen over in Mistletoe. They both continued to dig in to their meal until Dante decided to seize the moment and inquire about something that had been on his mind.

"So, what's the story with Lucy?" Dante asked. "I'm surprised she's still single. Has she been in any serious relationships over the years?" Dante tried to toss the question out casually. He'd been dying to ask Lucy some more personal questions, but given their history, he hadn't been too confident about asking. Since Troy seemed a bit more relaxed this morning, maybe he could fill Dante in.

Troy glowered at him. "Why are you asking about Lucy?"

There was a definite tone in Troy's voice that made Dante want to retract the question. He should have asked Nick instead. Dante stabbed one of the link sausages with his fork and shoved it into his mouth. After swallowing, he shrugged and said, "Just good old-fashioned curiosity. You got a problem with that?"

Troy's mouth had settled into a hard line. "Lucy's a good woman. She held her head up high after you left her in the lurch. Don't come riding back into town and mess with her head. She doesn't deserve that."

Dante slammed his fork down. "I'm not messing with her head. Chill out, will you? You're just looking for a fight." He should have known better than to bring up Lucy. Troy would take the side of a cactus if Dante went up against one.

"I'm not looking for anything. Lucy's my friend and I care about her," Troy said in a heated voice.

Dante narrowed his gaze as he studied his brother from across the table. "Friends? The two of you haven't ever gotten together, have you?" Dante asked as jealousy threatened to choke him. He dreaded the answer. Dante couldn't imagine Troy going that low with his ex-girlfriend, but stranger things had happened. Dante had an actor friend named Raynaldo who had walked in on his wife and one of his costars doing the horizontal tango. Their idyllic marriage had been shattered by her infidelity. The tabloids had run amuck with the sensationalized details and the whole world had tuned in for the details.

Troy met his gaze across the table. "Never. Not once. She's like a sister to me. I just don't want to see her get hurt again. In a few weeks you'll be heading back to California. And if you get involved with her she's going to be the one to suffer for it. You're living completely different lives. She's a hometown librarian in New England. You're a megastar living in La-La Land. Those two things don't compute."

Dante didn't have a good response to Troy's comment. The scorching kisses he and Lucy had shared the other night had left him wanting more of her. More kisses. More conversations. More Lucy. He'd never completely gotten her out of his bloodstream despite all the distance and the years standing between them. He wasn't sure he ever would.

Tension simmered in the air between them. It didn't take much to set off a firestorm between them, Dante realized.

"Now this is what I like to see," Mimi announced as she strolled into the kitchen and stood by the table beaming at her sons. "My two handsome boys getting along like biscuits and gravy." Dressed in a pink turtleneck sweater and a pair of jeans, she looked radiant. He hoped she was bouncing back a little bit from her deep mourning. After spending more than a year depressed and adrift, she now seemed upbeat and a bit more joyful.

"I made a plate for you, Mama. It's sitting on the stove," Troy said as he motioned in the direction of the covered plate he'd set aside for her. Mimi brought her food over to the table and joined them. A big smile was plastered on her face.

He had to give it to Troy. It might seem like a small thing, but cooking for their mother was a way to nurture her. Troy had been taking care of their mother for years. He'd moved back into the house in order to give her support and a shoulder to lean on during their father's illness. He'd never left. Dante felt a stab of guilt once again for being MIA. He'd never told his brother how thankful he was for him taking care of the home front while he'd been building his career in Hollywood. At some point, he needed to put his gratitude into words.

"Isn't it nice sitting together like this? I wish your sisters could be here with us," Mimi said. "I'm trying to get them to come for Christmas. That will be really special. A West family reunion. We can go sleigh riding and trim the tree together."

There was something comical about the way she made it sound, as if they were little kids again. Dante grinned and met Troy's gaze from across the table. Troy also seemed to find it humorous because he couldn't suppress his chuckle. Pretty soon the two of them were laughing in unison.

"What's so funny?" Mimi asked, looking back and forth between them. "On second thought, it doesn't matter. I'm just happy to hear laughter instead of fighting."

The three of them continued to eat breakfast while making small talk about town events.

"I hate to eat and run, but I need to head over to the set," Dante said, jumping up from his chair and placing a kiss on his mother's cheek. "I'll see you later, Mama. Thanks for breakfast, bro." He headed toward the sink and began to wash his plate and utensils before his mother called out, "Just leave them in the sink. I'll take care of them."

After grabbing his coat and saddlebag, Dante was out the door. As he settled into the driver's seat, his mind replayed his conversation with his brother. Troy was right. He didn't have anything to offer Lucy other than a few weeks of his time. With his focus on making the film, it wouldn't be much to speak of at all. They'd kissed the other night, and it had been way more than a peck on the cheek. The attraction between them still blazed like an out-of-control fire. Perhaps he should stick to making amends with Lucy rather than stoking the flames of their youthful romance.

Maybe from this point forward he could focus on becoming her friend again.

Friends didn't have random make-out sessions.

Who was he kidding? It was stupid of him to think there wasn't more between them than friendship. When he wasn't with Lucy, Dante was thinking about her. Her voice ran around in his head. He'd even had a few dreams about her that woke him up in the wee hours of the morning.

He was headed over to the library this morning to shoot his first scenes there. Although he knew Lucy would be busy working, he was hoping their paths would cross. He still had a long way to go in making up for the past, and it felt like he was running out of time.

* * *

Lucy had been trying to shake off her nervousness all morning, to no avail. Dante and his team were filming at the library today and, so far, she'd managed to steer clear of the mayhem. Thankfully, they were shooting in and around the southern wing of the library, which was separated from the main library area where she was working with patrons.

Although she'd heard noises during the morning hours, it was surprisingly not as much of a disruption as she'd imagined. For the most part it was voices carrying from that area to hers. Considering the big check the library was getting from Dante, Lucy didn't have a single complaint. The library would be able to greatly enhance its programming and hours. Just thinking about being open an extra day of the week filled Lucy with excitement. Money flowing into the library's coffers felt like a dream come true. She couldn't ignore that Dante's return had been beneficial to Mistletoe.

Despite her curiosity, she hadn't ventured over to the set. A part of her didn't want Dante to think she was overly interested in his project while another part of her wasn't sure she could withstand seeing her past reflected in the film. Dante being back in town was already unleashing a torrent of memories.

"What's all the ruckus, Lucy?"

Lucy swung her gaze up from the computer at the sound of her name. Seth Clifton, one of her regular patrons, was standing in front of the circulation desk, juggling a stack of books. He was a rather curmudgeonly figure in Mistletoe. He had a tendency to be a bit sharped-tongued, but Lucy took it in stride since she knew he'd led a sad life. With his mane of white hair and a disheveled beard, he had a distinctive appearance.

She grinned extra hard at Seth. Lucy had made a vow to herself to put a blissful smile on her face regarding the filming taking place on the premises and reassure all the patrons that it was a short-term project. "Something really exciting is happening. A film is being made here."

Seth sucked his teeth. His brows were knitted together in a fierce frown. "What do you mean?"

"As you probably know, Dante West is back in town making a movie. He's selected our library as one of his filming locations." Lucy tried her best to inject her tone with sweetness and light, along with a healthy dose of en-thusiasm. It wasn't hard to tell that Seth wouldn't be pulling out the welcome wagon for Dante and his crew.

Seth's frown deepened. "Do you mean to tell me that my tax dollars are being spent on this nonsense?"

"Umm, well honestly, the library is getting a sizable amount of money from Mr. West in return for him being able to use the space," she said in a neutral tone. She wasn't defending Dante, but it was only fair to look at the situation with all the facts at hand. Surely Seth was in support of a hefty donation to the library.

He rolled his eyes. "Everybody just bows down when some Hollywood jerk comes back to his roots. Phony balo-ney is what I say. Where's he been all this time? Kissing up to those folks in La-La Land."

Whoa. She'd been under the impression that the whole town was in love with Dante West, but Seth sounded down-right hostile. He wasn't being fair, considering Mistletoe was getting a large cash infusion from Dante's production company.

"Come on, Seth. That's not very nice. He's a hometown success story."

Seth snorted. "Nice. It wasn't very nice when he ditched you and this town for greener pastures."

Eeek! Lucy struggled to speak. Had the entire town known about her and Dante? It was wild that Seth knew about their teenaged romance. "I-I'm surprised you remem-ber that we dated. It was such a long time ago."

"I sure do. You moped around like a lovesick puppy

when he dumped you and left Mistletoe. Frankly, it was one of the saddest things I've ever seen in my life. You used to push around that library cart as if it was the only thing you had to hold on to." Seth made a tutting sound that grated on Lucy's nerves.

She didn't need or want his pity. And he was totally exaggerating about the library cart! As if that had ever happened. She drew herself up to her full height and smiled at him through gritted teeth as she handed him back his library card and pushed his stack of books toward him. "You're all checked out, Seth. Be careful on the walkway. It's a bit slippery."

"I'll be fine, Lucy. Steer clear of that Hollywood Romeo." He wagged his finger at her. "Don't play the fool twice."

Her mouth swung open. What was it with this town? The fact that people even recalled her high school romance with Dante was fairly shocking. It had been nearly a decade ago! Frankly, they all needed to get a life and butt out of her business. And if she wasn't a public servant she would have told Seth off in no uncertain terms. He needed to mind his business and hold his tongue.

She was nobody's fool. Oftentimes, she was written off as the sweet-natured librarian, when in reality she had a lot more pluck and grit than anyone ever gave her credit for. No one had the right to write her story except Lucy herself.

By the time evening rolled around, Lucy could see crews packing up equipment and driving away from the parking lot. She no longer heard any noises emanating from the other side of the library. Lucy tried to stuff down her disappointment that Dante hadn't sought her out. She was being ridiculous! He was directing a movie, for goodness' sake. Why would he have time to leave the set just to check in with her?

The kiss they'd shared the other night had seriously messed her up. She shivered just thinking about it. Dante was an amazing kisser. He'd been all heat and fire. Clearly, he'd been practicing a lot since their days together. Jealousy nipped at her. Back in the day they'd been young adults with limited experience in the kissing department. Over the years they'd both matured and grown, and now he left her wanting more.

"Hey, Lucy. Do you want me to stick around and help you lock up?" Denny's voice jolted her out of her thoughts about locking lips with Dante. She felt her face flushing at the heated memory.

"Thanks for asking, Denny. I'm all set. Maybe you could walk Nora to her car and give her a hand with her books." Lucy knew her coworker, Nora Letts, had a crush on Denny. If only Denny could see what was right in front of his eyes. Nora was kind and a bit on the shy side, but she was adorable. Perhaps Lucy could push the two of them together.

Denny looked over his shoulder. Nora was standing a few feet away, struggling with her bag. Denny sighed and called out to her. "Hey, Nora. I'm heading out now. Let me help you." Nora's face lit up with pleasure as Denny strode over and reached for her bag. As he walked out, Denny cast a backward glance at Lucy filled with longing.

*Please, please. Let some magic happen between Nora and*

*Denny.* More and more, Denny was popping up throughout the day to check in on Lucy at her various workstations. She viewed him as nothing more than a friend and a coworker, so she hoped he didn't consider her as a potential romantic partner as Stella imagined. If Denny did have feelings for her, Lucy knew she couldn't reciprocate. Her heart didn't pitter-patter when he was nearby. And the last thing she wanted was for Denny to get hurt. He was one of the good guys.

Seeing Dante again reminded her of what it felt like to be enthralled with someone. That rush of adrenaline. Butterflies floating around in your belly. Your heart thumping like crazy in your chest. Sweaty palms. Getting excited when they were in your presence.

All of a sudden, Lucy felt herself break out into a sweat. No, she couldn't be falling for Dante all over again. No way. Not this time, when she'd sworn she wouldn't have anything to do with him. She was almost nine years older now and no longer a kid with stars in her eyes. She'd grown and matured over the years. She knew better!

She didn't think she was mistaken. All the sensations she was feeling at the moment were exactly the same as she'd felt the first time around. Surprise. Nervousness. Wonder. Fear. Giddiness. They were swirling around inside her like confetti flying through the air. She hadn't gotten over Dante, and the realization was terrifying. All this time she'd thought that she had moved past their relationship, but she'd been terribly mistaken. Her feelings for Dante were alive and kicking her butt. And with him back in town, they would be impossible to deny.

At least the library was quiet now. Normally at this hour she had the place all to herself. It was sheer perfection as far as she was concerned. Her special time alone with the library, her thoughts, and Ella Fitzgerald. Lucy went over to her phone and studied the choices on Spotify. What was it going to be tonight? She sighed in satisfaction as she cued up the music. The strains of "Have Yourself a Merry Little Christmas" began to float through the space. Lucy started tapping her foot to the beat. As the tempo picked up, Lucy swayed back and forth to the music as she belted out the words. *Someday soon we all will be together if the fates allow. Until then we'll have to muddle through somehow."*

A slight shuffling sound caused her to whirl around. Dante was standing twenty feet away with his gaze glued to her. So much for thinking she was the only one left in the building! Dressed in a nice-fitting pair of dark jeans, a pullover long-sleeved tee, and a New England Patriots baseball cap, he looked like the old Dante. Although he could never look like a regular guy, he didn't look like a big Hollywood star either. There were slight shadows under his eyes, which hinted at long work hours and not enough sleep. She felt a slight pang in her heart at the sight of him.

"Dante! I had no idea anyone was still here." Embarrassment threatened to swallow her whole. Dancing all by herself in an empty library to Ella Fitzgerald must look all kinds of silly to Dante. She was now kicking herself for not making sure everyone had left the premises before she'd started to let loose. This was the first time they'd seen each other since their out-of-this-world smooch session. She wasn't sure if she was imagining it, but a slight tension hung in the air. Even from a distance she could feel the flicker of attraction.

"I'm sorry if I startled you. I didn't want to leave without seeing you and saying hello. The shoot worked out really well." The smile on his face spoke volumes about how he felt about his workday. She was so happy for him.

"I'm glad to hear it. I meant to pop over and take a peek, but things got so busy," she said. "I'll definitely make a point to stop by tomorrow, if that's okay. I mean, if it's not all right I'll steer clear."

"You're welcome any time, Lucy. You know that," Dante said in a low drawl.

She wished she wasn't so flustered by his presence. Why couldn't she be calm, cool, and collected? It was just Dante after all. Once she cut through all the hype and the action-hero label, he was still someone she'd known all her life. Someone Lucy had dearly loved.

Lucy ran her fingers through her hair and shifted from one foot to the other. The jazzy music was still playing, and she was torn between turning it off and allowing it to fill the silence between them. Before she could make up her mind, Dante moved toward her, quickly erasing the distance.

"Can I have this dance?" he asked, holding out his hand to her. His voice was smooth and sexy. Lucy hesitated a moment before nodding and slipping her hand in his. The thought of being so close to him unnerved her. Dante swung her into his arms and placed one hand at her waist while holding her hand in his. His moves were graceful as he whirled her around the makeshift dance floor. When he pulled her close so that there wasn't even an inch between them, Lucy sighed and rested her head against Dante's chest, breathing in the masculine scent of him. She felt protected in Dante's solid embrace, as if he could shelter her from all the bad things that might come her way.

When the music ended they were still holding on to each other and moving to their own silent rhythm. She stopped dancing and looked up at him, searching for something in the depths of his brown eyes. Did he feel the same romantic pull toward her that she felt for him? Was he regretting ever having left Mistletoe? And her?

"What are we doing?" Lucy whispered.

"Dancing." His voice sounded huskier than usual.

Lucy licked her lips. "It seemed like a lot more than dancing."

"Would that be so bad?" Dante asked, sliding his hand down her arm. She felt goose bumps rise up on her flesh. His touch sent her soaring, as if everything in her world had gone from black and white to vibrant color.

"I don't know," Lucy said. "We've been down this road before and it didn't end well." To say the least. Lucy had been bruised and emotionally wrung out after things had ended between them. She never wanted to feel so broken ever again. Nor did she want to hope for something that might never come to pass. But being around Dante made her want him. Want things she thought she'd buried years ago.

"I won't hurt you again, Lucy. I promise. Last time I was young and full of way more pride than I could handle," he admitted. "I know who I am now."

It made her sad to think she might have expected too much of him back then. Dante had been brash and cocky and tender. In her eyes he'd been some kind of wonderful. But he'd also been young and impetuous. How many people would have run off to Los Angeles without a place to live and a decent amount of money in their bank account? Dante hadn't been thinking clearly when he'd left, and the ripple effects of his life in California had led to him being homeless. That took a little sting out of her being left behind. She couldn't imagine what he'd been through, and although she wanted to know everything, a part of her was glad he hadn't given her the nitty-gritty details. It would shatter her to know how badly he'd suffered.

"I'm happy about that, Dante," she said. "What you're doing here in Mistletoe is a good thing." She smiled at him. "You're putting us on the map. And giving our economy a huge boost."

A famous movie star returning to his hometown to film a movie had created a renewed interest in tourism. Mistletoe had already experienced a large uptick in revenue as a result of Dante's presence. All the restaurants in town were servicing more customers. The Knightsbridge Inn was booked solid for weeks, along with countless Airbnbs. Now that their boiler problem had been fixed, the inn was accommodating a full house of guests. Mistletoe offered unique experiences for tourists such as sleepovers at the famous Holly Hill Lighthouse and glassblowing workshops with Jules Winchester, a famous local artist. Other producers were also scoping out Mistletoe as the setting for future films, following Dante's lead. Hopefully the surge in tourism would continue after Dante headed back to California. She needed to keep reminding herself that he wasn't staying on in town permanently. His life was on the West Coast, thousands of miles away from Maine.

Pretty soon he would be nothing but a memory.

"If I'm being honest, I came back for you, Lucy."

His confession served as a knockout punch to her equilibrium. Lucy felt her knees wobble. She sucked in a big dose of air to steady herself. Had she heard him right? She was the reason for his homecoming?

Just as Lucy summoned the courage to ask him to elaborate, he leaned down and pressed his lips against hers, surprising her with the sudden gesture. She couldn't have pulled away if she tried. She didn't want to. His lips swept over hers lightly at first—like gossamer wings—until a few seconds later when the pressure intensified. She tilted her face upward and slanted her mouth against his. His lips tasted like pure sweetness.

"Dante," she said, murmuring his name against his lips.

His lips wandered to the sensitive spot at the base of her throat. Dante rained kisses on her skin, leaving a fiery trail in his wake. *This type of intimacy*, she thought, *is what I've been missing out on all this time.* Feeling so close to another person that you weren't sure you could breathe without them. She was falling…tumbling, plummeting, disappearing into the abyss. It felt so good, but this was what she'd been afraid of with Dante's return.

The sound of a door slamming shut caused them to break apart with both of them still breathing heavily. Lucy turned toward the sound of the loud noise and saw a woman holding a vacuum cleaner. She'd completely forgotten about the cleaning service scheduled for this evening. As usual, being around Dante turned her brain into scrambled eggs.

"Hey, Annie," she called out, waving at the owner of Clean and Shine. A few times a week the cleaning crew came in to make the library sparkling and tidy.

Annie's eyes widened as she looked back and forth between Lucy and Dante. Crap! This was a one-way ticket to gossip town. She could tell by the stunned expression on Annie's face that she'd seen them kissing.

Dante waved at Annie, who looked as if she might pass out at the sight of him. The older woman slowly moved toward the conference room, turning around several times to brazenly gawk at them before fading from view.

Lucy moaned and covered her face with her hands.

"You okay?" Dante asked, reaching out and pulling her hands away from her face.

"I'm fine," she said, "but I have to warn you that we might be the talk of the town tomorrow. Annie is probably already texting her friends and spreading it all over Mistletoe that she caught us kissing." She knit her brows together. "It's possible the story might even be embellished."

Dante grinned. "That doesn't bother me for myself, but I'm sorry if it's going to be a problem for you. It kind of reminds me of the past. If you remember, we set tongues wagging back in the day. The girl next door and the rebel. People didn't know what to think about the two of us," he said with a chuckle. "It was perplexing enough when we were best friends, but when we started dating they nearly lost their minds."

"Including my parents," Lucy added, cringing at the memory of how overprotective they'd been when her friendship with Dante had segued to romance their junior year. Although they'd always loved Dante, neither one had been prepared for their intense high school romance. Dante had been more experienced than Lucy since he'd been dating since ninth grade. Her parents had both worried about him smashing her heart into little pieces, which is exactly what he'd done in the long run.

Dante looked down at his watch. "I'd love to stay and talk some more, but I have to head out. I need to rewrite a few scenes for tomorrow. Don't forget to stop in tomorrow afternoon to watch the shoot. No excuses will be accepted." Dante's tone sounded firm. He was staring at her with an expectant expression.

Lucy didn't bother arguing with him. No matter how busy things got tomorrow at the library, she would make time to watch a little bit of the filming process. She had to admit it was pretty exciting to have a movie made in Mistletoe. Someday when she was old and gray, Lucy could tell her grandkids about the achingly handsome movie star who'd come back to Maine to make a movie.

"I accept," she said, her eyes fixated on his wide, kissable lips. Now that she'd had a taste of Dante's swoon-worthy kisses, she didn't know how to stop wanting more of them. "I'm really looking forward to it," she admitted. "Now I can see what all the fuss is about." She flashed him a cheeky grin.

"I'll see you tomorrow, Luce," Dante said as he turned on his heel and strode toward the door.

As soon as he'd left the building, Lucy immediately felt his absence. He was raw energy—like the tide crashing against the shore. And every time she was with him Lucy felt as if she was dreaming. She needed to float back down to reality. *Quickly.* Bit by bit, she was unraveling. Instead of steering clear of her own personal kryptonite, she was making out with him at every opportunity that presented itself. She was falling deeper and deeper into the rabbit hole.

She ran her fingers over her swollen lips. It should have been one and done. She hadn't planned to kiss Dante again, but when it came to him, she had zero willpower. All he had to do was look in her direction and Lucy was putty in his hands. She wrapped her arms around her middle. Little by little she was being pulled back into Dante's life and she was placing her heart in the danger zone. All the warning signs were flashing in her face. If she wasn't careful she would soon become a member of the Lonely Hearts Club. Again.

Lucy shook her head. She wasn't going down this road with the man who'd stomped on her heart once before. It was way too risky, and she wasn't a woman who took chances. She knew her aversion to risk was all tied up in the heartache she'd experienced. Maybe that was why she'd spent most of her time safe and sound in a library. Perhaps it had become a fortress against having her heart trampled on.

Moving forward she had to be on her toes with Dante. It was okay to maintain a cordial friendship with him, but anything more would be reckless. Sharing kisses with Dante was off-limits for obvious reasons. The more she kissed him, the more Lucy wanted to be with him. She needed to try to nip these feelings in the bud while she still could. According to town gossip, he was leaving town right after Christmas and heading back to his glamorous Hollywood life. This time around, she vowed, he wasn't taking her heart along with him.

# CHAPTER TEN

As promised, the very next day Lucy carved out some time in her schedule to drop by Dante's shoot. She wasn't showing up for Dante's benefit, she told herself. As head librarian it was her duty to be knowledgeable about everything taking place within the library's walls. It was a historic moment, in fact. And it was only fitting for her to observe the action. If the Free Library of Mistletoe was going down in movie history, Lucy wanted to be a witness to it. For history's sake, of course.

The scene being filmed was an amalgamation of all the times Lucy and Dante had hidden among the library stacks, sharing stolen kisses in the middle of their study sessions. It was lighthearted, and Lucy imagined it would evoke romantic and heartwarming feelings in filmgoers. The sweet and tender emotions depicted by the leads brought a tear to her eye. It felt as if she'd walked back in time to a more innocent phase in her and Dante's lives when falling in love had been the easiest thing in the world.

Seeing these scenes being brought to life made Lucy wonder about the ending of Dante's film. In real life, their parting had been full of angst, anger, and broken promises. She snorted. Not exactly a happy ending for a movie.

When the scene wrapped, Dante made a beeline for Lucy. Although she'd tried to shrink into the background as she watched, clearly he'd spotted her. Maybe he'd heard her clapping enthusiastically once he'd yelled cut. She'd been so transfixed watching the scene unfold that she hadn't been able to resist cheering them on once it was done. She felt awestruck about all of Dante's accomplishments. Regardless of the way things had gone down between them, he was a hometown boy who was doing amazing things with his life. He'd come a long way since the days of high school theater productions.

"You made it," he said, his face lit up with pleasure. "So, what's the verdict?"

"I think it may go down as the best scene ever filmed at a library in cinematic history," Lucy raved. Of course she was exaggerating a little, but she wanted to hype him up a teeny bit. She didn't want to sound like she was fawning over him—something told her women did that all the time—but he deserved her kudos, especially when she'd always been so critical of him. And of course she thought the scenes were all fantastic because it was her library being showcased.

Dante's eyes widened. He pressed his hand over his heart. "Such high praise. I'm honored."

Lucy's eyes felt as wide as saucers as she studied the lights, cameras, crew, and actors assembled in the library's south wing corridor. They'd just finished filming in the study room. That particular space had always been one of Lucy's favorites because of the glorious stained-glass windows, the ornate wall sconces, and the gleaming mahogany bookshelves. It was by far the most sumptuous space in the building. This area of the library had been the vision of the town's most generous benefactor, Miss Prudence Merriweather. Back in the early 1900s she had commissioned a local architect, Ezekiel Jones, to build the room as a tribute to her late parents who'd perished in a boating accident. The result had been breathtaking in more ways than one. Ezekiel and Prudence had fallen in love and enjoyed forty-two years of wedded bliss.

Lucy couldn't help but think of their love story whenever she entered this magnificent space.

It was a bit jarring to realize that she wasn't in California at a fancy studio or a glamorous set. All the magic was taking place at her beloved library. It was way more thrilling than she'd initially imagined. Seeing the characters come to life under Dante's instructions had been surreal. All the cast and crew showed such respect and admiration for Dante, which said a lot about his directing skills. For the first time, Lucy could really see that Dante had been destined to follow this path.

"How did you learn to do all of this?" Lucy asked Dante, her voice full of awe.

Dante let out a throaty chuckle. "It took some time. I've been shadowing directors every single film I've made. Luckily, I worked with some really generous directors. And my good friend Chet Thibedoux has been my mentor for years. I don't know if you've heard of him, but he's one of the most accomplished directors in the world."

The name was vaguely familiar to Lucy, but she didn't know much about him. "It sounds familiar," she said. She would never admit it to Dante, but he was the only celebrity she'd ever seriously followed. Every now and again Lucy looked him up to see what he was up to in his career. It had always made her feel rather foolish, as if she was clinging to the past.

"I've worked with most of the cast and crew before, which is great because I went into the project knowing that they're all hard workers. I couldn't be happier with how it's all turning out." He rubbed his hands together gleefully. "I don't want to jinx it, but we could have a hit on our hands."

If the rest of the film was as captivating as what she'd seen, Dante didn't have a thing to worry about. She had a good feeling in her gut about the movie's success. It could end up being a classic movie like *The Notebook* or *Love and Basketball*.

Lucy glanced over at the actors who were assembled in a small group. They were sharing a lively conversation. She almost did a double take at the sight of one person in particular—Missy North.

The woman was radiantly beautiful. With her big black lashes, flawless honey-colored skin, and Coke-bottle physique, Missy exuded sex appeal. Lucy had seen her face plastered on the covers of celebrity magazines enough times to recognize her. Missy had gained fame as a cast member of the reality show *30 Days to Love*, in which six single females were placed on a remote island in Tahiti with twenty men. Over the course of the thirty days, each woman was supposed to find the love of her life. Missy became the breakout star of the reality show when she'd made a fiery speech during the finale about not needing a man to be content in her life. Since the airing of the finale, she'd exploded in the world of pop culture, earning six-figure endorsements along with television and movie roles. A person had to have been living under a rock for the past few years not to recognize her.

Missy had a rumored past with Dante and now she'd shown up as a member of his cast. Lucy wondered if something romantic was going on between them. Not that it was any of her business, she quickly reminded herself. Despite the kisses they'd shared, Lucy and Dante weren't an item. Far from it. She was still working on forgiving him for the way he'd ended things with her. Although she had a better understanding of the intense situation he'd been faced with in California, she struggled to understand how pride could have cost them both so much. It still hurt.

She had to acknowledge that they'd come a long way in the short time he'd been back in town. At least now she didn't hate his guts. Her stomach no longer churned at the thought of him being given a hero's welcome in Mistletoe. Perhaps his return would finally give her the resolution she craved.

Dante jerked his chin in the direction of the actors and crew members.

"Would you like to meet some of them?" he asked. His eyes were bright with excitement, his expression animated. For a second he reminded her of a pint-sized version of himself. Dante had been an adventurous and bold child. Even as a kid he'd been full of personality.

Lucy didn't hesitate to say yes. She recognized a few of the main players, and the idea of meeting them was exciting. This wasn't an opportunity that was likely to ever come her way again. She might as well embrace it with gusto.

"Missy, this is Lucy Marshall. She's the head librarian here and an old friend."

"Lucy, it's great to meet you," Missy said, flashing a perfect Colgate smile. For a moment she was mesmerized by Missy's amazingly white teeth. Veneers? Caps? She felt a bit catty wondering, but it was rumored that Missy had undergone lots of plastic surgery during her rise to the top. Either way, she was stunning.

"Nice to meet you as well. Welcome to Mistletoe," Lucy said, reaching out and shaking her hand. Lucy couldn't help but notice her expensive manicure—gel tips and all. Lucy loved getting pedicures, but because she used her hands so much as a librarian, manicures felt like a waste of money. Missy's nails made her look glamorous and sophisticated. Lucy tried to stuff down the feelings of envy flickering inside her.

"It's a lovely town. I'm only here for two weeks to film, but I'd love to explore it," Missy said. She leaned over and lightly jabbed Dante in the elbow. "I'm hoping Dante will show me around during some downtime."

Dante frowned and made a face. "Downtime? What's that?" he asked with a laugh. "I'm working my butt off." Missy laughed along with him. Lucy couldn't help but notice Missy's relaxed vibe around Dante. She couldn't seem to take her eyes off him either. It made Lucy feel slightly uncomfortable for reasons she didn't want to examine.

From what she'd witnessed so far, Dante was a babe magnet. Matter of fact, he'd always attracted attention. Back when he'd been a high school football star, Dante had been the object of endless female worship. He'd been athletic and gorgeous, not to mention popular. All the stars had been aligned for him to go on to bigger and better once he left Maine.

But back then he'd been Lucy's man, and everyone had respected their status as a couple. The rest of the girls had simply looked. No one had ever tried to get between them.

As Dante introduced her to the rest of his cast and crew, she found herself feeling really impressed by the people he was surrounding himself with on the project. They seemed solid and kind. All of them looked her in the eye and didn't talk down to her as if she was a nobody. She'd always believed that people in the movie industry were stuck up and snobby. It was wrong to have judged people without even meeting them.

"I better get back to work," she said to Dante. "This was really cool though. I'll never be able to view the library in the same way ever again." Lucy knew she was beaming but she couldn't seem to stop smiling.

"Hey, would you like to grab dinner tonight?" Dante

asked casually. He grinned at her and seemed very relaxed as he leaned against the doorjamb. "I'll be wrapping up filming in a few hours. I'd love to check out that burger place down the street."

A date? Was Dante asking her on a date? Pure adrenaline began racing through her veins. *Easy there, Lucy.* They were back to being friends, so most likely Dante just wanted to hang out. No strings attached.

"I promised Tess that I'd pick up a Christmas tree with her at Sawyer's." Lucy made a face. "She's been nagging me about it for weeks."

"You're a great big sister. You seem to spend a lot of time with her."

"She makes it easy." She sighed. "My mom was diagnosed with MS last year after a lot of health issues began showing up." Lucy massaged the bridge of her nose. Talking about her mother's health condition was painful. "Her symptoms have gotten worse lately, so Stella and I have made a point to spend more time with Tess so my dad can focus on getting my mom through this rough patch."

"Aww, Luce. I'm so sorry to hear that. Your folks were always good to me." Compassion radiated from his voice.

Lucy nodded. "We're all hoping it goes into remission, but for the moment, I'm happy to pitch in with Tess. It's the least I can do."

"Mind if I join you guys? You might need an extra pair of hands to carry the tree inside your house. Not to mention I'm treating for burgers and fries afterwards."

She knew Tess would be ecstatic at the idea of Dante

joining them on their hunt for the perfect Christmas tree. Having him take them out to dinner would cause her sister's ten-year-old heart to skyrocket into orbit. But did Lucy really want to spend more time with Dante? Was it smart to hold her hand so close to the fire?

"Sure thing," she said, the words slipping past her lips before she could rein them in. Ugh. She couldn't even explain why she hadn't been able to turn him down. *You need to live a little before he leaves Mistletoe*, a little voice buzzed in her ear.

"Great!" Dante said, grinning down at her. "Why don't I swing by and pick you up at six?"

"Okay. We should probably take my truck to transport the tree, but we can figure it out later," she said. "I'll see you tonight."

"It's a plan," Dante said as Lucy turned on her heel and made her way back down the corridor toward the main wing.

Lucy settled herself behind the main desk and began to check her work-related emails. She jotted down notes in her notebook and tried to focus on scheduling shifts and ordering books for the library's catalog. She let out a little squeal of excitement as she read the message from Marjorie Brown accepting her invitation. Marjorie was an up-and-coming author of multicultural children's books with whom Lucy had been trying to schedule a book reading at the library for almost a full year now. This was the part of her job that she loved the most—bringing talented writers to the Mistletoe community.

She bit the end of a pencil as her mind wandered to thoughts of this evening. She needed a foolproof strategy so she didn't end up getting too close to him. With Tess being present, her little sister would serve as a buffer between them. It would work heavily in her favor. She was not going to kiss Dante tonight. Nope! Even though kissing him made her feel as if she was soaring above the clouds, she knew it would only lead to trouble.

*Well, maybe that's the type of trouble you need in your life*, the little voice whispered. Lucy sighed. Part of the reason she'd been so annoyed at Dante's return was because of what he'd always represented to her. A walk on the wild side. He'd brought out the spirited side of her personality. But if she was being completely honest with herself, her life had become a little too uneventful. She missed being spontaneous, unpredictable. Dancing with Dante in the rain and kissing him under the glow of a blue moon.

*Admit it*, she told herself. *You would kiss Dante again in a heartbeat, if given the chance.* Sure, it could lead to heartache, but maybe it would be worth it to have a holiday fling with a movie star. She would remember it for the rest of her days. It was a story she could pass down to her grandchildren if she ever had any.

Being practical hadn't gotten her anything but a big fat dose of loneliness. Despite the fact that she was surrounded by family and a host of friends in Mistletoe, she ached for something more. She didn't want to have peaked romantically at nineteen years old. The heart was a muscle and she needed to exercise it, whether it was with Dante or somebody else. For a little while at least, she was going to wade into deeper waters. If it accomplished nothing else, Lucy might get back a part of herself she'd lost over the years.

If Dante tried to lay one on her tonight, Lucy was going to lean in and kiss him for all she was worth. And she wasn't going to regret it one little bit.

# CHAPTER ELEVEN

That night, Dante showed up at Lucy's house a few minutes before six o'clock. The idea of doing something in preparation for the holidays filled him with the type of pure joy he rarely experienced. Sometimes he got tired of being Dante West, the famous actor. It was refreshing to simply be Dante. Lucy didn't have stars in her eyes when she looked at him, and he didn't have to worry about putting on a show for her. He would wager that his status as an A-list celebrity meant very little to her. They were on track to becoming friends again, and he wasn't going to mess things up by kissing her. Even though he wanted to do it more than anything in this world.

Sparkling white lights lit up the front of Lucy's house. They dangled down from the roof like little icicles and hung off the railings of her wraparound porch, lending the home a festive air. It was yet another thing he missed about the Christmas holidays in Maine. California couldn't compete with gently falling snow, *snow* tubing, and an entire town lit up in holiday splendor. Once Lucy had a decorated Christmas tree standing in front of her bay window, the house would look perfect for the holidays.

For the entire ride to the tree farm, Tess peppered him with questions about his life in California and all his famous friends. Do you know Lady Gaga? Do you live in a mansion? Did you always know you were going to be famous? Dante didn't mind being grilled by her. She was spunky and spirited, bringing to mind a younger version of Lucy.

When they pulled into Sawyer's, the place was lit up with so many lights that it made the decorations on Lucy's street look like child's play. Christmas was on everyone's mind, judging by all the customers lined up to purchase trees. There was an electricity pulsing in the air that he vividly remembered from his younger years. He didn't know how to explain it, but just being back in Mistletoe at this time of year made him feel hopeful, as if anything was possible.

"Hey there!" Lou greeted them as they walked past the entrance. "Back so soon? Are you checking out the lay of the land for the scenes you'll be shooting? I just signed the contract you sent over."

"Not this time. Tonight is pure pleasure. Lucy is looking for the perfect tree," Dante explained. "And we're determined to find it. Isn't that right, Tess?"

"Yes!" Tess shouted as she raised her arm into the air with gusto. "We won't go home without one."

"You heard it from Tess's lips, Lou," Lucy said. "We're highly motivated buyers."

"Well then, I'll let you get to it," Lou said with a big grin. "If you need me just whistle."

"You got it, Lou," Dante said, clapping him on the shoulder.

Just as they began to look over the first batch of trees, Tess spotted a friend standing nearby with her parents. It wasn't long before the girls were talking a mile a minute with their heads together. It didn't take a genius to figure out they were hatching some sort of plot.

Tess came running back over to where Lucy and Dante were standing. She began to jump up and down. "Can I please go with Delia to get some cocoa and sugar cookies?"

"Already?" Lucy asked. "What about picking out my tree?"

"I trust your judgment," Tess quipped, her gaze darting back to Delia, who was beckoning her over.

"Do you want us to come with you?" Lucy asked, sounding a bit miffed.

"We're not babies, Lucy," Tess said in a huffy tone. She rolled her eyes for good measure.

Lucy frowned at her. "What did I tell you about rolling your eyes?"

"I'm sorry," Tess said. "I lost my head."

Dante stifled a chuckle. He could see the corners of Lucy's mouth twitching, but she managed to keep a straight face. "How about twenty minutes and then we'll meet you over there. Don't wander anywhere else, Tess Marshall. I mean it. I don't want to have to hunt you down if you're not where you've said you'll be."

"Thanks, Lucy," Tess said, tightly wrapping her arms

around her sister's waist. "I promise to stay put. I can't wait to see what you pick out." She turned toward her friend and after joining hands, they ran toward the tent.

"Wow. So much for her helping to pick out the tree. I was sold down the river for a cup of hot chocolate," Lucy said with a shake of her head.

"I think we might have done the same at her age," Dante said. "Matter of fact, I know we would've."

"You're right. She's a pretty good kid for the most part."

Lucy was smiling. She was proud of her little sister and it was written all over her face. Dante wanted to tell her to hold on to their relationship and never let it go. For the hundredth time since he'd been back, Dante wished he and Troy hadn't fallen out. He missed their closeness. His life would be so much richer with his brother in it.

"She is. Shall we walk among the trees?" Dante asked, holding out his arm to Lucy. With a grin she looped her arm through his and they began strolling through the rows of trees, eyeballing the large assortment. There were dozens and dozens of trees—balsam, evergreen, Fraser firs. Trees stretched out in rows for as far as the eye could see. A full moon hung in the sky, casting a lovely glow over the tree farm. Dante sniffed the air. It smelled like snow. Being born and bred in Maine gave him a sixth sense about impending snow. Sometimes, you could just smell it hovering in the atmosphere.

All of a sudden, Lucy stopped in front of a tall, robust-looking tree. A balsam fir from what he recalled. The needles were dark green and it had a near-perfect shape.

The branches were strong and sturdy. Back in the day he'd been an expert on local trees when he worked at Sawyer's. Of all the trees he'd worked with, the balsam had the best Christmas tree scent.

"Oh, it's magnificent," she said, crossing her hands in front of her as she gazed up at the massive tree. "But it might not fit in my living room. I can't go more than eight feet."

"I'm sure they can cut some off at the bottom," Dante said, trying to get a good look at the bottom of the tree. He bent down and examined the base. "It looks like several inches can be shaved off. It might just work," he said.

"Woot. That's great news," Lucy said, excitement etched on her face.

"Let me go get Lou," Dante offered. "I'll be right back."

As he walked away to find Lou, Dante felt himself grinning. This trip to Sawyer's tree farm was the perfect outing to deepen his connection to Mistletoe. The place was full of heartwarming memories—some of the happiest of his life. They harkened back to a time when his dad was alive, he was still tight with Troy, and Lucy was his best friend. Being here allowed him to relive those golden days and pretend as if nothing had changed when he'd left Mistletoe on the first bus out of town.

* * *

With snowflakes beginning to gently fall from the velvety night sky, Lucy couldn't imagine a more beautiful Maine evening to pick out a Christmas tree. The fact that Dante was her sidekick made it even more special. It was strange how things could change so much in a matter of weeks. It wasn't as if she'd forgotten their tangled past, but at least now they were working on reestablishing their friendship. That's where it had all begun back when they were kids.

She just had to remind herself not to get swept up in the blissful feelings that came along with this special time of the year. It would be so easy to get caught up in the romanticism of Christmas. Lucy stuffed her mittened hands in her pockets and gazed up at the inky night sky lit up by a glorious moon and glimmering stars. If Christmas had a smell, this was it. The heady scent of Maine Christmas trees hung in the night air. Fresh pine needles and peppermint. Vanilla and cinnamon. The aroma of impending snow drifted in the wind.

Once Lou came back with Dante, it was official. She was the proud owner of a magnificent balsam Christmas tree. She felt giddy with excitement just watching Lou tag the tree. She could picture it sitting in front of her bay window shimmering with colored lights and shiny ornaments.

"We're going to cut it down and wrap it for you, all right? You can pick it up out front in about twenty minutes," Lou said. "In the meantime, go enjoy yourselves," he said with a wink.

Lucy wasn't sure what to make of Lou's wink, but Dante didn't seem taken aback by it. Perhaps she was being a tad paranoid since Mistletoe had its fair share of gossips. Lou was a good-natured man who was simply being playful with them. Or perhaps he'd picked up on her emotions.

Sometimes she wondered if she was wearing her heart on her sleeve with Dante. Could everyone in Mistletoe see that she still had feelings for him? Or did people still link the two of them because of their romantic history?

"Let's check out the sleigh rides for old time's sake," Dante suggested. "Maybe we can take Tess and her friend for a ride if the line isn't too long."

"Sounds like a plan. I'm sure they'd love that," Lucy said, walking alongside him in lockstep. They strolled in companionable silence with neither one feeling the need to fill up the quiet with conversation. This didn't happen often for Lucy. And it felt nice to simply enjoy the ambiance of the tree farm. It was one of those wintry Maine nights where the weather wasn't unbearably cold and the air held the promise of even more snow.

Suddenly, Dante grabbed her by the hand and pulled her behind a cluster of trees. Surprised by the swiftness of his movement, Lucy let out a little squeak. Dante placed his gloved finger over her lips.

He began to whisper. "Paparazzi. I spotted them coming toward us." His eyes had a startled appearance and he was breathing heavily.

"Are you sure? Here in Mistletoe?" It was crazy to imagine they had followed Dante to Mistletoe, Maine, then tracked him down at a local tree farm.

Dante's expression was intense. "Trust me. I've had a few run-ins with them over the years. We're on a first-name basis. They're definitely looking for me. And I don't want you to get dragged into the crosshairs."

They both squatted down behind a cluster of trees to make themselves less visible. Lucy could see that Dante was rattled. He'd never been one to get shaken up easily, so this seemed like a big deal.

"I can't believe they followed you here." Clearly, Dante's movie-star life wasn't all glamour and glitz. Being stalked by paparazzi seemed incredibly invasive. And a bit terrifying.

"I should have been ready for this. They're pretty relentless. It's part of my everyday life back in Los Angeles, but I didn't really think they would follow me all the way to Maine." He let out an aggravated sound. "Anything to make a quick buck."

"I can't imagine anyone being proud to make their living that way," Lucy said. Even though her position as head librarian might appear ordinary to some people, it was an honest living. She was proud to work in a profession that helped educate and inform the public. It was horrific that anyone could justify stalking someone to make money.

"Do you mind if we just sit here for a few minutes?" Dante asked as he peered between the trees, clearly looking to see if the paparazzi was still in sight. "Hopefully they'll go away when they don't see me."

"Of course not," she said, settling down into a seated position next to him. "I'm a happy camper since we found my tree. We should probably find Tess in about ten minutes or so. I know she's fine, but I still have my big-sister hat on."

"I like watching the two of you together. It reminds me

of how I used to look out for Troy even though we're so close in age." He let out a ragged sigh. "I really need to settle things between us. I miss him."

"So, what are you waiting for? You're only in town for a limited amount of time. If you're going to make things right, you shouldn't squander what little time you have."

"You're right," Dante said. "There's just so much I need to make up for. When my dad got sick I wasn't around. I always told myself I'd come running if things got bad, but everything spiraled so fast with his illness."

"And you didn't get the opportunity to do it," Lucy said in a soft voice.

"No. And I never got a chance to say goodbye." Dante's voice trembled as he spoke, pure emotion taking over. "It still feels like a gut punch to have missed out on my dad's final moments. Nothing can ever make up for that."

"He knew you loved him. And he was proud of you."

Dante shook his head. "I'm not sure of that. I never saw any evidence of it when he was alive."

"Well, I'm one hundred percent certain. He bragged on you every opportunity he got. Every time I went to his store he talked my ear off about you. He used to rattle off the titles of your movies like nobody's business. Your dad didn't hesitate to chastise me if I hadn't seen it." She chuckled softly. "He had a lot of your press clippings hanging on the walls. Honestly, I can't imagine how he could have been any prouder of you."

\* \* \*

Dante felt like the wind had been knocked out of him. The idea of his dad having a sense of pride in his accomplishments was a staggering concept. If it was true, it would be a game changer for him. "Seriously?" he asked Lucy, knowing all too well she would never lie to him, especially about this.

"Yes," Lucy said with a nod. She began to chuckle. "I think he even framed that *People* magazine cover from a few years ago when you were named Sexiest Man Alive."

He let out a sound of surprise. "He did what?"

Lucy nodded. "You heard me. He papered the walls of the store with your accomplishments. And he was happy to tell everyone all about your career." She wrinkled her nose. "Honestly, at times I just wanted to tell him to take it down a notch, but he was such a good man I didn't have the heart to hurt his feelings."

Dante made a face. "Let me guess. Troy took those things down? Because I certainly didn't see any of them when I swung by there."

Lucy shrugged. "If he did, it was probably out of anger. That's why you need to squash whatever this ugliness is between you. There's no reason that the two of you can't be a united front. Trust me, if my mother's illness has taught me anything, it's that we need family in our corner. You've already lost your dad, Dante. Isn't that enough?"

Dante struggled to speak past the huge lump in his throat. Lucy had dropped a bombshell on him. He'd never imagined that his dad had felt pride in any of his accomplishments. Because his father had opposed him leaving

Mistletoe to carve out a career in California, Dante hadn't believed he'd ever approved of what he'd built for himself. Hearing this from Lucy's lips was life changing. It would probably give him the closure he'd been wanting ever since they'd lost him.

For the first time in a long time, his heart felt less weighed down. With one anecdote, Lucy had set him free. It put so many things in perspective. His father had been a complicated man who hadn't fully been able to communicate with his son, but he now knew that he hadn't been ashamed of Dante's choices. It made all the difference in the world.

"Thanks, Luce," he said, reaching out and grazing her cheeks with his gloved hands. "You have no idea what this means to me."

"I'm glad I could help," she murmured, her eyes locked on his.

Before he knew it, Lucy was leaning toward him and placing her lips against his own. For a moment he froze out of pure shock. Since Dante had been back in Mistletoe he'd kissed Lucy twice, but both times he'd been the one to initiate the kiss. It both shocked and humbled him to have her making the first move. Her lips felt warm and soft against his. A light perfume mixed with the scent of the various trees filled his nostrils. He reached out and placed his hand on the back of her neck in an effort to anchor her to him. Dante kissed her back eagerly, plundering her lips with his tongue. Lucy let out a little sigh as her mouth opened and the kiss deepened. He felt Lucy's mittened hands grasping the collar of his winter parka. It was as if both of them needed to get closer to each other at all costs. All the yearning of the lost years between them had manifested itself into this one smoking-hot kiss.

"Mommy. Daddy. There's someone back there hiding."

Dante felt like someone had thrown a bucket of cold water on him when the sound of a child's voice rang out, interrupting the most heavenly kiss on earth. A little kid had spotted them! She was peering through the gap and pointing at them. There was every possibility that they could be discovered making out behind the Christmas trees.

Lucy's eyes were practically bulging out of her head. Their faces were still so close together he could see the tiny freckles on the bridge of her nose. Like everything else about her, they were beautiful.

Once the family moved on down the row, both of them burst out laughing. The corners of Lucy's eyes crinkled as she chuckled.

"That was close," Dante said, grinning at Lucy. "I'm not sure we could have explained that one." He wouldn't have cared for himself, but he didn't want Lucy to experience any embarrassment or become the object of town gossip. It was the same reason he hadn't wanted the paparazzi to spot them together. Photos of him and Lucy would be splashed all over the tabloids within twenty-four hours if they managed to snap pictures of them. Lucy would be branded as Dante West's latest fling and her whole life would be turned upside down. He couldn't let that happen. She wasn't just anyone. Lucy owned a large chunk of his heart.

Lucy's cheeks were flushed. "You're right. It would have

been awkward. And I happen to know that family too," she said sheepishly. "I think we should go to the tent and find Tess. Our time is up."

"Let me see if the coast is clear," Dante said, peeking out between the trees. From what he could see, no paparazzi were lurking around. It was highly possible that they were somewhere at the tree farm, but he and Lucy couldn't hide all night long, even though he didn't have a single problem with the concept. He enjoyed being alone with her. During those rare moments it almost seemed as if they hadn't been apart all these years. Their bond was still intact.

As they made their way to the tent, Dante kept his eyes peeled for any glimpse of the paparazzi. Thankfully, they were nowhere in sight. He let out a relieved sigh. Lucy seemed very protective of her reputation as town librarian, and he didn't want anything to tarnish it. Tabloid pics of him and Lucy would put their rekindled friendship back in the danger zone. Friendship? Who was he kidding? His feelings for Lucy went way deeper than friendship, and the kiss they'd just shared was proof. But what good would come of telling her? He was determined not to hurt Lucy this time around. He'd already done far too much damage in the past.

As soon as they stepped inside the tent, Tess came running over to them.

"What took you so long?" Tess asked. "I was beginning to think you guys got lost among all the trees."

Lucy reached out and lightly tugged at one of her sister's braids. "We didn't get lost, Tess. We did, however, find the most amazing, beautiful, wondrous Christmas tree. You're going to love it." Lucy sounded as exuberant as a child. Tess's face lit up, matching her sister's joy.

"Can we decorate it tonight? Can we please? And, Dante, can you help?" Tess pleaded. Dante didn't envy Lucy at the moment. With her warm brown skin, endearing smile, and adorable pigtails, Tess was the type of kid it would be hard to say no to.

"Not tonight, Tess," Lucy said. "That usually takes hours. Don't worry though. We'll come up with a plan to decorate it."

Tess hung her head and stuck her lip out. "No fair," she mumbled.

"So, who's ready for burgers and fries?" Dante asked in an upbeat voice as he looked back and forth between the Marshall girls. At the same time both Lucy and Tess shouted their approval. Tess's wide grin touched his heart as the little girl slipped her mittened hand in his. Lucy mouthed a thank-you as they headed over to the lot to pick up their tree.

*I could get used to this*, Dante thought. The strange idea flitted through his mind, throwing him a bit off balance. Being back home had been a positive experience so far, but Mistletoe was no longer his home. Years ago he'd decided that in order to make it big in Hollywood he needed to leave his Maine hometown. As a result, he'd carved out an incredible life for himself in California. There was no turning back or giving in to sentimentality. Mistletoe was in his past, not his future, even though Lucy made him yearn for things he hadn't thought of in years.

# CHAPTER TWELVE

A few days later, Lucy was at town hall helping to final-
ize the plans for Mistletoe's annual holiday bash. The
Christmas Frolic was a one-hundred-year-old town tradition
that celebrated community, the holiday season, and Maine.
Lucy loved being a part of the Mistletoe planning committee, especially since this year some of the proceeds were
earmarked for the library. Little by little, Lucy's goal of gar-
nering financial support for the library was coming to
fruition.

At the moment, she could barely focus on the matter
at hand. Thoughts of Dante danced in her head like sugar-
plums. Their paths hadn't crossed since their night at the
tree farm and Lucy keenly felt his absence. It was such a
strange feeling to go so long without him being in her life,
but now she was accustomed to seeing him. It may have
been her imagination, but it was almost a physical ache. It
was making her feel a bit off-kilter.

There were so many things left unsaid between them. They'd barely scratched the surface. Lucy couldn't shake the feeling that she and Dante were rebuilding what had been broken between them years ago. But it was hard to hope for anything solid to develop since Dante was only in town for the short term. Lucy knew how she felt about him, and it explained so much about why she'd had such a hard time moving on. Dante had been her once-in-a-lifetime love, and those feelings had never really died. Embers had been simmering under the surface, and with his return, a full blaze had been reignited.

All the kissing and touching they were doing didn't mean they were together, she reminded herself. Not in the truest sense of the word. All it demonstrated was that there were huge sparks whenever they were near each other. Dante hadn't said a single thing about how he felt about her. And she would feel like an utter fool if she expressed her feelings only to find out he didn't feel the same way.

As soon as the meeting ended, Lucy quickly gathered up her belongings so she could go back to the library. After she said her goodbyes and headed toward the door, Lucy felt a tug on her arm. Turning around, she came face-to-face with Violet Stewart, a local artist and historian who considered herself a town matriarch. With her vibrant red hair, glittering emerald eyes, and animated demeanor, Violet commanded attention everywhere she went.

"I was at my Daughters of Mistletoe meeting this morning and I heard the most outrageous rumor." Violet raised her eyebrows and sent Lucy a knowing look. Lucy wanted to let out a snort. The women's group was nothing more than a haven for town gossips. They were supposed to be working on town history projects and exploring genealogy trees, but Lucy suspected not much work was being done other than flapping their gums.

Violet edged closer to her. "I'm not one to gossip, but I think it's only fair to tell you that certain town residents are saying you are having an affair." She lowered her voice to a whisper. "With Dante West."

Lucy steeled herself not to react to the outrageous claim. "I really have to get back to work, Violet." Maybe if she didn't take the bait, Violet would leave her alone.

"You were spotted at the library," Violet said, pointing a finger at Lucy. "Necking with a movie star. And here I thought you were a Goody Two-Shoes."

Necking? Lucy hadn't heard that expression since her grandmother was alive. She felt as if she'd been transported to the 1950s.

She shook her head. "Don't believe everything you hear, Violet. I'd be careful about passing on rumors. It might come back to bite you in the you-know-what."

Violet put her hands on her hips. An expression of outrage appeared on her face. "Lucy Marshall! I wasn't spreading any talk about you and Dante. I was merely letting you know what folks were saying about the two of you. I thought you'd appreciate the heads-up."

Lucy was working hard not to say something she might regret. Mistletoe had far too many busybodies walking around town spreading dirt. Even though aspects of the story were true, Lucy hated being the subject of gossip. Violet had a knack for making her rumors sound disreputable.

"Be careful," Violet warned. "Dante was always a sweetheart, but he's a celebrity now." She winked at Lucy. "He's probably got a few ladies waiting for him back in California. Don't let him break your heart..." Violet trailed off and Lucy had a gut feeling she'd stopped herself before uttering the word *again*.

Lucy smiled through gritted teeth. Although she was annoyed, she couldn't really be too upset. The possibility of having her heart shattered was her biggest fear about reconnecting with her ex. She tilted her chin up and didn't bat an eyelash as she responded, "Don't worry about me. Mama didn't raise any fools."

"Glad to hear it," Violet said with a bob of her head. "See you at the Christmas Frolic," she trilled, her voice carrying. With a wave of a few fingers, Violet was gone. Lucy huffed out a tightly held breath. She'd tried to keep her cool, but Violet had gotten under her skin.

"Maybe you need to get your own romance going so you can stay out of mine," Lucy muttered.

She felt a gentle arm being placed around her shoulder. "Don't give her a second thought, Lucy. She's blowing everything out of proportion, as usual." When she turned her head, Eva Langston was by her side with a sympathetic expression. "There was a little chatter, but nothing outrageous. They were basically saying you were getting it on at the library."

Eva was the owner of Casablanca, the classic movie

theater on Main Street. Blond and statuesque, Eva was one of the kindest-hearted people in town. She'd been Lucy's friend since she'd arrived in town five years ago and purchased the old theater. Eva had worked diligently to fix up the place and restore it to its former glory. With a new name and marquee, plush red leather seats, and an expanded concessions area, Casablanca was a favorite spot in town.

Lucy threw her hands up. "I love Mistletoe, but the rumor mill is so out of control. It makes my head spin."

Eva nodded. "Tell me about it. I just found out I have a secret husband in Cape Cod. Seems someone forgot to tell me about him." She winked at Lucy. "I wonder if he's tall, dark, and handsome?"

Lucy chuckled along with Eva. "So much for Mistletoe being a sleepy little New England town. If you scratch the surface, there's a lot more to it."

"Do you have time to grab a hot cocoa? We can dish some more at the Coffee Bean," Eva suggested, her hazel eyes twinkling.

"I'd love to chat more, but I have to head back to work. I'm swamped." It would be lovely to catch up with her friend, but her schedule wouldn't allow it. Not today anyway.

"Why don't I walk with you?" Eva asked as she looped her arm through Lucy's. "We can discuss setting up for the Christmas Frolic...or talk about a certain gorgeous hometown celebrity who happens to be your ex."

Lucy let out a groan. "Not you too. All anyone wants to talk about is Dante."

Eva smirked at her. "Can you blame us? He's the hottest

thing to hit this town since sliced bread." Lucy giggled at the comparison. It was great to have a friend who could make her laugh at the situation. She was so tired of worrying about her every conversation with Dante. Between her own doubts and the endless town chatter, Lucy had a lot to worry about. Eva was a judgment-free zone.

As they stepped outside into the wintry air, Lucy and Eva strolled past the shops and paused to gaze longingly at the gingerbread houses in the window of Sweet Temptation, the best bakery in Maine. The establishment had the best cakes Lucy had ever tasted. And if she wasn't running late she would step inside and order a six-pack of red velvet cupcakes with cream cheese icing. Just looking at the display made her stomach grumble in appreciation.

"So, is there anything going on with you and Inferno?" Eva asked as they walked toward the library. "As one of your best friends, I really need the scoop. And I pinky swear not to tell a soul." She held out her pinky and Lucy wrapped her own around Eva's.

Lucy paused for a moment before speaking. Telling Eva might take a huge weight off her shoulders. "As you know, I dated Dante for a few years back in high school. It was a pretty intense relationship. We had plans for a future together, but he headed to California without me. It totally blindsided me."

Eva cringed. "Ouch."

"Exactly. It hurt more than I can put into words. And now he's back in Mistletoe, famous and finer than ever. At first I was angry at him, but now…"

"Now you're falling for him," Eva said.

Lucy stopped in her snowy tracks and glanced over at Eva. Were her feelings so obvious?

"Am I right?" her friend asked, her brows furrowed.

Lucy nodded as they continued walking. "Yes, you're right. No matter how much I've tried not to fall for him, it seems as if my heart has a mind of its own." She shrugged. "I don't know what it all means though. We're really good at kissing, but I have no idea what he's feeling toward me. And it's driving me a little bit crazy." By this time, they'd reached the library and Lucy knew her time with Eva was up.

"Well, maybe you should find out how he feels," Eva said, reaching out and pulling Lucy in for a hug. "Ask him, Lucy. Point-blank. Period. Put on your big-girl panties and get some answers."

* * *

A few days later, Lucy decided to take action. Eva's words had issued a challenge to her that she found hard to ignore. *Put on your big-girl panties.* She wasn't a teenager anymore and if she wanted answers from Dante she needed to go get them. Although he was still filming at the library, Lucy barely saw him. When he did have a few minutes to chat it was always casual and brief. It left her with an empty feeling in the pit of her stomach.

Lucy had been informed by a crew member that shooting was going to conclude early this afternoon because of a script change. Filming would resume in the morning. By this time, the crew members knew Lucy by name and she knew most of theirs as well. As soon as she got back to her desk, Lucy busied herself with colored paper, scissors, and gel pens. During a lull in the day, Lucy did a little reconnaissance mission to figure out Dante's whereabouts. One of his crew members pointed her toward a small office in the back of the library where Dante was working. By this time, most of the cast and crew had taken off.

Lucy spotted Dante through the partially open door. He was seated at a desk poring over a thick notebook. She knocked firmly on the wooden surface, willing herself not to chicken out.

"Hey there, Lucy. Long time no see." He beckoned her in with a wave. Seeing Dante's eyes light up at the sight of her felt amazing.

"You look wiped out," Lucy said. Maybe her timing wasn't so good after all. Dante appeared a bit worse for wear. A five-o'clock shadow graced his handsome face. "Did you pull an all-nighter?"

"It's pretty intense trying to keep things running smoothly on a set," Dante explained. "I did manage to get a few winks last night, but I'm looking forward to sleeping in over the weekend." He ran a hand over his face.

She chewed the inside of her lip. "My timing might be way off, but…" Her voice trailed off, swallowed up by her own discomfort. She was making a bold move with Dante, and for the life of her she didn't know if she was making a fool of herself or not.

She slid the invitation across the desk until it landed in front of him.

"What's this?" Dante asked as he fingered the piece of colored paper with his name scrawled on it in cursive.

"Open it and find out."

Dante couldn't hide the smile on his face as he opened it up and looked at her invitation. He swung his gaze up to meet hers. "You're inviting me to the movies? Tonight?"

"I heard through the grapevine you were wrapping up early today, but if it's not a good time I'll take a rain check."

Dante gaped at her. "Are you kidding me? I've dreamed about going back to see a flick at the Regal. That's where I learned about cinema and started dreaming about being a part of the film industry. I'll never forget going to see *The Godfather* and *Star Wars*."

"Actually, it's not the Regal anymore. My friend Eva bought it and renamed it Casablanca. I'm sure you can guess why. But trust me, you won't be disappointed. She spruced the place up and added some cool features while maintaining that classic aesthetic."

He nodded. "Casablanca is a cool name for a movie theater." He stroked his jaw. "So, what movie is playing tonight?"

She felt a huge smile tugging at her lips. "Why don't we meet there at quarter to six and you'll see it on the marquee." She reached out and ran her fingers along the stubble on his jawline. "That way you can go home and take a shower and shave. Even rest up a little."

"It's a date," Dante said. The words rolled easily off his tongue.

"I'll see you then," Lucy answered, turning on her heels and heading back to her own office. She could feel her cheeks getting flushed and she imagined there was a certain pep in her step. She had a movie date with Dante tonight, and everything felt right in her world.

At quarter to six, Lucy stood in front of the Casablanca movie theater wearing a thick wool coat with a faux-fur trim and her most fashionable winter boots. Dante was right on time to meet her. Even from a few feet away she could see he was cleanly shaven and rested. He walked toward her with a huge grin on his face as he pointed up at the marquee.

"I love it. *Butch Cassidy and the Sundance Kid.* One of my favorites."

"How could I forget? We saw it together more than a few times." Lucy giggled. "Every time you started quoting the lines everyone else in the theater got upset."

"Thanks for doing this, Luce. I didn't realize how much I needed some downtime." Lucy felt herself wrapped up in Dante's arms as he went in for a hug. Being in his arms felt like heaven even though the embrace was brief. They both knew that the movie would be starting shortly. She felt Dante's hand loop around her waist as she gave their tickets to the theater attendant.

After stopping at the concession stand for sodas, popcorn, and M&M's, they headed into the theater. Although it was fairly empty, Lucy saw a few acquaintances who did a double take at the sight of Dante. For once she didn't care about town gossip. There was an easy rhythm between her and Dante. Nothing felt forced or contrived. They were simply enjoying each other's company and having fun.

For the next two hours they were mesmerized by the adventures of Paul Newman and Robert Redford. At certain points in the movie they whispered back and forth while sharing a big tub of popcorn. When the final credits rolled, the audience was cheering with Dante hollering the loudest.

"I think I ate too much popcorn," Dante said with a groan as they left the theater and headed outside.

"Why don't we walk it off?" Lucy suggested. "It'll do us both some good. This area looks so festive and bright this time of year."

"Great idea." He interlocked his hand with hers as they walked down Main Street. It felt like old times going to the movies and then holding hands as they took in the sights of downtown Mistletoe.

"Do you remember cutting class and sneaking into the movies?" Dante asked as they walked.

She looked over at him, admiring his strong jawline and nice profile. "Of course I do. Every single time I thought we would get suspended. I was so worried about getting a ding on my perfect record."

Dante threw his head back and chuckled. "I didn't have a pristine record to care about."

"No, you sure didn't," Lucy agreed, covering her mouth with her hand as she laughed. Always the rebel, Dante had pushed past boundaries. He'd been an original. She would bet it was one of the reasons he'd beaten the odds to become a successful actor.

They crossed the street and headed toward the town green. From where they were standing, they could see the town gazebo lit up with brightly colored string lights. Set against the darkness, the effect was breathtaking. They stood in silence for a few moments and soaked in the beautiful scene.

"So are you busy on Saturday?" Lucy asked, breaking into the silence. "If not, I would love it if you could help us out by doing some shifts at the Christmas Frolic. I'm on the planning committee and I'm basically going to be there all day. We could use another set of hands."

"We're actually ahead of schedule with filming, so I can definitely make some time to help out."

"It will mean a lot to the town having you there." Her voice softened. "And to me."

Dante placed Lucy's face between his hands and stared deeply into her eyes. His expression was intense. "Whatever you need, Luce. I've got you. I care about you. And even though I'm here to make my film, I want to spend as much time with you as I can. When I'm with you, I feel like I'm my best self. It's been a long time since I've felt that way."

Lucy felt fluttering in her belly. She'd wanted to know how Dante felt about her. And here it was. His feelings mirrored her own. It wasn't words of love or any promises about the future, but it showed her that she wasn't wasting her time. He did have feelings for her.

"I feel the same way, Dante." She didn't need to say anything else, she realized. Things were good between them. She was starting to be hopeful. Perhaps she'd been wrong about him smashing her heart into little pieces.

Maybe, just maybe, this time around they would get things right.

# CHAPTER THIRTEEN

Dante made his way through the downtown area of Mistletoe as he headed toward the town green for his shift at the Christmas Frolic. Mistletoe resembled a picture-perfect postcard of a quaint New England town getting ready to celebrate the most joyful time of the year. Last night's snowfall had cast its wintry magic all over town, and the smell of Christmas hung in the air—peppermint, pine cones, and evergreens. Everywhere Dante looked it appeared as if someone had sprinkled Christmas cheer all over his hometown. Tinsel and candy canes and decorations galore. He wouldn't be surprised if he saw a fleet of reindeer flying down from the sky led by Santa Claus himself.

Memories came flooding back to him. He'd been attending the annual Christmas Frolic ever since he was a toddler. It had been one of his dad's favorite Mistletoe traditions. Every year he'd entered the pecan pie eating competition and participated in the Christmas cookie extravaganza. His dad had baked a mean iced sugar cookie that had won him a multitude of ribbons. Although he'd always tried to act as if he was nonchalant about his wins, they'd all seen the evidence of his deep pride. Those were some wonderful memories he held deep in his heart.

Being here today made him feel connected to his dad, which was one of the reasons he'd agreed to help Lucy today with the event. The other reason was Lucy herself. Dante would do just about anything to make her happy. He was crazy about her. With no filming taking place today, it provided him with a rare opportunity to be a part of the holiday action.

He walked through the town green, smiling at all the special holiday touches. The ice sculptures were magnificent— angels, Christmas trees, and a nativity scene. He'd never seen so much tinsel in his life. The gigantic evergreen tree sat squarely in the center of all the activity. Later on tonight, the townsfolk would gather and decorate the tree as a community. A choir would be singing carols and handing out candy canes to the kids. Excitement hummed in the air even though the event didn't start for a few hours.

He spotted Lucy exactly where she'd said she would be. She was standing at the Santa's Village display dressed in the most adorable elf costume. If all Santa's elves looked this enticing in their costumes, Dante would have volunteered ages ago. Lucy was pacing back and forth with her lips moving a mile a minute. Was she talking to herself? If so, she was having a rip-roaring conversation.

Before he could even greet her, Lucy threw her hands in the air and began talking up a storm.

"We have a problem," Lucy announced. There was more than a hint of drama in her statement. The look of panic on her face didn't match the uplifting holiday vibe surrounding them.

"What is it? How can I help?" Dante asked. He was eager to assist in any way possible. Coming back home reinforced the fact that he was a member of the Mistletoe community. He knew the importance of this event. It was the highlight of the Mistletoe holiday season. Dante was ready to roll up his sleeves and get to work.

"Santa has food poisoning. We need a replacement for this afternoon," she said. "If we don't have a Santa Claus in the village there's going to be trouble with the kids who are expecting him. I can't stand the thought of them being disappointed."

"This afternoon?" Dante let out a low whistle. "That's short notice. Maybe I can make some calls to a few old friends." His mind was scrambling to come up with a suitable person for the job. Someone older. A portly physique would be beneficial as well as a pleasant attitude.

Lucy bit her lip. "We don't have time for that. Santa has to be in his suit and primed for action in less than an hour. We usually like to take some pictures beforehand for the local paper."

"Oh, wow. That's a bummer for the kids. What kid doesn't want a meet and greet with Santa?" He vividly remembered being eight years old and not being able to sleep the night before Santa's town visit. He'd written a list the length of his arm and presented it to the man in the red-and-white suit with the utmost optimism.

"Well, it doesn't have to be if a certain hometown hero steps in," Lucy drawled. The smile that broke out on Lucy's face made him weak in the knees. She could move mountains with that mesmerizing smile. He was sure of it.

Hometown hero? Wait a minute. She couldn't possibly be talking about him. The hopeful expression etched on Lucy's face answered his question. She wanted him to get dressed up in a red-and-white Santa suit, don a white beard and mustache, then listen to Christmas wish lists?

"Me? Are you serious? No, Lucy. I can't do it." Dante vigorously shook his head. He needed to nip this idea in the bud before it spiraled out of control. There was no way he was suiting up to play Santa Claus. The idea of working with kids made him nervous. It wasn't at all in his wheelhouse. He'd done it once before as a struggling actor trying to make ends meet and it had been disastrous. Dante had roasted in the hot California sun wearing the heavy, itchy Santa suit. He'd been a complete failure at the job, managing to make several kids cry while others had accused him of being a fake Jolly Old Saint Nicholas.

Within seconds her expression morphed into a familiar one. Every time Lucy wanted something from him back in the day she'd given him a mournful, wide-eyed look. From what he remembered, it had worked wonders.

Lucy folded her hands prayerfully. "Please, Dante. It's for the kids. It's town tradition to have Santa sit front and center at the gazebo on the town green. Don't you remember how much we loved it when we were kids? All you would have to do is listen to what the kids want for Christmas and utter a few ho ho hos. Easy peasy."

Dante grimaced. "I don't have very much experience with little kids. To be honest, they kind of scare me," he admitted. "I just don't think I can do it convincingly."

Lucy let out a wild hoot of laughter. "You perform some of your own movie stunts, don't you? Yet a bunch of little kids terrifies you?"

"Basically," he said. "I won't know what to do if they cry or have a tantrum." He shuddered at the thought of it.

Lucy swatted him with her hand. "You can charm birds from the trees. I don't think you'll have any trouble with small children. They're all going to be so excited about Christmas and the presents that'll be under the tree. We can't disappoint them. It's tradition."

"We?" Dante asked with a raised brow.

She did a little twirl. "I'm one of Santa's helpers. Come on. How can you resist my elfin charms?" Dante swept his gaze over Lucy's formfitting costume. She did look pretty enticing. Now if Lucy wanted to sit on his lap he wouldn't have a problem with it.

"Wait a minute. What about Nick? He actually has a kid, so he's got experience. Or Troy. He has those broad shoulders that would fill out a Santa suit nicely," Dante suggested. At this point he didn't care who he was throwing under the bus. Anyone but him.

Lucy frowned. "I already called Nick. No answer." She

made a face. "And when I called Troy, he suggested that I ask you."

Dante let out a shocked sound. "He said that? What a punk. He's been doing that ever since we were kids." Dante shook his head in disbelief. "Always pointing the finger in my direction."

Lucy folded her arms across her chest and tapped her foot. "I know you and Troy have major sibling issues, but can we focus on the current crisis at hand? Will you or will you not suit up as Santa Claus for the Christmas Frolic?"

Seconds ticked by during which Dante felt completely immobilized. He really really really didn't want to be Santa, but with every passing moment his options were becoming extremely limited. He would look incredibly mean-spirited if he didn't say yes. Especially since Christmas was coming soon. He would seem like a Grinch.

He heaved a tortured sigh. "All right. I surrender. Suit me up."

Lucy let out an earsplitting shriek. She rushed at him, throwing her arms around him in a gigantic bear hug. Having her in his arms was a pretty big consolation prize for taking on this gig. He liked the way she fit perfectly into the crook of his arm.

She looked up at him, her brown eyes twinkling. "I knew that Mistletoe could count on you."

"You did?" he asked. He didn't want to say it, but he'd been seconds away from flat-out refusing. Had her faith in him been restored by this act of kindness?

"Yes! You wouldn't have come back home if you didn't believe in this town."

"True. Most of all, I believe in you, Lucy. If anyone else had asked me to do this I wouldn't have agreed." He was being completely honest with her and he hoped Lucy could see his sincerity. She was opening up to him little by little and peeling back the layers. They'd come a long way in the short time he'd been back in Mistletoe. She'd surprised him the other night by inviting him to the movies and then asking him to help out today at the Christmas Frolic. She was thawing to him. Although the past still loomed over them at certain times, Dante was convinced that they'd managed to turn a corner.

"But you did say yes, so now you have to quickly get suited up," Lucy said, clapping her hands together. "The line to see Santa is always huge, so you should get a little hydrated after you put the costume on. You might feel a little stuffy inside the suit, so if you need a break you can just give me the high sign."

Ugh. Costumes were usually stifling and smelly. In the fledgling days of his acting career he'd worked as a character at a theme park. Dante shuddered at the recollection of how dirty the outfits had been. He hoped this one had just been picked up from the cleaners. Lucy pulled him by the arm to a makeshift dressing room behind the Santa's Village area. She reached into a garment bag and pulled out a red-and-white Santa suit that looked as if it had seen better days.

"Ta-da!" she said in a spirited voice as she held it

up. Immediately Lucy scrunched up her nose and sneezed, followed by a flurry of sneezes.

Oh, great. The outfit was giving Lucy a case of the sneezes. That really didn't bode well. Dante reached for the costume. It was in decent condition although it reeked of mothballs. The smell was quite potent. "This thing needs to be Febrezed or something," Dante said. "It reeks."

"Sorry about that. The costume came from someone's attic. It should air out now that it's out of the bag." Lucy's expression was sheepish. There was no way she truly believed the smell would fade. It was so strong it made his eyes tear up. Hopefully none of the kids would pass out from the stench.

"Why don't you put it on? Here are the accessories," Lucy said, handing him a plastic bag. "Come out when you're done." Lucy drew the curtain closed and he could hear her boots shuffling as she walked away.

Dante grunted and began taking off his clothes so he could put the Santa suit on. After a few minutes of tugging and adjusting, he finally shimmied into the outfit. He patted the stretched-out stomach area of the costume and frowned. Hopefully Lucy had a little stuffing to fill out the stomach to make him look authentic. Lastly, he put on the beard, mustache, and tiny pair of glasses. Too bad he didn't have a mirror so he could look at himself. With a tortured sigh he pulled the curtain back and stepped out. Lucy was sitting a few feet away from him looking at her phone.

"Ho ho ho," he said in a weak imitation of the various Santa impersonators who'd made his holiday dreams come true. Lucy swung her gaze up in response to his greeting.

She stood up and walked over, her eyes roaming from head to toe. Almost instantly, her face crinkled up and she began to giggle. Within seconds the giggle turned into a deep chuckle. Before long she was clutching her stomach and letting loose with huge belly laughs. No words were coming out of her mouth. At one point she was laughing so hard she had to lean over at the waist to catch her breath. Several times she tried to compose herself, but each time she ended up cackling with laughter.

"Oh, goodness. I'm so sorry. I don't know what came over me, but—" She clapped her hand over her mouth as more giggles emerged.

He should have known better than to put the Santa suit on. He'd only done it to make Lucy happy, but he wasn't thrilled about looking like a fool. "I look like an idiot, don't I?"

"No, you don't. I promise," she said, patting him on the shoulder. "You look like a perfect Santa Claus."

"Ha! You shouldn't tell lies, Lucy Marshall. Your laughter spoke volumes."

"I'm sorry for laughing. Honestly, it was more because of the irony of a hot movie star putting on a Santa suit than anything else. You look like a very respectable Old Saint Nick. I promise."

Dante could feel a grin stretching from ear to ear on his face. "So you think I'm hot, huh?"

Lucy shrugged. "You're okay, I guess."

"Too late. You said I was hot." He stroked his jaw. "They don't call me Inferno for nothing," he teased.

"You did not just say that!" Lucy said, letting out a groan.

"Hey, you were the one who said I was hot," Dante said, grinning. "And it's too late for you to take it back."

She slapped a hand against her forehead. "Are you ever going to drop this?"

"Nope," he said with a grin. "I'm having way too much fun with it."

She rolled her eyes. "Well, you know you're hot. It's not like they give Sexiest Man Alive to celebrities who aren't serious eye candy. I'm sure a million people have told you so over the years."

He took off his Santa glasses and locked gazes with her. "I've had my fair share of compliments, but it means more coming from you, Lucy."

They were standing so close to each other that Dante could see the little caramel flecks in her brown eyes. If he moved an inch closer, he could easily kiss her. As it was, her perfectly shaped pink lips were offering an invitation he was finding hard to ignore. Lucy tilted her face upward. Her eyes were bright and filled with joy. He didn't want to do a single thing to dampen her spirit. This moment wasn't about him getting close to Lucy. It was about suiting up as Santa to help the Mistletoe community.

"So what's next?" Dante asked, taking a step away from her. He saw a momentary flash of something that resembled disappointment in Lucy's eyes. She quickly recovered by shuttering her expression.

"Are you ready to take some promo pics? I promise not to tell the photographer your identity. It's better to just call you Santa."

"I'm good with however you want to handle it," Dante said. And he meant it. He hated to see actors who considered themselves above certain roles or community service endeavors. He never wanted to be perceived in that negative light. If Dante West dressing up as Santa would help Lucy and the town of Mistletoe in any way, he was all for it. He owed his hometown a huge debt of gratitude. He wouldn't ever have risen so high as an actor if it hadn't been for his family and this town. Being back here cemented it, bringing the situation into clear focus. As for Lucy, there really wasn't anything he wouldn't do for her, even if it took a little coaxing.

"Let's maintain a little mystery," Lucy said. "That way we won't run the risk of the kids hearing at some point that it was you in the costume. Does that make sense?"

"Sounds good to me. Let's go take some photos," Dante said, clapping his hands together. Even though he was dreading this gig, excitement thrummed in the air. So many townsfolk were milling around with smiles on their faces—especially the kids—their joy felt infectious.

The photo shoot was fun, especially since Lucy was in most of the pictures as Santa's very special helper. In one shot she was sitting on his lap and pressing a kiss against his cheek. In another he hoisted her over his shoulder and her pert backside was facing the camera. He made a point to ask the photographer to send him that particular photo. He planned to frame it and put it in a special place at his home in Los Angeles. The thought shook him a little bit. It was the first time he'd thought of Lucy and the future.

At noon sharp, kids started lining up for a visit with Santa. Lucy had walked him through everything, and his nerves had finally settled down. He wasn't sure why he was putting so much pressure on himself. If he couldn't play Santa Claus, he wasn't much of an actor, he reminded himself. Maybe it was because he knew how special this experience was for the kids here in town.

For the next hour straight, Dante used every ounce of his acting talent to portray the best Santa Claus the town of Mistletoe had ever seen. He channeled every single movie he'd ever seen with Santa in it. *Miracle on 34th Street* had always been his favorite. The actor who'd played Santa, Edmund Gwenn, had even won an Oscar for his role as Kris Kringle.

The first hour passed in a blur as dozens of kids sat beside Santa's throne and recited their Christmas list wishes to him. Every type of kid stopped by—shy ones, funny ones, energetic ones, nervous ones, loud ones, and even a few bratty ones. With Lucy standing nearby as his elf helper, it made playing Santa Claus way more fun than it would have been otherwise. Whenever there was a short break in the action, they made jokes and snapped pics on Lucy's cell phone. When he finished up with each child, Lucy would walk them back to their parents while Dante beckoned another child to come visit with him.

Then Tess was standing at front of the line decked out in a blue winter coat with a red-and-white candy-cane-striped dress with matching leggings on underneath. He wasn't an expert on kids, but he thought she might just be the most adorable one he'd ever known. Dante beckoned her forward as Elf Lucy escorted the previous kid back to their waiting parent. Tess came forward and sat down on the bench next to him.

"Hi, Dante. How's it going?" Tess asked, peering up at him.

"Ho ho ho. The name is Santa Claus, my dear. What's your name?" Dante asked, startled by Tess's rapid discovery that it was him inside the Santa suit.

"I know it's you, Dante," she said in a matter-of-fact tone. "Don't worry. I don't believe in Santa Claus anymore."

"Aww. That's a bummer. Did I do something to give it away?" A terrible thought crossed his mind. "Did you just find out right now? Am I the reason you don't believe in Santa Claus anymore?" His heart was beating fast waiting for Tess's reply. Lucy might skin him alive if he was the reason her baby sister no longer believed in good old Kris Kringle.

Tess giggled. "Of course not. I found out ages ago, but everyone in my family wants me to believe, so that's why I'm here. I'm doing my part to keep the magic of Christmas alive."

This was awkward. He wasn't sure if he was supposed to try to sell her on the Santa thing or pat her on the back for uncovering the truth. This was the reason he hadn't wanted to play Santa. A moment like this needed a more seasoned Santa, one who was actually good at playing the role. He really didn't want to crash and burn again, especially not at this special event.

"So, what's on your wish list for Christmas?" he asked, hoping to focus on something positive and cheery. If she didn't believe in Santa Claus, he would bet his last dollar she still believed in presents under the tree. What kid didn't want to wake up on Christmas morning and rip open a mountain of gifts?

Tess grinned. "There's only one thing I want. A puppy of my own. If that happens, it'll be a real Christmas miracle."

"So what kind of dog are you hoping for?" he asked.

"I love cocker spaniels and chocolate Labs," Tess said. A dreamy expression passed over her face. Dante made a mental note to mention Tess's wish for a Christmas puppy to Lucy. He would love to see Tess's dream come true.

He wagged his gloved finger at her. "Anything's possible at Christmas. Don't stop believing."

Tess squinted at him. "Isn't that a famous song?"

He patted her on the head. "It is indeed. A rather iconic song at that."

She rolled her eyes. "Are you telling me you actually believe in Santa Claus? For real?"

Dante paused a moment before answering. He didn't want to straight-up lie to her, but he wanted her to see all the possibilities. "I believe in goodness, especially during Christmas. I believe that there are so many people out there who want to perform miracles for other folks just so they can see them smile. I believe that this time of year we see the beauty in people's hearts more than any other time. If that's not the spirit of Santa Claus, I don't know what is."

Tess grinned at him and tugged playfully at his beard. "Thanks, Santa. You're the best."

She jumped up and bounded past Lucy, who eyed her curiously. "What did you say to her?" she asked in a low voice. "She looked like she was floating on air."

Dante shrugged. "That's between her and Santa," he said with a smile tugging at the corners of his lips.

"Well played," Lucy said with a grin. "I didn't think she believed anymore."

He winked at her. "I wouldn't be too sure of that. She asked Santa for a puppy. Any possibility of that happening?"

Lucy winced. "That would be a question for my parents. I can pass it on, but with all of my mother's physical challenges these days, I'm not sure it would work out. Puppies are amazing, but they're a lot of work."

"Sorry. I didn't even think of that," Dante apologized. Leslie's medical condition had ripples.

Dante glanced at his watch. His Santa gig was almost over. It hadn't been as painful as he'd envisioned. The kids had been cute, and for the most part, well-behaved. And he'd been a pretty fine Santa, if he did say so himself.

He stood up and stretched his legs. "What do you say I treat us to some fried dough over at the concessions stand? My stomach is starting to growl."

"Wait. There's one more," a voice called out from the crowd.

A brown-skinned woman with long flowing braids was pushing a sweet-faced little boy in a wheelchair straight toward him. The child couldn't have been more than seven years old. With mahogany-colored skin and big brown eyes, he was adorable. He was grinning so much it threatened to overtake his entire face.

Dante quickly sat back down. "Ho ho ho. What's your name, son?" he asked in a booming, Santa-esque tone.

"I'm Jimmy," the boy announced. He pulled out a long list from his jacket pocket. "Don't worry. I won't read the whole thing. Just the highlights."

Dante felt a smile tugging at his lips. "You're my last visitor, so take your time, Jimmy. Lay it on me."

For the next fifteen minutes, Dante listened as Jimmy read his list, then told him a few knock-knock jokes. He also inquired about the weather in the North Pole and the health of his reindeers. The kid had the type of personality that made Dante want to sit and listen to him all day long. When his mother returned to the stage to signal an end to his visit, Dante leaned down and hugged him.

"See you on Christmas Eve, Santa. I'll be tracking your path on radar. Fly safely," Jimmy said, waving as he left.

"Wow. That kind of blew me away. He's some kind of kid," Dante said, turning toward Lucy. "It brings everything into perspective." Meeting Jimmy made him feel ashamed about his earlier attitude about playing Santa. He'd done such a small thing, yet it had brought such joy to the kids. That's what Christmas was all about. Spreading joy and making dreams come true. Giving without the expectation of getting anything in return.

Lucy shook her head. "He's an amazing kid. Jimmy comes into the library all the time and checks out the most fascinating books. He's a robotics fan and has aspirations of working for NASA in the future. I have no doubt he'll make it happen."

Dante's gaze trailed after Jimmy as his mother wheeled him away. He spotted Troy enthusiastically greeting them at the end of the ramp. Even from a distance, Dante could see the huge grin on his face. His first gut impression was that his brother had never looked happier, and Dante felt a tightness in his chest at the realization. More than anything, he wanted Troy to be joyful in his life.

"Jimmy's mother, Noelle, is dating Troy. They've been going strong for almost two years now," Lucy explained. "From what I've seen, Troy is really close to Jimmy. His father passed away when he was a baby, so Troy is like a surrogate dad to him."

Dante watched as Troy placed a kiss on Noelle's temple, then high-fived Jimmy. From this angle they resembled a loving family unit. Troy tenderly placed his arm around Noelle and they disappeared into the crowd. Watching it unfold caused an unsettled feeling in the pit of his stomach. That's how far apart he and his brother had drifted. Dante wasn't even aware that his brother had a serious girlfriend. They were miles away from the days when they'd been each other's confidantes.

"Are you okay?" Lucy asked. "I think we're all done here."

"Yeah," he said. "I can't wait to get out of this itchy suit." He reached into the costume and scratched the area by his shoulder.

"You really showed up today for the town," Lucy said. "Just think of all the kids who'll go to sleep tonight dreaming of a magical Christmas morning."

Lucy's remark served as a reminder that Christmas was rapidly approaching. Time was beginning to slip through his fingers. He still had goals to accomplish before he left town. Being back in Mistletoe provided a rare opportunity for him to try to heal old wounds. He wasn't even close to making up for the past, he realized. Not by a long shot.

# CHAPTER FOURTEEN

Lucy headed toward the backstage area with Dante trailing behind her. The event had gone off without a hitch. Dante had been a good sport and played his role to perfection. She could tell he'd been incredibly moved by his interaction with Jimmy. She had enjoyed watching him and Tess talking like they were best buddies. Whether he realized it or not, he had a knack for communicating with kids. Perhaps they recognized the gigantic size of his heart. Dante had always been a big marshmallow on the inside, something she sensed very few people were aware of because of his tough-guy Inferno persona. The nickname and image had always surprised Lucy because it didn't resonate with the Dante she'd known. He'd been her own personal teddy bear—tender and sweet. And from what she'd seen, he still was.

"So, do I get something nice in my stocking for putting this ratty suit on?" Dante asked in a teasing tone as he held up a bedazzled stocking.

Lucy chuckled. It was still hilarious seeing him in the Santa getup. He didn't look at all like himself. No one had known that it was Dante underneath the costume, which made it all the more comical. She knew a lot of celebrities would have used this event to portray themselves as do-gooders in their community. She respected Dante for keeping his role under wraps and for agreeing to help out in a pinch. More and more Lucy was beginning to realize that Dante hadn't changed all that much despite his celebrity status. He was still a giver.

"Hey! You're getting the best gift of all," Lucy said, making her voice sound like spun sugar. "The knowledge that you've made so many children happy beyond their wildest dreams."

"Come on. You can do better than that," Dante urged. He wiggled his eyebrows suggestively. His eyes radiated a playfulness she couldn't ignore.

Was he daring her to do something? She'd seen this impish expression on his face a million times before. More often than not he'd been up to no good, pushing her out of her comfort zone and getting her to try new things. Whether she was cutting class with him to go to the movies or sneaking out of the house at night to meet him at the lake for skinny-dipping, Lucy had always felt invigorated by their adventures. Although Dante had changed over the years in terms of his focus and drive, he still possessed the same audacious spirit. That was one of the reasons she'd fallen in love with him back in high school. Somewhere along the way, she'd lost her own sense of adventure.

But now she was standing before him, wanting to be as bold as the old Lucy, the one who'd taken chances. What was it about Dante that made her want to hold her hand over the fire?

What was the harm in doing something unexpected? She took a step closer to him until there was no distance between them.

Lucy yanked down his beard and mustache, then stood on her tiptoes and placed a kiss on his sweet lips. Although she'd meant it to be a quick peck, Dante had other ideas. She felt his arms encircling her waist and drawing her closer. His lips moved over hers powerfully as the kiss intensified from tenderness to a red-hot blaze.

"Lucy!" a voice rang out, interrupting their impromptu kiss. She didn't even have to turn around to know who'd walked in on them.

"Hey, Stella," Dante said, looking past her shoulder. When Lucy turned around, Stella was standing a few feet away glaring at both of them. Her mouth was a thin, hard line. She acted as if she hadn't heard Dante's greeting. She locked eyes with Lucy, sending her a message of disapproval.

"Why don't I go change out of this getup," Dante said, beating a fast path toward the dressing room. Once he was gone, Lucy spoke up, hoping to dispel the friction vibrating between her and her sister.

"Hey. I was looking all over for you," Lucy said. "I could have used another elf to help me out with Santa's Village."

Stella scoffed. "Really? I'm surprised you had the time. You seemed pretty tied up with Santa Claus."

*Zing!* Stella was definitely throwing out barbs. Lucy was trying not to let Stella's foul attitude get to her. Maybe she was just having a bad day, she reasoned. She was willing to cut her some slack. Her sister had lived through her own personal nightmare this past year and the holiday season could be bringing it all to the surface.

"Dante was a really good sport. He stepped in and really saved the day," Lucy explained. "He was a big hit with the kids."

Stella frowned. "So you've forgiven him?" Her voice was as frosty as a February morning in Maine.

A thick tension hung in the air between them. Lucy wasn't sure what was upsetting Stella, but she was giving new meaning to glacial vibes. Her sister was one of the sweetest people she'd ever known, so it was odd to see her like this.

Lucy shifted from one foot to the other. "I've decided life is too short to harbor grudges. It's not that I've forgotten anything that happened, but I just don't see any point in being enemies," Lucy explained in a halting voice. She wanted to tell Stella that she was falling for Dante again, but the expression on her sister's face urged her to tread carefully. Stella looked like she might explode.

"And the two of you are hanging out now? Hooking up?" she snapped.

Lucy sucked in a shocked breath. It wasn't like Stella to act like this. She had no idea what had set her off.

She resembled a fire-breathing dragon. It validated Lucy's decision not to tell her the truth about Dante. Clearly, Stella couldn't handle it.

"We're just having fun with no strings attached," Lucy said, trying to keep her voice light. "It's not like I'm expecting anything. He's leaving town right after the holidays."

"Oh, that's rich," Stella sneered. "Guys like Dante always have fun, usually at other people's expense."

Lucy winced. It hurt to hear Stella trash-talk Dante. He didn't deserve it. He wasn't the same person who'd treated her so badly years ago. Stella didn't know what she was talking about. Things were much different now.

"Shh. He might hear you," she cautioned her sister. Lucy really didn't want Dante to hear any negativity flowing from Stella's lips. It would be humiliating, especially now that she and Dante had truly connected in a meaningful way.

Stella made a tutting sound. "A few weeks ago you wouldn't have cared about that. Back then you were dead set against him even coming back to town. I can't believe you caved so quickly."

"Stella, I know that when Dante came back to town I wasn't happy about it, but in the past few weeks we've talked through a lot of things and I understand a lot more than I did back then. It's not black and white. And he's not this evil guy who went out of his way to ruin my life."

Stella dug into her purse and pulled out her cell phone. After a few taps she held it up to Lucy. "Is he a good one though? Check out the headline in *Hot Tea*."

Lucy took the phone and studied the image staring back

at her from the gossip site. It was Dante standing close to Missy, who was looking up at him with straight-up infatuation and a healthy dose of lust in her eyes. The headline read: *Dante West Resurrects Affair with Reality Star.* Just seeing it on the screen created a jarring sensation throughout her body. Was Dante romantically involved with Missy? No way. She'd seen them in each other's company and Lucy hadn't picked up on any romantic vibes. Was she simply seeing things through rose-colored glasses? Or were the tabloids making up juicy stories? The other night at Sawyer's tree farm the paparazzi had been trailing Dante so they could snap some photos and slap on a fake headline. It could have been Lucy's own face plastered online if they hadn't hidden themselves behind the trees. Lucy thanked her lucky stars it wasn't her being blown up all over the internet. Being in the tabloids wasn't a good look for a town librarian.

She shook her head and looked away from Stella's cell phone. "That's just tabloid fiction. It happens to all famous people. Dante's no exception. Fake headlines sell magazines."

Stella seemed incredulous. Her mouth hung open in what Lucy could only assume was stunned disbelief. "I can't believe you're dismissing what's right in front of your eyes. You're determined to think the best of him at all costs."

"Dante was never a player, Stella. As I said, we're just enjoying spending time together. And that's fine by me." Lucy didn't dare tell Stella that she had feelings for Dante. It was best to downplay things.

"What's going to happen to you when he packs up his fancy equipment and heads back to California? What happens when he sets fire to all the plans you made for the two of you and marries someone else?"

Lucy gasped. "Stella, who are you talking about? Dante or Rafe?" she asked in a soft voice.

Dr. Rafe Santos had been Stella's fiancé and the man she'd thought she was going to spend the rest of her life with. A week before their dream wedding he'd told Stella that he was calling it off because he didn't believe she was his soul mate. Stella had been heartbroken and humiliated. Six months later Rafe married his high school sweetheart and brought her back from Virginia to Mistletoe. He and his wife purchased the sweet Victorian home in the center of town that he and Stella had talked about buying for themselves. Although Stella had gracefully picked up the pieces of her life, her heart had been shattered. Ever since then, Lucy had harbored fantasies about punching Rafe in the nose until he bled profusely. She considered it an act of the highest restraint that she hadn't done so.

Stella froze. Her mouth opened, and although she was clearly trying to speak, no words came out. Instead, big fat tears began falling down her face as her body was wracked with heart-wrenching sobs.

"Stella! Oh, my sweet, sweet girl," Lucy crooned as she held her sister in her arms. For their entire lives, it had always been Stella holding Lucy up when she fell down. Now it was her turn to comfort her big sister. Lucy knew Stella had suffered, but she'd been blind to the fact that it was ongoing. Stella was such a strong person and she'd fooled Lucy with her stiff upper lip. It hurt her to realize how wrong she'd been.

"I-I thought I was over it, Lucy. I really did," Stella said, sniffling and dabbing at her eyes with the hem of her jacket sleeve. "But it comes back in waves, like a tsunami that completely drags me under."

Lucy reached out and wiped a stray tear from her sister's face. "Hey, it's all right. You're allowed to be sad. It's okay that you're still grieving all that you lost. You thought he was your forever and then he wasn't. It was all ripped away from you. You've been so brave holding it together all of this time." And perhaps that was part of the problem. Stella had been so stoic throughout her ordeal. Lucy's heart had broken for her sister when she'd had to tend to all the details of canceling her wedding. Now, at least, she was dealing with the grief and pain.

Stella's eyes were red from crying. "I saw them earlier and Rafe dropped a bombshell. They're having a baby. Did you know that?"

Lucy sucked in a shocked breath and shook her head. She hadn't heard the news. She wasn't sure how much more Stella could take. To lose her fiancé and have him marry someone else so quickly was a stab in the gut. Everything else was just plain torture.

"I didn't mean to project my heartache on to you and Dante. I just don't want to see you get hurt all over again. It's bad enough that I'm walking around with an empty cavity where my heart used to be. I don't want you to join me." Stella's voice was laced with so much anguish it made Lucy think she might break down in tears herself. She hated Rafe with everything she was worth for shattering her sister's heart and breaking her spirit.

"Stella, I'm going to be fine. It's you I'm worried about. I want you to lean on me whenever you need to cry or vent. Or punch a wall if need be. I've done it a few times myself."

Stella began to chuckle. "I won't be punching any walls. That sounds really painful. With my luck I'd break my hand."

Lucy laughed along with her. "Well, it's all right if you do. I've got your back. And in case I haven't made it clear, Rafe is the world's biggest fool, bar none. I know it might be difficult to hear, but he did you a major favor by calling things off. This way you can move forward and find the one."

The one. Ever since they were teenagers Lucy and Stella had talked about finding that one magical person who would be their forever. In their endless conversations they'd fantasized about dream weddings, tropical honeymoons, and white picket fences. Sadly, it seemed that neither one of them was even close.

"Let's hope we both find him," Stella said. "Unless of course you already have." Stella locked gazes with her, issuing a challenge with her words that Lucy wasn't sure how to respond to. Years ago she'd thought of Dante as being her one, but she hadn't gone down that road in a long time. They were friends now . . . with kissing privileges.

Suddenly, Dante reappeared minus the red-and-white Santa costume. Lucy hadn't ever been so happy to see anyone before in her life. It saved her from having to get real by answering Stella's loaded question.

"Hey, I hope I'm not interrupting anything," Dante said, holding up the Santa suit. "I can't tell you how happy I am to give this back to you."

Lucy laughed and took the suit off Dante's hands and placed it back in the garment bag. "Don't forget to add this gig to your acting résumé, Dante. You were a picture-perfect Santa. You're going into the master list for next year," she teased. She knew it was highly unlikely he would be back in Mistletoe this time next year, but she wanted to see him squirm a bit.

Dante winced and shook his head. "I'm not sure I'll ever be ready for a repeat performance. It wasn't as bad as I thought it would be, but I'll pass."

The look on Dante's face was comical. He'd been such a lifesaver earlier by stepping in and playing Santa. Dante had singlehandedly rescued the Santa's Village event. She'd been so desperate to find someone to assume the role, Lucy had even considered donning the Santa suit herself. She knew without a shadow of a doubt it would have been a hot mess.

"How would you ladies like to walk around the festival with me?" Dante asked, looking back and forth between them. "I'm thinking some holiday baked goods and poutine fries."

Lucy darted a glance at Stella. She still looked shaken

by her run-in with her ex-fiancé. And walking around the town green with the most famous face to ever grace Mistletoe wouldn't give Stella the privacy she needed. As much as Lucy wanted to stroll around the Christmas Frolic with Dante—maybe hold his hand or sneak a kiss—her sister came first.

"I think Stella and I are going to talk some more," Lucy said. "Maybe we'll catch up to you later on."

"Okay, then. More Yule log cake for me," he said, rubbing his stomach as he strode away from them. Lucy watched him as he walked off. Her stomach twisted a little at the sight of him leaving. She knew soon enough he'd be taking off for good and all these moments they'd shared would be nothing but memories.

Although she'd been tempted to walk around the holiday fair with Dante, she knew Stella needed her far more than Dante ever would. Not to mention that she was a bit leery after seeing her sister's heartbreak up close and personal. It served as a reminder that being romantically involved with Dante made her vulnerable. Even though she kept telling herself that she was just going to live in the moment and enjoy their relationship until he headed back to California, Lucy wasn't being honest with herself. If she lived to the ripe old age of one hundred and four, Dante West would always own a piece of her heart. And the very idea of losing him a second time hurt like hell.

# CHAPTER FIFTEEN

As Dante wandered around the Christmas Frolic, he couldn't help but wish he had Lucy by his side. He understood that Stella needed some TLC. He wasn't sure what was going on with her, but her puffy eyes and tear-stained cheeks spoke to her fragile state of mind. The Marshall sisters had always shared a tight and loving bond. It was nice to see nothing had changed in that regard. He truly envied them. Earlier today when Dante had spotted Troy in the crowd, he'd yearned for things to be different between them.

Along the way several people paused to talk to him and a few kids asked about his upcoming movie, *Fatal Implosion*. It would be the last film in the popular franchise and fans were already clamoring to see it. When he went back to California he would be busy promoting the film, sitting down for interviews and traveling to premieres. In addition, he would be finishing up this film he was directing. He still hadn't come up with a title for the movie. All the internal memos referenced it as the Mistletoe project. Dante had been waiting for the perfect title to pop into his brain, but so far, it eluded him. Maybe he was being too sentimental about it.

As he walked past the gazebo, Dante ran straight into Lucy's parents, who were walking around with Tess. Dante enjoyed a mini reunion with the Marshalls. When he was a kid, their home had always been wide open to him. He'd eaten more meals at their dinner table than he could recount. At Christmas, Dante had helped them trim the tree and he'd always left a gift for Lucy underneath it so she could open it up on Christmas morning. Before parting ways with him, they reminded him not to be a stranger and invited him to pop over to the house before he went back to California. Just knowing he was still welcome made him a bit emotional. After things had gone so terribly wrong between him and Lucy, he'd figured that Leslie and Walt had written him off. It was gratifying to know they hadn't.

After saying his goodbyes to the Marshalls, Dante continued to explore the event. He grinned as he passed the pie-eating competition. This year it was pumpkin and apple, two of his personal favorites. The sight reminded him of his dad and how much pleasure he'd taken in being a part of Mistletoe's holiday celebration. Dante could picture him sitting at the table stuffing his face with pie and grinning from ear to ear when he won the contest. For the first time in years he could think of his father without guilt swallowing him up whole. Not all the memories of him were painful.

"Dante!" a high-pitched voice called out his name as he stood in line at the concessions stand. When he turned toward the sound, he spotted Missy standing about twenty feet away waving wildly at him. Unsurprisingly, she was smack-dab in the middle of a crowd of teenagers signing autographs. He could tell she was in heaven, judging by the look on her face. Missy loved being a celebrity far more than she enjoyed the craft of acting. She was a good person, but somewhere along the way her priorities had shifted.

Missy had poor impulse control. On several occasions she'd put the moves on him, even though he knew for a fact she wasn't single. He'd always let her down gently, telling her he didn't want to cross any romantic lines with her because they were colleagues. He was halfway telling the truth. Although Missy was attractive and sweet, she wasn't Dante's type at all.

Lucy's face suddenly appeared before his eyes. She was, and would always be, his very definition of beauty. With her sepia-colored eyes and toasted-brown skin, she radiated like the sun. He could easily picture her twenty years from now with slight crow's feet surrounding her eyes and strands of silver by her temples. She'd always be a knockout.

Before he knew it, Missy was beside him, clutching on to his arm. "Dante. I'm so happy to see you here. Come join us. We're about to take a sleigh ride." Dante looked behind her where a group of his cast and crew had congregated. He waved, happy to see them enjoying their downtime. The next few days would be filled with intense shoots and long days and nights, so it was nice they could experience the festival and get a taste of the town's holiday vibe.

Suddenly, Nick strolled up, providing a convenient out for him with Missy. It wasn't that he didn't want to hang out with his cast and crew, but after spending so much time on set, Dante needed a break. He wanted to revisit the Christmas Frolic through the lens of his childhood and reconnect with old classmates and teachers. He wanted to figure out how he could continue giving back to his hometown.

"Hey, Nick!" Dante said, effusively greeting his friend with a pat on the back.

"Hey there, Santa," Nick said with a wink. "Miles can't stop talking about his visit with Mr. Claus."

Dante put a finger to his lips. "Shhh. I'm trying to keep the mystery going."

Missy knitted her brows together, clearly unaware of what they were talking about.

"Nick, this is Missy North," Dante said. "He and I grew up in Mistletoe. We used to play football together."

"I'm Nick Keegan," Nick said, reaching out to take Missy's hand in his. "It's nice to meet you." Missy turned her attention to Nick and flashed him her best Colgate smile.

Dante couldn't remember Nick ever looking so awestruck by a woman other than Kara. Maybe his friend was ready to stick his big toe in the dating pool after all, although he knew Missy wasn't exactly available. She was keeping it on the down low, but Missy had gotten married a year ago. Despite some bumps in the road between her and Scott, they were still hitched.

"This town sure has its fair share of handsome men. There must be something in the water," Missy quipped, her eyes roaming over Nick's physique in full admiration. She turned her gaze to Dante. "I'll take a rain check on the sleigh ride."

"You saved me," Dante said in a relieved voice as Missy walked away.

"From what?" Nick asked, his gaze trailing after Missy. "She doesn't look like the sort of woman a man needs saving from. Have mercy!"

Dante shook his head. The awe on Nick's face was comical. "You have no idea. Proceed at your own risk."

Nick laughed. "No, thank you. I know better than to pursue a woman who only has eyes for you. I learned that lesson back in high school."

Nick had had a crush on Lucy back in the day, but he'd gotten over it once she and Dante had become an item. There had been no hard feelings and his friendship with Nick had never wavered. Shortly thereafter, Nick had fallen for Kara. And they'd all been happy and coupled up. At least for a little while. Every now and then, Dante wondered what his life might have been like if he had stayed in Mistletoe. Would he have been stuck working at the family hardware store? Or would he have gone to college like Lucy? Perhaps he would have ended up with Lucy and forged new dreams. Although he loved the life he'd built in California, he regretted missing out on the possibility of a life with Lucy. Was he just being sentimental? Or was it something more?

"Speaking of Lucy, how's it going between you two? I know you've been filming at the library." He made a face. "Town chatter has been in overdrive since you came home."

"It's been going pretty well," he admitted. "I won't say all is forgiven, but we've managed to forge something new out of the ashes. I guess you could say we're friends." Dante didn't want to tell Nick he'd reignited a romance with Lucy without her okaying it. Clearly she hadn't wanted her own sister to know the truth. He couldn't really blame her, considering that she would be facing the rumors head-on once he finished filming in Mistletoe. The very thought of leaving caused a funny feeling in his gut.

"Friends, huh?" Nick said with a snort. "In case you didn't know, something happens to your face when you talk about her." Nick pointed to Dante's eyes. "Right there. There's a special light in your eyes. That's the only way I can explain it. But it's there."

"You've been watching too many of those romance movies you like so much," Dante said, rolling his eyes.

"Hey! It wasn't me who loved those movies. It was Kara. I just watched along with her," Nick protested. "Haven't you ever heard of Netflix and chill?"

"Whatever you say, Nick," Dante said, chuckling as he shook his head. Nick was a huge fan of romantic movies and it had permeated his relationship with his wife. His friend was a romantic soul at heart. Dante believed he wasn't the type of man who should walk through life alone.

Nick's eyes focused on something behind Dante. "Hey, Lucy. Your ears must be burning," he said, his eyes twinkling.

"Hey, Nick. Dante. Were you guys talking about me?" Lucy asked as she walked up. She looked back and forth between them. Dante shot Nick a dirty look.

"I was just telling him about the great Santa Claus experience and how I was the jolliest Kris Kringle this town has ever seen," Dante fibbed. "I told him you killed it as Santa's favorite elf."

"Aww. That's nice of you to say," Lucy said. He could tell she was pleased at the compliment by the way she was beaming. "It was a lot of fun. It really set the tone for a wonderful festival."

"I feel bad that I missed it. Our sitter took Miles. I just got off work, but he raved about it as soon as I saw him," Nick said. "Great job, guys."

"Don't forget it's your turn as Santa next year," Lucy said, looking at Nick pointedly.

"Why don't we just ask Dante to come back and suit up again?" Nick asked, playfully slapping Dante on the shoulder.

"That is so not happening," Dante muttered, making sure Lucy didn't hear him. Nick had to stifle a laugh with his hand.

"Did you guys get food yet? I'm starving," Lucy said, peering around Nick to check out the concessions area.

"Not yet," Dante said. "I think I ran into everyone I've ever known on the way over here, all the way down to my nursery school teacher, Miss Botts."

"That's how small towns are," Lucy said. "Plus, you've been gone for a long time. I imagine folks are wondering if you'll ever come back."

Dante wasn't sure if Lucy was simply stating the facts or dinging him. She had a pleasant expression on her face, but there was a slight edge to her voice. He shouldn't be surprised. It wasn't as if he could sweep back into town and instantly patch everything up with his magic wand.

"I better go find Miles so he doesn't overdose on Christmas goodies. We'll catch up to you guys at the tree lighting ceremony," Nick said, practically racing away from them. Nick had clearly sensed something off in Lucy's tone and he'd chosen to get out of Dodge. That was pure Nick. He avoided confrontations at all costs.

Dante didn't bother telling Lucy he would definitely be coming back to Mistletoe. Talk was cheap. He would simply show her through his actions that he wasn't going to be MIA any longer. Being home in Mistletoe was restoring something inside of him he never imagined he'd get back. And he never wanted to lose it again.

"Is Stella okay? She looked pretty broken up earlier." He wasn't trying to pry, but perhaps Lucy's mood was tied up in Stella's sadness. It made sense with them being so close.

Lucy quirked her mouth. "Not really, but she will be. Someone kicked her heart around a little bit and it's going to take some time to heal those wounds," she explained. "I managed to cheer her up a little bit, but she wanted to make an early night of it. I tried to convince her to stick around for the tree lighting, but her heart wasn't in it."

"I'm sorry," Dante said. "Not just for what Stella's going through, but for what I put you through as well. I can't say it enough."

Lucy simply nodded. Hurt lurked in the depths of her eyes. Even though he'd made progress with Lucy over the past few weeks, he was beginning to realize that he couldn't erase how he'd made her feel. The damage was done. It didn't matter that his heart had been broken as well. He'd been the one to set everything in motion, so he had to take ownership.

It wouldn't be surprising if Stella's situation brought back memories of her own heartbreak. Maybe that's what he was sensing lurking under the surface with Lucy.

"I ran into your parents a little while ago," Dante said, changing the subject. "It was great to see them looking so well. They looked like a couple of teenagers."

Lucy's face lit up. "They do, don't they? Rest and relaxation has helped my mom so much. She has a doctor's appointment soon and we'll find out if she's in remission."

"I'll think good thoughts. Care to get some food?" He sniffed the air. "It smells delicious."

"Sure," Lucy said, rubbing her stomach. "I could go for some apple cider and cheesy fries. Oooh, and maybe a pecan twist. And a hot dog and corn fritters."

"Good thing you're not hungry," Dante teased as they got in line. He liked a woman who enjoyed her food. Lucy's love of food had given her curves in all the right places, and he thoroughly approved.

A few minutes later they'd ordered enough food to feed half of Mistletoe. Each of them carried a tray to a nearby table they'd been lucky to claim from a family who'd just finished eating. In keeping with the holiday theme, all the tables were decorated with garlands and candy canes. In the center sat a beautiful crimson poinsettia. The entire town green had been transformed into a true winter wonderland.

Everywhere he looked there were reminders that Christmas was rapidly approaching. Vendors were selling beautiful handwoven stockings that reminded him of the ones he'd had as a kid. Gaily decorated pine wreaths were scattered around the area. The town tree stood majestically in the center of the activity, drawing everyone's attention to its splendor. He loved the vibe in his hometown—festive, fun, congenial. He'd never found such community in California. Only Mistletoe managed to evoke these warm and fuzzy holiday feelings.

"There goes your mom, Dante," Lucy said, dragging him out of his thoughts. She was gesturing toward a nearby tent where his mother was standing and surveying the festivities. She looked festive in her red parka and green leggings, accompanied by a pair of reindeer antlers.

"Mom," Dante called out as he stood up and waved in her direction. Surprisingly, she heard him above the din of the crowd and quickly made her way over.

"Hey, guys," Mimi said, eyeing the massive amount of

food spread out on the table. "You've got the right idea. I'm famished."

"Come and join us," Lucy said, beckoning his mother to sit down. "We have plenty of food to share. I think our eyes were bigger than our stomachs."

"Don't mind if I do," Mimi said, letting out a sigh of relief as she sat down. "I've been volunteering in the holiday craft tent since this morning. My feet are killing me."

Dante jumped up. "Let me go get you something to drink, Mama."

By the time he ordered another apple cider, corn fritters, and some more cheese fries, then returned to their table, a few more friends were seated with them. Nick, Miles, and the Marshall family were now a part of the group. Dante couldn't be happier as he watched the lively conversation and animated faces. This was what being back home was all about. A place where everyone knew his name. And it had absolutely nothing to do with his fame. He'd grown up in this small New England town and he was one of their own, no matter how far he'd roamed.

When he sat back down next to Lucy, a funny feeling spread through his chest, as if someone was squeezing his heart. At first he couldn't place the sensation, but then it dawned on him. It was sheer happiness exploding inside of him. Although he'd been back in Maine for weeks now, it wasn't until this very moment that he truly felt as if he was home.

# CHAPTER SIXTEEN

Lucy felt a little guilty about being so happy when Stella was probably sitting at home feeling miserable. Nothing she'd said in five separate phone calls could convince her sister to join them at the festival. She was determined to lay low tonight.

"I'm all right, Lucy. I promise. I'm just not fit to be cheery and holiday-ish right now. I hate missing the event, but the thought of running into Rafe is unbearable."

"If you want company I can be there in a flash," Lucy had told her.

"Honestly, I'm good. Go forth and spread some holiday cheer around town. Enjoy yourself. I'll call you tomorrow."

She'd left it at that. If Stella needed her she wouldn't hesitate to leave the Christmas Frolic, but she had the feeling she wouldn't hear from her sister tonight. In the meantime, Lucy was going to enjoy the tree lighting and participate in decorating the town's tree.

"Come on, Lucy," her mother urged as she ended the phone call. "The tree lighting is about to start." She was leaning on a cane for support and holding on to her dad with her other hand. Her mother winced as she took a step. Lucy knew the symptoms of her mother's MS were aggravated by long hours on her feet. Lately she brought her cane along with her to give her support when she was fatigued.

Lucy bit her lip. She wasn't sure how her mother was going to be able to stand up during the lighting ceremony and help decorate the tree. It broke her heart that she was experiencing so many health issues related to her MS. Even though she'd shown signs of improvement, it was a sneaky disease that tended to rear its ugly head at the most unexpected times.

Dante made his way through the crowd carrying one of the plastic chairs from the concessions area. "Now you can get off your feet and enjoy a front-row seat," he said to her mother, then placed it right in front of the tree.

"This is so thoughtful of you, Dante," Leslie said, moving toward the seat. When she sat down a look of relief passed over her face. Her dad shot Dante a look of gratitude.

"Thank you," Lucy said to Dante. "I should have thought of it myself, but I'm really grateful that you stepped up." Lucy wanted to give Dante a standing ovation for finding a way to make things more comfortable for her mom.

"It's my pleasure," Dante said. "As kind as she's always been to me, it's the least I can do to make sure she has a comfortable spot to watch the lighting ceremony."

Mayor Finch stood in front of the tree and announced the

official start of the Christmas tree lighting ceremony. "May this tree fill our community with joy and unite us in our quest for peace all over the world. Let there be light!" With a flourish, the mayor gestured toward the tree as it became illuminated.

Just as the lights on the Christmas tree blazed into being, Dante turned to look at Lucy. A warmth in his eyes caused heat to spread through her all the way to her booted toes. The lights bounced off the tree, giving Dante's face a special glow. He looked happy. She wondered if her own expression mirrored his. She felt more at peace in this moment than she could ever remember. With Dante by her side it felt like old times. Tender, sweet memories came rushing back to her—moments she hadn't thought of in years. She felt Dante's gloved hand reach for hers and her heart swelled. For some it might be a small gesture, but it was one of the ways Dante had shown affection when they were together. It had always given her a thrill, and now was no exception.

As Lucy stood in front of the magnificent town tree as the lights shimmered and twinkled, she knew that she didn't want to be anywhere else in the world during the holidays. Mistletoe might be a small dot on the map, but it radiated pure Christmas charm.

"Not even my recollections can do this justice," Dante said, looking up at the tree with an expression resembling awe. "Maybe it's because I've been away for so long, but it seems grander. Bigger. Better. Yet at the same time it's just as I remember it."

"Mistletoe outdoes itself every year," Lucy said. "You're right. It gets better and better. Maybe we value it more as time passes by. I hope this town tradition never ends."

"Dante!" Tess called as she came running toward them clutching an ornament in her hand. "Can you lift me up super high? I want to put this right in the center."

Lucy watched as Dante hoisted Tess above his head so she could place her ornament exactly where she wanted it to sit. It was a beautiful miniature sled ornament, which didn't surprise Lucy at all because of Tess's love of sledding. Lucy had selected her own favorite town ornament from the collection—the Maine lobster—and was just looking for the perfect spot to hang it. She looked the tree over and noticed an empty patch on the side where no ornaments hung. She quickly walked over and hung up the lobster, stepping back a few paces so she could see how it looked. Just seeing it hanging among the other ornaments caused Lucy to grin so hard her cheeks ached a little bit.

"It looks fantastic, kiddo." She heard the deep baritone of her father's voice, as well as the touch of his hand on her shoulder. Lucy turned around to see him gazing at the lobster ornament with a grin on his face. "You and your holiday lobsters. It wouldn't feel like Christmas without them," he said with a chuckle.

Lucy was known for finding interesting holiday decorations featuring lobsters. Ornaments. Wreaths. Light-up lawn displays. Kitchen towels. Aprons. You name it. She'd purchased it. There was something about the lovable crustacean that she found irresistible.

"Thanks, Dad. Are you having fun?" she asked, looking up at him. With his salt-and-pepper close-cropped hair framing a handsome, russet-colored face, Walt Marshall was a distinguished-looking man. He was also an absolute sweetheart. His devotion to her mother served as an inspiration for Lucy. Because of him, she knew there were men out there who were vow keepers and committed to marriage for the long haul. It gave her hope of one day finding that same devotion.

"I am," he said, dangling his own moose ornament in the air. "It's so nice to see your mother enjoying herself. She's been through so many ups and downs with her illness. She doesn't walk around advertising it, but she's been in a lot of pain. It's improved lately, but she's my personal shero. Smiling through the tough times."

Lucy looped her arm through his and nuzzled her face against the fabric of his wool coat. "Oh, Daddy. I want to be the two of you when I grow up. I'm always struck by how you stand by each other, no matter what. I can only hope to find something half as wonderful."

"You will, baby girl. Just be sure you're ready to receive him when he comes." With a wink he left her side and headed back toward her mother, who was busy hanging up a few ornaments of her own at the bottom of the tree.

Her father's comment caused her to frown. Did he think she wasn't ready for love to come into her life? Was he giving her some kind of warning? His words were something to think about.

A few minutes later, Lucy made her way back toward

the spot where she'd left Dante and Tess. They seemed to be getting a kick out of being in each other's company. For someone who claimed not to be at ease around kids, Dante sure looked like a pro. And Tess clearly thought Dante wore a Superman shirt under his winter coat.

"Lucy! Look at this one," Tess cried out. She was holding up an ornament with Dante's face on it next to fiery flames and the word *Inferno*. As far as ornaments went, it was a hot mess. In a million years she couldn't imagine someone wanting to hang it up on their tree. Except maybe Dante's mother.

Dante took the ornament from Tess's hand and held it up to scrutinize it. "This is the first time I've ever seen this. It's hideous." With his mouth twisted and his brown cheeks flushed, Dante couldn't have looked more mortified if he tried. "I need to talk to my agent about my licensing agreements. This is not okay."

Lucy burst out laughing. "That must be a collector's edition."

Dante's eyes threatened to bulge out of his head. "Collector of what? Cheesy ornaments? Tacky tree trimmings?"

"I wish we had one for our tree," Tess said, hero worship shimmering in her brown eyes. "Can you look on eBay for me, Lucy?"

Dante bent down so he was face-to-face with Tess. "Just take this one. You'll be doing me a huge favor."

"Tess will not be engaging in any five-finger discounts, Dante." She sent Dante a pointed glance. Although he was probably kidding, Tess seemed to be hanging on his every word. Lucy had a hunch she would follow his lead in a heartbeat.

Clapping rang out as the last of the ornaments were hung on the tree. Lucy took a picture of the final product so she could show Stella tomorrow. By then she imagined Stella would be curious to see photos of the town celebration. Music began to play over the loudspeaker. Christmas music! Couples paired up on the makeshift dance floor as they danced to the upbeat rhythms of holiday favorites.

"I'd almost forgotten about this part, although I don't know how I could have. It's pretty incredible," Dante said. "I remember how much fun my parents had grooving to Aretha Franklin and Frank Sinatra. And us kids would always find a way to make special requests and then we'd take over the dance floor." He threw back his head in laughter. They were standing so close she could see the little crinkles on the sides of his mouth as he chuckled. "I remember doing some awful hip-hop moves."

A hundred different memories came floating back. The magic of being whirled around the dance floor by her father as snow gently fell from the sky. Her first slow dance with a boy she liked—Dante. Tonight would be near perfect if she could hit the makeshift dance floor with him once again.

"It wouldn't be a lighting ceremony without dancing," Lucy said, tapping her foot along with the beat of John Legend's "Merry Christmas Baby."

"Dance with me then," Dante said, holding out his hand to her as Tess looked on. Her little sister was practically squealing with delight. She looked as if she might push Lucy onto the dance floor herself.

Lucy shook her head. "I don't know. It's one thing to dance at night in the library when no one's around, but I don't want to make a fool of myself. I'm not much of a dancer."

"Don't worry. I've got you," Dante said, pulling her into his arms. "Don't sell yourself short, Luce. Just pretend it's the two of us at the library dancing to Ella Fitzgerald."

Lucy followed Dante's instructions and simply gave in to the joy she always experienced when she was dancing. It was freeing to do something she loved so much without feeling self-conscious. What was the worst thing people could say about her? That she had two left feet? It certainly didn't feel that way as she moved around to the beat.

Of course dancing with someone as graceful and rhythmic as Dante made it all feel effortless. The way he swung his hips was way sexier than she wanted to think about for any prolonged period. Lucy felt stares in their direction. Most were well-meaning and a product of curiosity, she imagined. A few local friends gave her a thumbs-up that made her wonder if they approved of her dancing skills or her famous dance partner. She didn't want to do anything to cause people to think she and Dante were an item again. Fielding those type of questions was way too much pressure.

As the tempo slowed down and the strains of "This Christmas" by Donny Hathaway began to play, Lucy stopped moving. This was slow dancing music. She wasn't sure if she wanted to dance cheek to cheek with Dante with the whole town looking on. Their tangled past still hung over them, serving as a flashing neon sign for the townsfolk. It was hard to imagine tongues wouldn't be wagging about them. But hadn't she decided to live a little and not worry so much about what other people thought? Wasn't it time she stepped out of the little box she'd created for herself?

"Don't leave me hanging," Dante said in a low voice. His eyes were twinkling just as brightly as the town tree. He was like a magnet, constantly pulling her in. Even when she tried to resist, it was impossible. So why even bother?

Just standing this close to him caused her pulse to race like crazy. She could see little puffs of air coming out of his mouth because of the frosty weather. He looked adorable and she wanted nothing more than to warm up his lips by placing her own on his.

Lucy leaned in to him, fitting against his chest as if she was meant to be there. Dante tightened his arms around her. She let out a deep breath she'd been holding. Being in his arms felt like safe haven even though she knew it was foolish to lower her guard. That's when a person tended to get blindsided. She hated being a bit jaded, but her past with Dante had taught her a few life lessons she couldn't easily forget. But with every kiss, every time he took her hand in his, every dance, and every lingering look, Lucy felt as if she was tumbling back down the rabbit hole.

Was it so out-there, ain't-never-gonna-happen, in-her-wildest-dreams impossible that she and Dante could permanently find their way back to each other? Or was she being delusional in even daring to allow it to cross her mind? The world he inhabited was a far cry from their quaint hometown. Lucy had seen the pictures of him splashed across the pages of *Us Weekly*. Vacations in Saint-Tropez on supersized yachts. Attending the Met Gala in New York City with A-listers like JLo and Lady Gaga. Dinner dates with Rihanna. Skiing in Zermatt, Switzerland. In her wildest imaginings, Lucy couldn't place herself in any of those locales. At heart, she would always be a small-town girl.

She raised her head and locked eyes with Dante. He lowered his head till she felt his lips brushing against her ear. The steady rise and fall of his chest was soothing. A woodsy smell rose to her nostrils. She breathed him in, loving the masculine scent of him. She had the feeling she was wearing her heart on her sleeve with every look in his direction.

"What if we really give them something to talk about?" Dante whispered, his lips lingering for far too long on the sensitive lobe of her ear. His mouth was twitching and a look of mischief was etched on his face.

She swallowed, almost afraid to ask him what he meant. Dante had always liked pushing the envelope. Even though he was now an adult, Lucy could still see the spirited young man peeking out. "I'm scared to ask," she said. "Remember, I'm the town librarian. I do have a reputation to uphold."

"Don't worry. I won't tarnish your character," Dante said, flashing her a wide smile.

Dante started moving faster to match the increasing tempo of the music. His moves were becoming more intricate and a bit out of her league. Lucy wasn't sure she could keep up, but he led her through the steps by tightly holding on to her and showing her the way. For the first time in her life, she knew what it meant to be led around the dance floor.

He spun her around, making her dizzy.

"Whoa," she said, tightly gripping the collar of his coat so she didn't fall on her butt. "Easy there, Fred Astaire. I'm not exactly Ginger Rogers."

"You are to me," he said, smiling at her in a way that made her feel light-headed. And she knew it had absolutely nothing to do with the dancing.

Dante lowered his head down and pressed his lips to hers. They had a slight sugary taste. Remnants of the pecan twist, she reckoned. It caught her completely off guard as his mouth tenderly moved over hers. Everything else faded away until there was nothing but the two of them. Lucy kissed him back with gusto, despite the prying eyes she sensed were watching them. This, she realized, was living in the moment and relishing her renewed connection with Dante. Kissing him was like fireworks on the Fourth of July. It was heat and flashes of light and pure wonder. Pure magic.

"See. That wasn't so bad, was it?" he asked as the kiss ended along with the song.

"Are you kidding me? You just threw shark bait into the water," Lucy whispered.

Awareness pricked at the nape of her neck. A quick glance around confirmed that all eyes in the crowd were focused like laser beams on her and Dante. It seemed as if everyone she'd ever known in Mistletoe was gaping at them. Teachers. Her pastor. Neighbors. Friends. Her family. Dante's mother. Nick and Miles. A cheer rose up in the crowd and people started enthusiastically clapping. Heat rose to her cheeks. She hadn't expected all this fanfare.

Dante threw back his head and chuckled. "We're getting a standing ovation."

"Spoken by a true actor," Lucy said. "You really do love the spotlight, don't you?"

Just then Mimi walked up and held out her hand to her son. "I think you've set tongues wagging enough for one night. Why don't you take me for a spin on the dance floor? It's been a while."

Dante took his mother's hand and said, "Let's do this, Mama."

Lucy stood on the sidelines watching as Dante twirled his mother around the dance floor. They looked incredibly sweet together. Mimi was so petite and bubbly. The height difference between mother and son was about a foot, which was an adorable visual.

Lucy made a point to stand in an area out of sight of prying eyes. It was nice to watch the action unobserved. She let out a little squeal of surprise as she clapped eyes on Denny and Nora. They were dancing to the holiday music, and from the looks of it, having a grand old time. A romantic at heart, Lucy saw a lot of possibilities for them as a couple. There was something so magical about this time of the year. Anything was possible. Although Lucy really did believe in holiday magic, she wasn't holding on to any fantasies about her and Dante.

Something was nagging at her. A bothersome feeling that she wasn't enough for a man like Dante. Ever since he'd left Mistletoe, Lucy had asked herself if Dante had viewed her as unworthy of his time and attention. Otherwise, why wouldn't he have worked harder to keep her in his life? He was now a celebrity who could be with any woman of his choosing. According to Dante, that woman was her. And it felt oh so amazing to be wanted. Wonderful and terrifying at the same time. But she couldn't stop worrying when the rug would be pulled out from underneath her again.

# CHAPTER SEVENTEEN

As the Christmas Frolic came to an end and the evening
sky began to turn a gorgeous shade of velvety black,
the crowd thinned out on the town green. Tired babies were
asleep in their mothers' arms. Couples were walking hand
in hand. Lights were extinguished. Quiet settled over Mistletoe as the dark of night set in, even though the town tree
continued to shine.

Dante stayed around to assist in breaking down Santa's
Village and to help transport boxes and concession items
to nearby vans. When it was time to head home, Dante
couldn't find Lucy. Had she left without saying goodbye?
Or had they simply not crossed paths? It had been a wonderful evening, full of amazing moments. He would have liked
to tell Lucy how he felt about this spectacular day and
closed out the evening by holding her in his arms.

On the drive home, his mind wandered over the day's
events. The Christmas Frolic had been enjoyable on so

many levels. He's gotten to spend time with his mother, Nick's and Lucy's families, as well as Lucy herself. Playing the role of Santa had allowed him to do something for Lucy, who was always doing things for everyone else. She wasn't the sort of person to ask others for help, so filling the gap when she'd needed someone meant a lot to him.

As soon as Dante walked in the house, he heard a commotion coming from the back. His mother's voice rang out sharply. He followed the sounds down the hall until he reached the kitchen.

"What's going on?" Dante asked, immediately sensing a panicked vibe in the room. Troy was standing next to their mother with a distressed expression on his face.

"A pipe burst in the basement of the hardware store. One of the employees happened to be there using the photocopier after hours, so he alerted me. I called the emergency plumbing service, but it may take them a while to get there. Can you head over there with me? We can try to bail as much water as we can before they get there."

"Of course. Let's go. Grab some buckets from the garage and a wet vac if you guys have one."

"While I do that, get Nick on the phone," Troy said. "Maybe he can help us out."

Dante quickly dialed Nick, who promised to meet them at the shop in ten minutes. Thankfully, Miles was at a sleepover with his best friend. Troy and Dante hopped in Troy's truck and they raced over to the hardware store. Nick arrived moments after they pulled up in the back lot. He jumped out of his car with a bucket in each hand.

In the basement, Dante was up to his knees in water, as were Troy and Nick. They worked nonstop for a solid hour, bailing out buckets of water and tossing them out the back door like a well-oiled machine, until the emergency service arrived. By the end, the muscles in Dante's arms burned from repetitively filling and heaving buckets of water. He was sweaty and grungy. And he'd worked up an appetite. But he wouldn't want to be anywhere but here aiding his brother and helping to rescue the family business from water damage.

"I can't thank you enough, Nick," Troy said, shaking his hand and pulling him into a tight hug.

"We really appreciate it," Dante added. Nick helping them out didn't surprise him at all. He was loyal to a fault and one of the best friends he'd ever had. Dante wasn't even sure anymore if he had friends in California who truly had his back. And what did that say about his life in Los Angeles?

"That's what friends are for," Nick said. "I'm here anytime you need me."

Dante heard that a lot in his line of work, but not many people meant it. Not like Nick did. With each and every passing day Dante was connecting the dots and realizing his life wasn't all it could be. There were things missing from his world—things he was finding all around him in Mistletoe.

Once they were back at the house, Dante and Troy both headed off to take showers. Their clothes were sopping wet and emitting a foul odor. After he got out of the shower, a knock sounded at his bedroom door. When he opened it, Troy was standing there.

"I'm heating up some pizza if you want some," Troy offered. "It'll be ready in a few minutes."

"I'll be right down," Dante said, feeling pleased at Troy's invitation. They'd united for a common cause: to save the hardware store from disaster. And it felt like they were brothers again. Dante couldn't put into words how happy it made him. He'd been carrying the weight of their estrangement on his shoulders. Suddenly, he felt much lighter.

As he arrived in the kitchen, Troy was taking the pizza from the oven. He'd already set the table with plates, utensils, and mugs for two. The kettle on the stove began to squeal.

Troy divvied up the pizza with a pizza cutter and brought the pan over to the table. He poured hot water in each of the mugs. "Hot cocoa," Troy announced. Dante stirred the drink and moaned as the smell of chocolate rose to his nostrils. He took a huge swig, allowing the warmth to comfort him. The hot shower had been nice, but standing in water for over an hour had chilled him to the bone.

Troy sat down across from him and placed a few slices of pizza on his plate. "You did a good thing playing Santa Claus today," Troy said. "It meant a lot to everyone."

"Thanks. I heard you suggested me for the job," Dante said with a raised eyebrow. "Remind me to return the favor someday." Dante bit into a slice, relishing the flavor as it landed on his tongue.

Troy let out a hearty chuckle that seemed to emanate from deep down inside of him. Dante had always loved his brother's laugh. It was great to hear it again. "I couldn't do it myself. Jimmy would have figured out it was me. That kid deserves to believe in Santa Claus for a few more years at least."

Dante nodded, feeling moved by his brother's words. "Lucy told me about you and Jimmy's mom. Her name is Noelle, right? The two of you look good together," he acknowledged. "And Jimmy is an amazing kid."

"The best," Troy said. "They've been through a lot, so my goal is to make their lives better. Noelle is the most wonderful woman I've ever known. I really feel lucky to have found her."

Dante cupped his hands around his mug. "It sounds serious." He couldn't remember the last time his brother had spoken about a woman with such reverence.

"I suppose it is. Noelle makes me want to be a better man. I want to take care of them."

Dante leaned forward in his seat. He splayed his hands on the table. "You're good at taking care of people. Way better than I am," Dante admitted. "You took care of Dad when he was sick and now you're Mom's support system. I never said thank you, but I want you to know how grateful I am."

Troy locked gazes with him. "That's good to hear. For so long it seemed like you didn't care. I know you sent money and took care of the medical bills, but you weren't around much."

"I always cared, Troy. That never changed."

Troy focused on his mug, idly stirring the contents with a spoon. "That's what put a wedge between us. When Dad was sick all I wanted was for you to be here with us, but by the time you came it was too late."

"And I've had to live with that knowledge. Trust me, it's been painful. I shouldn't have listened to him when he told me to finish the movie I was making overseas. My place was here with my family."

He swung his gaze up. "You talked to him about it?" Troy asked, sounding incredulous.

"Yeah. Numerous times. But I should have known better. He was sick, and I should have jumped through hoops to come back to Mistletoe. If I'm being honest, I was afraid."

"Of him being sick?"

Dante bowed his head. He hadn't told a single soul about his fears. It had been difficult to admit even to himself. "Yeah. There were so many years when we were at odds, so it was scary to suddenly feel as if he was slipping away from me before I could make things right. To be honest, I didn't have a clue how to make it happen."

Silence stretched out between them.

"I know you think he didn't believe in you, but he did," Troy said, looking down and fiddling with his fingers. "He just couldn't stand the thought of you leaving, so he tried to make you stay by not encouraging your acting aspirations. I think he was scared for you." Troy massaged the bridge of his nose. "I heard him talking to Mom one night about it. He'd heard a lot of stories about bad things happening to teenagers who went to LA to pursue their acting dreams. He didn't want you to become one of them."

Dante steepled his fingers under his chin. "That sounds like him, you know. He always did things to protect us. I always thought he was trying to clip our wings," he said, shaking his head, "but he wanted to keep us safe like any parent would." He let out a brittle laugh. "And he was right to be worried. California was a tough place to navigate. I struggled in the beginning."

Troy locked eyes with him. "I had no idea. You didn't tell us."

Dante nodded. "I know. That's my bad. I wanted to do it on my own and not bog everyone down with my problems, especially after the way I left."

"All the more reason to be proud of all you've accomplished. I should have said it before, but I'm proud of you. And I killed that article about you. I never really intended to print it. That was a draft copy you saw that day. I was just blowing off some steam."

Relief swept through Dante. He'd been hoping Troy had changed his mind about the article, but he hadn't wanted to ask. With the press still linking him with Missy and making up stories about an affair, a local article written by his own brother would have created a media frenzy.

"Lucy told me about the items Dad hung up at the shop. The articles. Press clippings."

Troy nodded. "Yeah. Of course. He was a proud father. Would you really expect any less of him?"

Dante ran a hand over his face. For so many years his

emotions had been bottled up. He and his father had never managed to air out their issues. They'd tiptoed around each other rather than bringing it out into the open. "We had a lot of unfinished business. There was a lot of stuff we didn't hash out. I really wish we had." He wondered if he would ever move past this profound regret.

"At least you were communicating. Talking. That's what matters most of all. He knew you loved him and vice versa. Beating yourself up isn't going to change anything, Dante. All you can do is to move forward."

"When did you get so wise?" Dante asked. Troy had matured over the past few years. No doubt it was a result of their father's illness and subsequent death. As caretaker and emotional support system, Troy had been as solid as a Maine oak tree. He'd filled a role Dante hadn't been able to.

"I was born that way," he said with a grin.

"You planning on putting those things back up on the walls?" Dante asked, trying to keep his expression serious.

"Are you kidding me?" Troy asked. "Not a chance. I figure you already have a big head from all those Hollywood folks stroking your ego."

Dante shook his head and chuckled. "I can always count on you to keep me grounded, Troy." It was nice to sit with his brother and share a pizza and some laughs. It was long overdue.

"Are we good?" Dante asked, holding his breath as he waited for Troy's response.

Troy sat back in his chair and folded his arms across his chest. "On one condition."

"Lay it on me," Dante said. He was eager to hear Troy's stipulation.

Troy grinned. "Jimmy really wants to meet Inferno. I told him that I might be able to hook him up with a meet and greet."

Joy swept over him. It wasn't a magic fix, but he and his little brother were on their way to being back on track. "Absolutely. Let's get him down to the set so he can watch us shoot some scenes."

Troy leaned back in his chair and folded his arms across his chest. "What I said to you about Lucy...I was dead wrong. If you want to start things up again with her it's none of my business."

"We're only hanging out. Nothing serious. Like you said, I'm heading back to California right after Christmas." He shrugged. "One of my main goals was to see Lucy face-to-face and apologize for the way I left town. She hasn't said it in so many words, but I think she's forgiven me. We've managed to get our friendship back."

"Just friends?" Troy shook his head. His mouth had a skeptical twist. "I saw the way she was looking at you today at the festival. She's in deep, Dante. And if you want to know the truth, I think you are too."

# CHAPTER EIGHTEEN

The library was a much quieter place now that Dante and his team had finished shooting there. Lucy no longer found herself distracted by the possibility of seeing him in the middle of her workday. On the downside, Lucy had gotten used to seeing Dante and watching the movie being filmed. It had livened up her world, much to her surprise. One thing had been abundantly clear throughout the entire process: Dante West was a genius. He managed to cull brilliant performances from his actors, and the scenes she'd watched always shone. Although he was a fine actor, Lucy thought he was an exceptional director. She had a feeling his film would be well received, and it might earn Dante some awards come Oscar time. His career could permanently change from actor to director.

Lucy smiled as she watched Denny and Nora leaving the library together. They were a full-fledged couple now, which made Lucy smile every time she saw them.

Right now they were holding hands as they called out their goodbyes to her and exited the library. She sighed. Seeing them together reminded her of the early days of her relationship with Dante. Lucy hoped they never had to weather any of the storms she and Dante had gone through.

A few minutes later Lucy locked up and headed out the front doors of the library. The ringing of the church bells sounded melodic and peaceful. They usually rang in the evening only to herald special occasions. Lucy had forgotten about the yearly gathering across the street at St. Mark's Church. It was a holiday candle ceremony to honor the memory of all the loved ones who'd passed away in the Mistletoe community. She'd always thought it was a beautiful way to honor those who were no longer with them. Lucy walked over to where people stood with candles in their hands. Although it wasn't a huge crowd, it was nice to see so many turn up to honor their loved ones. The flickering candles looked so beautiful set against the darkness of night and the blanket of snow on the ground. It was somber yet lovely.

"Here you go, Lucy." Miles, Nick's son, handed her a candle. With his pecan-colored skin and fine features, he was a carbon copy of his mother.

"Thanks, Miles," she said, wishing things were different for him and Nick. Kara had been such a force of nature. She'd been the foundation of their world. She imagined the ceremony provided them comfort at such a difficult time of the year. Although the holidays were always spectacular in

Mistletoe, it was heartbreaking for families who were grieving a loss. Her mind swung to the Wests. She wondered
if they were somewhere in the crowd holding candles
for John.

Lucy lit her candle and stepped toward the back of
the crowd as the ceremony began. Names were called and
families were allowed to light one of the bigger candles at
the front. Much to Lucy's surprise, Dante stepped forward
when his father's name was called. He stood among the
others as a prayer was recited and the candles were extinguished. As she turned to put out her own candle, she
spotted Stella's ex, Rafe, huddled up with his wife. Just the
sight of him filled her with distaste.

She couldn't even imagine how difficult it was for Stella
to constantly cross paths with him in their small town.
Lucy's hand clenched at her side. She had never had the
opportunity to tell him off after he'd ditched her sister at the
altar. At the time, Stella had been in a pretty fragile state
and Lucy hadn't wanted to make matters worse.

And now he was standing mere feet away from her with
a wide grin showcasing his pearly whites. Humph. He was
cheesing it up while her poor sister was still licking her
wounds. It didn't sit well with Lucy. Not one little bit.

With his tawny-colored skin and tall, thin frame, he'd
always reminded her of the actor Will Smith. Unfortu-
nately, Rafe possessed none of Will's charm and wit. Lucy
had never liked him, but for Stella's sake she'd tolerated
him and done her best to be kind and welcoming. Rafe
had been way too arrogant, nitpicky, and demanding of

her sister's time and attention. Lucy hadn't wanted Stella to marry him, but she'd never desired her to end up so crushed and broken.

"Fancy meeting you here," Dante said as he sidled up next to her. His greeting pulled her out of her thoughts about Rafe. With his navy peacoat and knit hat, he emanated a fashionable yet casual air. As always, he looked way too handsome for his own good.

"I thought you'd be filming tonight."

"We were shooting from the wee hours of the morning until about an hour ago," Dante said, running a hand across his face. He looked tired. "Just hanging out with my mom and Troy. We had dinner before coming over here."

Her eyes widened. "You're here with Troy?" she asked.

Dante nodded. "We made peace thanks to a burst pipe at the hardware store. There's nothing like several feet of water, buckets, and a basement to provide a bonding experience."

Lucy clapped her hands together. "How perfect. Peace during the holidays. That's wonderful. I'm so tickled for you guys."

Dante shoved his hands into the front pockets of his jeans. "We're still a work in progress, but at least we're talking and enjoying the occasional beer together. My mom is pretty stoked about it. We wanted to come light a candle for my dad."

Lucy was happy for Dante and his family. She'd always known there was a great deal of love in the West family. The bonds between them had frayed because of John

West's tragic illness and death, but those ties could never be permanently severed.

"I keep expecting my dad to walk into the room over at the house. It's a strange feeling," he said with a sigh.

Lucy knew Dante was now staying over at his mom's house. She imagined it had been the perfect setting for reconciling with his family. "That's a normal feeling. Memories are all around you in that house."

Distracted by the sight of Rafe placing a kiss on his wife's cheek, Lucy kept glancing in their direction.

"What's wrong?" Dante asked, narrowing his gaze as he looked at her.

"Nothing," she said, dragging her eyes away from Rafe. "I'm good."

He reached out and touched the space between her brows. "So what's this little frown line then?"

"A sign of aging perhaps," she quipped.

"Negative. You, Lucy, are aging like a fine wine." He winked at her in an exaggerated gesture. "And you're twice as sweet."

Lucy let out a tortured groan. "Yikes. You should have quit while you were ahead. That last part was over the top," she said, chuckling.

"So tell me what's up then."

"See that tall guy with the ridiculous-looking wool hat?" Lucy slid her gaze in Rafe's direction. Dante followed the trail of her gaze.

"Yeah. He looks like Where's Waldo."

Lucy smirked. "He's Stella's ex-fiancé."

Dante's eyes widened. "Ex-fiancé? What's the story there?"

"To make a long story short, he ditched her right before the wedding. He gave her some song and dance about them not being soul mates."

Dante let out a low whistle. "That sounds ugly."

Anger swept through Lucy. "It was brutal for Stella. Just picture canceling a wedding for two hundred of your nearest and dearest family members and friends, the Hawaiian honeymoon, then having to eat most of the costs. Not to mention dealing with a narcissistic would-be groom who quickly married someone else who is now preggers."

"That's awful for Stella, but why is this coming up now?"

She made a face. "Because he's here with his wife, so instead of basking in the cheer of Christmas, I'm fantasizing about hiding behind a tree and slamming him with some snowballs. He's the reason Stella's been upset. The baby announcement didn't go over well when he told Stella at the Christmas Frolic."

Dante wrinkled his nose as if he'd smelled something bad. "That's pretty heartless of him. Let me guess. His wife was by his side when he did it, right?"

"How did you know that?" Lucy asked.

He shrugged. "I know a lot of men like him."

Lucy looked over again at Rafe. Just the sight of him upset her. He was holding hands with his wife and making stupid faces. They looked as if they were right out of central casting as the picture-perfect couple. "Should I go ahead and do it? He wouldn't even know it was me." Just the thought of lobbing snow at Rafe put her back in the holiday spirit. Fa la la la la.

Dante vigorously shook his head. "Nah. I wouldn't suggest it. What if you hit his wife by mistake? That wouldn't be good for your town librarian rep."

Lucy bit her lip and swung her gaze back to Rafe. She sighed. "You're right. It's not worth the risk. She's not the one who's a big fat jerk."

"You can lob one at me if you like," Dante suggested.

"What? Why would I do that?" she asked.

"Because of what I did to you. I didn't leave you at the altar, but I left you hanging. I broke your heart."

Lucy hadn't been expecting a comment like that from Dante. His words pricked at her, reminding her that there were still unresolved issues between them.

"Go ahead. I deserve it. And I think it'll make you feel better."

She bristled. "I don't need to throw snowballs at you, Dante. I'm not mad at you anymore. It's dead and buried."

"Aren't you?" he asked, his head slightly cocked. "Just a little? Because I can feel it, right under the surface. Unless of course I'm imagining things."

"This is stupid," Lucy said, moving away from him and walking in the other direction toward the courtyard of the church. She didn't want to dredge this up now that they were together again. It hurt too much to rehash the past. Seconds later she felt him grasping her arm and turning her back around.

"Hey! Where are you going?" he asked.

She shrugged his arm off. "Away from you and this crazy idea. A snowball isn't going to change anything. The past is the past, Dante." She threw her hands up in the air. "I had to deal with having my heart smashed into pieces just like Stella is doing now. You're a little bit late with your snowball therapy."

Lucy moved away from him and began walking back toward the group. All of a sudden, she felt a whack on her back. As she turned around Dante was standing a few feet away with a snowball in his hand.

"Don't you dare!" she shouted, stomping her booted foot.

*Whack!* Another snowball hit her square in the chest. Icy particles splashed onto her face. Dante was grinning at her with his arms folded across his chest

"That felt really good," he said. "Wanna try?"

Lucy was so mad she was sputtering. Who did Dante think he was ordering her around and throwing snowballs at her? This was the most juvenile, annoying thing in the world. It was almost as if he was trying to set her off. Her anger spiked when she saw him scooping up another handful of snow. Clearly, he didn't know who he was dealing with. Back in the day she'd been an expert snowball thrower. How quickly he'd forgotten.

She bent down and hastily formed a snowball that looked more egg-shaped than round. Lucy wasn't looking for perfection. She just wanted to get him before he was able to get her again. She hurled the imperfect snowball in his direction. By some small miracle, it landed on his shoulder. "That's for making me think I wasn't worthy of a happy ending." Dante's mouth fell open. Guess he hadn't been expecting her to return fire. It served him right!

She grabbed some more snow and formed a perfectly rounded snowball. She hadn't done this in a while, but it was all coming back to her now.

"This is for writing me that ridiculous letter filled with all those false promises." She threw the snowball right at the center of his chest. He looked slightly taken aback. By her aim or her anger, she couldn't tell.

She bent down and scooped another handful of snow into a perfect icy sphere. She felt triumphant. "And this is for making me cry myself to sleep for months." Before she knew it, she was hurling snowball after snowball in his direction, all the while spouting different grievances she had against him. With each word she spoke, Lucy felt some of her long-held fury dissipating.

After a few minutes she was thoroughly exhausted and losing steam. She was spent, both emotionally and physically. She wasn't sure if Dante thought this was a game, but for her it had turned serious on a dime.

"This is for making me feel that I wasn't special." Her voice broke and the snowball landed with a plop at Dante's feet. Her shoulders heaved with exhaustion. She hung her head, not wanting him to see the tears misting in her eyes. She didn't want to come across as weak. Still, after all these years, Lucy still felt as if she wasn't whole. Because of him.

Suddenly, Dante was beside her, lifting her chin up so he

could see her face. Her lips were trembling and it felt as if she might burst into tears.

Dante looked devastated. A tremor ran along his jaw and his voice sounded unsteady as he said, "You were special. You'll always be special to me. Past, present, future. Forgive me if I ever made you feel that you weren't."

"It seemed like you just traded your life in Mistletoe for something better," Lucy said. She pushed out the words, making herself incredibly vulnerable. This was probably the rawest truth she'd ever laid on him. It sat at the core of all her issues with Dante. He'd swapped out their love story for fame.

"California wasn't better, Luce. It was an escape, and I built it up in my mind as a path to my dreams and a way to end the dysfunction with my dad. But it was disorienting and full of disappointment. Somehow I clawed my way through and made it as a working actor, but the odds weren't in my favor. Of the guys I lived with when I first arrived there, I'm the only one who's had any sort of success. Some have really fallen on hard times." He shuddered. "Los Angeles was a means to an end. Before I ended up there I viewed it as this magical place, but reality quickly slapped me in the face." He reached out and ran his palm down the side of her face. "I envisioned a future with you, Lucy, but I had doubts about being able to hold both of us down. It scared me and I let fear get in the way of us. The truth is, nothing can compete with Mistletoe. If I searched the whole world over, I'd never be able to find what this town and you have given me."

With every word he spoke, Lucy felt lighter. This was the type of honest conversation she'd needed to have with him. It was way overdue. Just getting it off her chest made all the difference. Everything she'd just yelled at him had caused her pain. By laying it at his feet, she was shedding layers of hurt.

Dante wrapped his arms around her and she felt his energy lifting her up. For so many years she'd held on to these feelings without fully being able to vent to the one person she'd needed to hash it out with.

"I wasn't trying to make you feel bad," Lucy said. "But I needed to get it out."

"I know you weren't. Being back home gives me a chance to face all the things I've been avoiding head-on. I'm not going to lie. It doesn't make me feel good to hear how badly I messed up, but I need to absorb it."

"Thank you. I think that I just needed to be heard. So I can put it to rest. Eight and a half years is a long time to carry this around," Lucy confessed.

"I still care about you, Lucy. Very much. I've told you a few times that you're the reason I came back to Mistletoe. That's the truth." His eyes were radiating emotion as they focused on her. She couldn't look away if she tried.

"Can I ask you why?" She blurted out the question. At this point, she really needed to know the answer. She knew he had feelings for her, but were they as intense as hers? Was she being ridiculous for even thinking they might have a future together?

"Six months ago I nearly died while filming a movie.

I performed a stunt I had no business doing. I was really lucky I made it out alive. I spent almost two weeks in the intensive care unit. Going through that experience showed me that tomorrow isn't promised. I knew I had to come back home to try and fix the things I'd broken."

Lucy was stunned. She hadn't heard anything about an accident and she had a hunch his own family hadn't known about it. Mistletoe would have been buzzing with the news. The whole community would have been praying for him.

She grabbed his hand and squeezed. "Dante. That's so frightening. I'm so sorry you went through that. I can't imagine what a toll it must have taken on you." Lucy shivered at the thought of Dante lying in a hospital bed, hovering between life and death.

"I'm grateful to still be here. I wrote this script because of you. The film mirrors our relationship right down to the heartbreaking ending. This is the only place I wanted to film it, and it's not just because I belong here. It's because you're here. My being back home is all tied up in you. You know I still care about you, Lucy. Very much."

Dante's words cut straight through to her heart. It had been shocking to hear him speak about his accident. It terrified her to think she could have lost him before they found each other again. Her heart couldn't seem to stop beating wildly at the way he'd spoken about her. His emotions were written all over his face and embedded in his voice. She was soaring...flying sky-high in a way she hadn't experienced since they were in love.

All this time she'd been incapable of truly letting him go.

There had always been a part of her that still belonged to him. She hadn't wanted to face it before, but here it was— the incontrovertible truth. He was imprinted on her soul. From the sounds of it, Dante hadn't been able to let go of her either. It wasn't just the past tying them together. It was the present as well.

When their lips met in a fiery kiss, it felt downright exhilarating, as if all the emotions they were feeling were rising to the surface. Lucy let out a sound of satisfaction as Dante's lips moved over hers. She kissed him back with equal intensity, plundering his mouth with her tongue. She reached up and placed her hands on his shoulders to steady herself against the sudden weakness in her knees.

This kiss was different from all the others. It felt like an unspoken promise between them. Lucy pressed against Dante as the kiss intensified. Moments later when they broke apart, Dante ran his fingers through her hair and sighed. "I hate to run, but Troy and Mama are probably wondering where I am." He jerked his chin in the direction of the church. "Looks like everyone is heading home."

Dante was right. The crowd had thinned out with only a dozen or so people still grouped together. From this distance she was able to spot Troy and Mimi looking around, presumably for Dante. She watched as Troy dug his cell phone from his pocket then tapped the screen.

"I think your cell phone is about to ring," Lucy said, smiling as Dante's phone began chirping the song "Last Christmas" by Wham!

He grinned at her before picking up the call. "I'll be right there, Troy," he said before disconnecting. Dante encircled Lucy by the waist, pulling her against him. He dipped his head down and placed a featherlight kiss on her lips. As he drew back, he said in a low voice, "I wish we didn't have to say good night so soon."

"Me too," she murmured, lacing her fingers through his. He leaned down and pressed his forehead against hers. For a few beats they remained like this until they reluctantly broke apart.

"I'm going to be tied up for the next few days," Dante explained, "but I want to see you, sooner rather than later. Maybe we can grab dinner or you can cook for me." There was a playful glint in his eye. "I could go for a big Maine dinner." He dramatically rubbed his stomach.

Lucy chuckled and gently pushed at his chest. "Or you can cook for me. I'll never say no to lobster and mashed potatoes. Or spaghetti and meatballs."

"Okay, maybe we can cook together. I'll call you, Luce. Can I walk you to your car?" he asked.

"That's sweet, but I'm parked right over there," Lucy said, pointing toward the library's lot. "Night, Dante."

"Good night, Lucy," he said as he walked in the direction of his family. Lucy watched as he met up with Troy and his mother. It was nice to see the three of them together. As they headed away from the church, Mimi stood in the middle of Troy and Dante. She looped an arm around each one of her boys in an endearing gesture. This, Lucy thought, was the true definition of holiday magic. Dante really had come full circle with his loved ones. For Mimi, having Dante home for the holidays and patching things up with Troy would no doubt be the best Christmas present she'd ever received.

Try as she might, Lucy couldn't stop herself from hoping something might come of this. If two people still had feelings for each other, anything was possible. He hadn't said the L word, but neither had she. But after tonight, Lucy couldn't ignore it any longer. The love she'd felt for Dante had never gone away. She'd simply buried it along with her heartbreak and humiliation. But now, against all odds, and with the enchantment of the holidays swirling all around them, she and Dante might just have another chance at being together. After so many disappointments in their past, Lucy was hesitant to believe that things between them could work out.

But it was Christmastime and the words Dante had shared with her tonight made her feel more hopeful than she'd ever dared to hope before. This Christmas, Lucy was getting the best gift of all. Dante himself, wrapped up in a big red bow.

# CHAPTER NINETEEN

Dante stood in front of Mistletoe Elementary School and admired the stunning brick façade of the hundred-year-old building. The school had been spruced up a bit since he'd been a student, but it still maintained its historic charm. Set against a blanket of snow, the school looked inviting and achingly familiar. As he walked up the stairs, Dante paused to admire the huge pine wreath hanging on the door. Once he stepped inside, a cascade of memories flooded him. Now that he was an adult, everything looked smaller. The lockers looked the same. He walked past number 304, the locker he'd used for years. He'd kept Star Wars posters inside along with stickers and trading cards.

He felt thankful that his assistant had reminded him about this engagement. His filming schedule was so hectic it was hard to remember what day it was sometimes. Without the reminder, Dante would have totally forgotten his promise to Tess.

As he made his way through the building, he easily spotted Tess, who was waiting for him in the hallway outside her classroom. She heaved a big sigh of relief when she saw him walking toward her. She was dressed in an adorable blue jumper with matching leggings and a pair of Mary Janes.

"Dante! You came! I was hoping you didn't forget." Tess wrapped her arms around his waist and grinned up at him. Not that he needed a payoff for stopping by Tess's school for the special program, but if there was one, this was it.

"What? How could I forget about today? It's the best invite in town."

The smile Tess had on her face made him feel ten feet tall. She grabbed his hand and brought him into the classroom where she began introducing him to her classmates and teacher. Dante spoke to the kids about reaching for your dreams and never giving up on them. After a Q&A session followed by punch and cookies, Dante headed out of the classroom to a chorus of thank-yous and hugs. The kids had made him feel like an actual VIP with their enthusiasm and interest in his career.

On his way out back down the corridor, he crossed paths with Stella. She was dressed in a pair of dark slacks and a cream silk top. He'd totally forgotten she was a second-grade teacher at this very school. The job fit her personality since she exuded a gentle vibe. It angered him to know she'd been dealt such a bad hand with her fiancé.

"It's official," Stella said. "Tess thinks you hung the moon. It was sweet of you to come today as her special guest. I know the school district can't wait to shout it from the rooftops."

"It was my pleasure. Something tells me Tess usually gets what she wants," he said with a throaty laugh. "I have to admire her pluck."

"You're not wrong about that," Stella said, shaking her head. Her steely-eyed gaze went straight through him, and her mouth was settled in a harsh, thin line. He had the distinct impression she was itching to say something that had nothing to do with today's school program.

"Dante, I have to know." She knit her brows together. "You and Lucy? What's going on there?"

"What exactly are you asking me, Stella?" he asked gruffly. Stella's disapproval bounced off her in waves. It made him feel antsy, as if something bad was about to crash down on him. It was best she got straight to the point for both their sakes. He was about to jump out of his skin.

"I would ask what your intentions are, but then I'd sound like someone from a century ago." She quirked her mouth. "Last time things didn't end so well with the two of you. I don't want to see Lucy hurt again. So, as her big sister, I'm just telling you to be careful with her."

A sigh slipped past his lips. Why did it seem as if everyone in Mistletoe was just waiting for him to mess up again? It stung way more than he wanted to admit, even to himself. "I don't blame you for being wary of me, but I'm not going to hurt her."

"I always liked you, Dante. And I rooted for you and Lucy. But that was before you turned Lucy's world upside down. I know what that feels like and I really don't want to see her get slammed again." Stella folded her arms across her chest. "Not by you. Not by anyone."

"Neither do I," Dante said in a quiet voice. He felt a little bit humbled by Stella's words. The love she felt for Lucy shone like a beacon. She was being protective in the same way Dante would be if he viewed someone as a threat to Troy's peace of mind. He didn't know what else to say to reassure her. How could you prove that you wouldn't hurt someone? It was near impossible to put into words the way he felt about Lucy.

"I've got to get back to class. Thanks again for coming," Stella said, nodding her head before taking off at a fast clip down the hall.

As he walked back outside into the brisk chill of a Maine morning, Dante felt a shiver run across the back of his neck. Something about his conversation with Stella was bothering him. He'd basically promised not to break Lucy's heart. It was a vow he intended to keep, but he was well aware that so many things were outside of his control. He hadn't even discussed anything with Lucy about the future, most likely because he didn't have a single clue as to what to say.

He felt things for Lucy he'd never experienced with any other woman, but was it crazy to try to make this thing between them official? With his hectic lifestyle in California, what could he offer Lucy? Her life was here in Mistletoe and his was on the West Coast. It was a lot more complicated than their feelings for each other.

Knowing he wanted to see her tonight, Dante pulled out his cell phone and messaged her. Hey there, beautiful. We're filming at MHS tonight. Maybe we can grab dinner afterwards? 7 o'clock?

A few minutes later she texted him back. Sounds like a plan. I've been craving spaghetti all day. Followed by a smiley face emoji. Dante grinned at his phone screen. He would meet up with Lucy tonight and they would talk about where things were going with them. Dante had a feeling Lucy's feelings mirrored his own. He was in love with Lucy. If she felt the same way about him, anything was possible. A smile tugged at his lips. Especially at this time of the year.

*  *  *

Lucy studied her reflection in the rearview mirror. "Not bad," she said, giving herself high marks for her makeup application. She'd carefully blended her foundation on her face after using a primer, then used eye shadow and an eyeliner to highlight her eyes. Her lips were a berry red. As a final touch, Lucy had applied mascara and bronzer to accentuate her cheekbones. Her hair fell around her face in soft waves. Most days Lucy was fairly no-frills regarding makeup, but since she was surprising Dante on set before their dinner date, she'd wanted to get a little bit more glammed up than usual. She was wearing a red sweater dress with black leggings. Cute but comfy.

By showing up for the actual filming, she was being

spontaneous, which had always been a bit difficult for her. Lucy liked order in most areas of her life. As a kid, the idea of coloring outside the lines had been shocking. Things like punctuality and following the rules were ingrained in her, although lately she'd been tempted to disrupt her orderly life and shake it up a bit. Lucy knew it had everything to do with Dante. He brought out this side of her.

Little by little, fun Lucy was coming out of the shadows. Dante had invited her to dinner and he'd let her know he was working this evening. He hadn't invited her to stop by the set, but it would serve as a sweet surprise. It was fitting that Dante was filming at Mistletoe High School. Much of their love story had played out within these walls. She didn't have to work too hard to figure out where all the action was taking place. Loud noises led her straight to the school gymnasium where cast and crew members were milling about. Lucy scanned the area for Dante, but she didn't see him anywhere in the crowd.

After a few minutes of searching, Lucy figured her best bet was to ask one of the crew members. Luckily, she spotted one of the cameramen she'd met during the library shoot.

"Hey, Sam. Remember me? We met over at the library," she said.

"Of course I do. Lucy, right?" Sam asked, smiling at her. "What can I do for you?"

"I was looking for Dante, but I can't seem to find him."

Sam looked around then turned back to her. "We're on a short break, so he might have gone outside for a little air. I would go down the corridor and look out in the courtyard."

"Thanks, Sam," Lucy said. She knew exactly the area Sam mentioned. The courtyard had been Lucy and Dante's lunch spot when they were upperclassmen. Lucy smiled remembering all the snowball fights that had broken out during lunch period with their friend group. Dante had always been at the forefront of the mischief with his impish grin and devil-may-care attitude. They'd shared some wonderful times over the years. She was looking forward to more in their future.

After rounding the corner, she headed toward the courtyard. Lucy peered through the window. When she caught a glimpse of Dante, her body tensed. He was standing in the courtyard locking lips with Missy. Lucy would recognize her anywhere with her long hair extensions and va-va-voom figure. Through a haze, Lucy saw Dante's arms around Missy. A hiss escaped her lips as she quickly retreated back down the corridor and away from the sight of them. Almost on autopilot, she made her way outside, through the lot and to her car. Tears stung her eyes. She rested her head on the steering wheel and slowly counted to ten before she revved the engine and took off. Lucy needed to get as far away as possible even though she knew the image of Dante and Missy would be impossible to forget.

She felt so incredibly stupid and humiliated. How had she allowed Dante to crush her spirit once again? Why would he do this to her?

What had she expected? Dante hadn't made her any

promises. He hadn't jerked her around. This time it had been all about her and the way she'd allowed her heart to rule her head. At twenty-eight years old she should have known better. Hadn't Stella warned her about falling for Dante all over again? Hadn't she seen all the warning signs about Missy? But Lucy had steadfastly ignored them. She'd gotten carried away by all the memories and the way he made her feel.

She let out a sob. Tears streamed down her face and she angrily wiped them away. Maybe she was just one of those people who would love only one person for her entire life. Perhaps Dante was that person.

She still loved him, and she'd foolishly let herself believe that there was a place for her in his life...and in his heart. Perhaps it had been the magic of the holidays. Or the memories that were hovering around them like ghosts of Christmases past. The truth was she'd never gotten over him. She'd loved him all this time. Oh, she'd stuffed it down into a little black hole where no one, including herself, could see it. But it had been there under the surface just waiting to make an appearance again. It had all come roaring back as soon as he'd returned to Mistletoe.

* * *

As soon as Dante felt Missy's lips against his own he went into full-blown shock. It was as if his brain couldn't process what was happening. Within seconds he placed his hands on her shoulders and pushed her away. Her mouth hung open with astonishment. She took a step toward him, but Dante held up his hand to ward her off.

"No!" he said sharply. "Stay where you are. That was way over the line, Missy."

"I was just trying to show you how much I admire you, Dante." Missy looked bewildered, as if she truly didn't understand where she'd gone wrong.

He clenched his teeth. "That's not how to do it. What if the rest of the crew had seen you kissing me? It's inappropriate to say the least."

"I've never had anyone complain about being kissed by me." Missy's inflection was teasing but completely unsuitable considering the circumstances. Was that a smirk on her face?

He frowned at her. "It's not funny, Missy. I'm the director of this film. I set the tone for what happens on set, and I'm not going to allow your antics to ruin my reputation. I have rules about being involved with cast members. Up until now I've given you a pass about being flirtatious with me, but this is too much. I'm not interested in you in a romantic way. Period. Point-blank. This is your last warning to keep things professional. If you try something again, I'll be forced to recast you and reshoot your scenes with another actress."

The moment the words came out of his mouth, Missy burst into tears. Her shoulders heaved with huge sobs. "I-I'm so sorry, Dante. I promise you it'll never happen again." She swiped at her tears with the hem of her shirt.

"It's no excuse, but Scott and I have been going through a rough patch. I had a miscarriage a few months ago and it's really taken its toll on our relationship." She took a deep breath before continuing. "I want to be respected in this industry, so moving forward I have to remember to act like a professional. I'm sorry I put you in such an awkward position."

Dante heard contrition in her voice, but he was a huge believer in actions speaking louder than words. "We'll see," he said in a clipped voice before turning away from Missy and heading back to the set.

On his way, he was stopped by Sam, one of his crew members. "Hey, Dante. Did Lucy find you?"

"Lucy? Was she here?" Dante asked, looking all around the area. "I haven't seen her."

"She headed toward the courtyard not too long ago," Sam said, pointing down the hall. "Maybe you just missed her."

Dante's heart seized. The courtyard? Was it possible she'd seen him with Missy and misunderstood the situation? Although he wanted to believe there was some other explanation for her to have disappeared, he couldn't think of a single one that made sense. Hoping to catch her before she left, he headed out to the parking lot and scoured the area for Lucy's car. After a few minutes he pulled out his cell phone and called her. When she didn't answer, Dante decided to text her. He was desperate to find out why she'd left without speaking to him.

A bad feeling settled over him as the minutes ticked

by with no response from Lucy. Other than a sudden emergency, he couldn't think of any reason why she would have vanished. Unless of course she'd seen him and Missy in the courtyard. And if that was the case, Dante knew it would blow up everything he'd been rebuilding with Lucy.

* * *

Lucy drove through town, gazing at Christmas lights and the festively decorated shops on Main Street. Despite the holiday cheer permeating the downtown area, Lucy felt dispirited. She continued driving as if on autopilot. Once she reached home she took a hot shower, changed into a comfy pair of pj's, then fed Astro. Perhaps sensing her mood, Astro turned his nose up at his dinner and refused to eat. When Stella called to chat, Lucy couldn't even pretend that she was fine. She'd been a sniffling mess.

A half an hour later, footsteps echoed noisily on the hardwood floors. Lucy was sitting in her living room on the sofa, nestled up with Astro.

Stella's voice washed over her.

"Lucy, what's wrong?" Stella asked. "You sounded absolutely wrecked on the phone. Did something happen with Dante?"

Lucy nodded. Although she didn't want to spiral any further, she knew it was best to just tell Stella and get it over with. Her sister wouldn't rest until she told her everything. It would be like ripping off a Band-Aid. It would hurt at first, but then the pain would fade. "You could say that. I saw Dante locking lips with one of the actresses in his film. He didn't see me, but I saw plenty."

Stella gasped. "The same busty brunette he's been pictured with in the tabloids?"

"Yes. One and the same. Busty, big lashes, oozes sex appeal. That's her," she said, choking back a sob. "It's not her fault, but I can't stand her at the moment."

"I hate her too," Stella fumed. "Who does she think she is sweeping into town and kissing your boyfriend?"

If she didn't feel so wounded, Lucy might have laughed out loud. Her sister had always helped Lucy fight her battles. This time was no different. "He's not my boyfriend," Lucy explained. "We never put a label on it, but we were together. And I thought it was something real." Now that she was saying it out loud it sounded ridiculous. Why hadn't she reined herself in? If she had, Lucy wouldn't feel as if someone had run her over with a semitruck.

"What a snake! He was hooking up with you and her at the same time. What is it with some men?" Stella asked. "Such colossal liars!"

"He didn't actually lie to me. He never said we were exclusive. But he told me that he cared for me." That was the thing! He hadn't made Lucy any promises. Even though she was upset with Dante, she knew deep down this wasn't like last time. He'd never told her he loved her. It wasn't his fault that she'd never stopped loving him.

"But he led you to believe you were. He—he made you

fall for him," Stella protested. Her face was getting flushed and she was clearly getting worked up.

"I did fall for him, but that was my own fault." More tears slipped past her eyelids. She wiped them away with the last of her tissues. "I don't think I'll ever allow myself to go down this road again. It hurts too much. I put myself out there and look what happened."

"What can I do?" Stella asked. "Even if it's just listening, I want to be here for you."

"I just need to get over him." She let out a brittle laugh. "I've been in this situation before. I never imagined I'd be licking my wounds all over again. Talk about a glutton for punishment."

Stella leaned in and placed her arm around Lucy. "Well, I'm not going to let you do it alone," Stella said. "We can pig out on ice cream and watch Hallmark movies. I can run out and get some mint chocolate chip and cookies 'n cream."

"That sounds amazing," Lucy said. "You might need to pick up a few boxes of Kleenex too. I don't think I've seen the last of these tears, and I'm fresh out of tissues."

"Done," Stella said. "I'll be back in a flash with more Ben and Jerry's and tissues than you can handle." Stella squeezed her hand and stood up before grabbing her purse and heading out the door.

Lucy settled into the sudden silence. She'd turned off her phone's ringer, not wanting to talk to anyone until she'd calmed down. A quick look at her messages showed several texts from Dante.

Where are you? I heard you dropped by the set.

I thought we had plans.

What about our spaghetti dinner?

About an hour later he'd sent a few sad-faced emojis. She resisted the impulse to send him a turd emoji in response. At this point, that's what he deserved.

*No, Lucy. You're better than that. Keep your head up.*

Instead of doing something petty, Lucy placed her phone down with a bang. Was Dante messing with her? Trying to meet up with her after making out with Missy was pretty low. She had no respect for that type of stuff. She was a big girl, but she still had feelings. Hadn't Dante promised never to hurt her again? That vow had lasted all of two seconds. She buried her face in her hands. She'd knowingly walked right back into the danger zone with her arms wide open.

*What a fool she'd been.*

She'd practically wrapped herself up as a Christmas gift with a big red bow and handed herself over to him. As the image of herself as a present danced before her eyes, she let out a wild cackle of laughter that almost had her questioning her sanity. There was absolutely nothing humorous about heartbreak. Lucy had made it way too easy for a player like Dante. He'd waltzed back into town with a lot of pretty words and endless amounts of charisma.

Now all she could hope for was to make it through Christmas without falling apart. She would put on a cheery smile and do her best to spread love and light throughout town, even if it killed her.

Déjà vu gripped her. She'd walked this path before and it felt worse this time. She should have known better than to think a librarian and a movie star would walk off into the sunset together.

When Dante left Mistletoe her heart would ache just as unbearably as it had eight and a half years ago. But this time around, Lucy had no one to blame but herself.

\* \* \*

Dante patted his stomach as he stared at the food laid out on the craft services table. He really needed to insist on having healthier food options for the cast and crew. Eating chocolate doughnuts, cookies, and sandwiches always felt good in the moment, but he'd put on a few pounds since filming began. After filming on this movie wrapped he would start running or working out on an elliptical machine to get himself in shape for his next film.

It didn't matter at the moment. It wasn't as if he could eat a bite since his stomach was tied up in knots. He still hadn't heard from Lucy, and his imagination was beginning to run wild. While a part of him feared that she had seen him with Missy, Dante had to stay positive and grounded about the situation. He was still in director mode. The entire production was counting on him to act in a competent manner. Even so, he'd had to stop himself from getting in his rental car and heading over to Lucy's house.

Making matters worse, he was still reeling from the kiss Missy had laid on him in the courtyard. Dante was furious at her complete lack of judgment. He really hoped she would get her act together, both professionally and in her private life.

It wasn't easy for Dante to confront people, but Missy hadn't given him a choice. It was something he'd had to deal with head-on rather than allowing it to go unchecked. Other than a few regretful looks in his direction, Missy kept her distance for the rest of the shoot. Dante felt fairly optimistic that she'd learned her lesson. He only had a couple more scenes to shoot here in town. Unless he ended up reshooting scenes, he would have a few days of leisure leading up to Christmas, which thrilled him. Between spending time with Lucy, Nick, Miles, and his own family, Dante planned to make the most of the holidays.

*If* Lucy was still speaking to him.

"Dante. You have a very important visitor." When he looked up, Sam was standing a few feet away with Tess at his side. "Nice to meet you, Tess," Sam said with a wide grin before walking away.

"Hey, Tess." Dante looked at his watch. It was almost seven. This time of year in Maine the sky turned dark at four o'clock. "What are you doing here? Isn't it awfully late for you to be out by yourself?"

Tess came rushing toward him at lightning speed and kicked him. Pain seared through his shin, and he howled in agony. Tess stood in front of him with her hands on her hips.

He reached for his shin and began massaging the area. "Ouch. What did you do that for?"

Tess was glaring at him as if he'd just canceled Christmas. She was huffing and puffing like a fire-breathing dragon. "You hurt Lucy!"

He kept rubbing his shin. "What are you talking about?"

"You made her cry. And she doesn't believe in love anymore. All because of you!"

Tess might as well have been speaking a foreign language. She wasn't making any sense. "She what? I have no idea what you're talking about."

Tears were streaming down Tess's face, and although he wanted to hug her, he didn't want to be kicked in his nether regions. He wouldn't put it past her. Pure fire was emanating from her eyes. "You made her think she was special! And now she saw you with that lady in your movie. And you're so stupid if you can't see that Lucy is the best you'll ever have." Tess began to sputter. "She's better than the best, matter of fact. She's one in a million."

His suspicions had been correct. Lucy had seen him with Missy and jumped to the worst conclusion.

He held his hands up. "Tess, you're preaching to the choir. I already know how amazing Lucy is. She's the reason why I came back to Mistletoe."

"Then why did you kiss someone else?" she asked. "That's exactly what Lucy said."

Dante clenched his teeth. Why hadn't Lucy stuck around and confronted him about it? If she'd stayed, Lucy would have seen him telling Missy off. It would have been very clear to her what was going on. But instead she'd taken off without a word and ignored his messages and their plans to meet up for dinner.

"I-I didn't kiss her, Tess. But that's not something I want to discuss with a ten-year-old. No offense, but this is grown folks' business."

"None taken," Tess said. "But I'm actually more mature than most kids my age. It probably comes from having two older sisters."

*Tell me something I don't know*, Dante thought. Tess was a thirty-year-old masquerading in a ten-year-old's body.

"Tess, let me give you a ride home. I'm sure your parents are looking for you."

"Okay. You can pop in next door and see Lucy while you're at it. Maybe get down on your knees and beg for her forgiveness." Tess's eyes glimmered with a hint of excitement. All this drama must be like catnip for her.

Dante held in a groan. He certainly wasn't taking advice from a little kid. And he wasn't begging either. The idea rankled him. He hadn't done anything wrong. Why was he being painted as the bad guy? Just because he'd made mistakes in the past didn't mean he was doomed to repeat himself. Perhaps Lucy would always view him as a screwup.

"Why don't you call home and let them know I'll be dropping you off?"

Tess shrugged. "I don't own a cell phone. My parents aren't getting me one until I turn twelve," she said matter-of-factly.

"That's probably a good idea," Dante muttered. He figured Tess could do a lot of damage with access to a cell phone. It made him shudder to even think about it.

"I'm sorry for kicking you, but I thought it was a good metaphor for you kicking Lucy's heart around," Tess said. Dante didn't even bother responding. Perhaps it was karma for how he'd acted in the past with Lucy. If that was the case, he might have a few more kicks to the shin in his future.

After dropping off Tess at home and making sure she made it safely inside, Dante slowly drove past Lucy's house. There were two vehicles in the driveway. He knew one belonged to Lucy. The house was lit up and the interior emitted a cozy glow. The Christmas tree they'd picked out at Sawyer's peered out majestically from the living room window. With snow blanketing the roof and the lawn, it resembled a picture-perfect postcard of a New England Christmas.

Dante didn't want to go inside and talk to Lucy. He didn't want to apologize for something he hadn't even done. Now, more than ever, he realized that the past was always going to hang over him and Lucy like a dark cloud. Clearly, she didn't trust him. She hadn't stuck around earlier to ask him any questions or to clarify what was going on between him and Missy. If she had, he could have easily explained the situation. He'd worked so hard to learn from the things he'd done wrong in the past. He'd genuinely loved Lucy, and it had been agonizing to lose her because of his own foolishness. But he'd become a better person over the years, and he wasn't one to lie or manipulate. Did she even know him at all?

Staring at Lucy's warm, inviting home made him yearn for things he might never have. The truth was, he wasn't sticking around Mistletoe once the holidays were over. Especially not now that he and Lucy were at odds again. Although these past few weeks in his hometown had been wonderful and productive, his life was far away from Maine.

Reuniting with Lucy was something he would always cherish, but it bothered him to think he'd somehow caused her pain all over again. That had been the last thing he'd ever wanted to do, and yet somehow, history was repeating itself. It didn't matter that he hadn't done anything wrong. The result was still the same.

He was losing Lucy all over again. And it hurt just as much the second time around.

# CHAPTER TWENTY

The last forty-eight hours had been rough on Dante. While he yearned to explain things to Lucy, another part of him felt resigned to the situation. Perhaps they were destined to be at odds.

Troy, Noelle, Jimmy, and his mother were visiting Dante on set at Sawyer's tree farm where he was filming today. The special visit gave his mood a perfect boost. Jimmy was all raw enthusiasm and infectious energy. He got a kick out of sitting in Dante's director's chair and being an extra in one of the scenes. The kid talked a mile a minute and always had a fresh supply of jokes. Troy and Noelle were joined at the hip, holding hands and whispering to each other. Although he was happy for the couple, his own feelings about him and Lucy left him raw. His mother kept bursting into tears and was dabbing at her eyes with a tissue.

"Your father would have been so proud at this huge step

you're taking," she said between sniffles. If she'd said that to him a few months ago, Dante wouldn't have believed it. But now, armed with the knowledge that Troy, Nick, and Lucy had given him, it filled Dante with an additional layer of contentment.

Try as he might to stay in the moment, Dante's thoughts kept drifting back to Lucy. Dante wished he'd knocked on her door the other night and talked things through with her. Another part of him wanted to bury his head in the sand and pretend things hadn't unraveled again. His goal in returning to his hometown had been to make things better with the people he'd hurt in the past. Now, with less than a week standing between him and heading back to California, there was a gaping hole in his plan to fix things.

Maybe some things would always stay broken.

He went on a coffee run with Troy so he could bring back specialty drinks and pastries, unique items that weren't provided by craft services, for the cast and crew. It was a small thank-you for all their hard work and dedication over the past few weeks. He was cautiously optimistic about the film. No matter how it was received by the public, Dante knew he'd put blood, sweat, and tears into the project, along with a huge chunk of his heart.

On the ride over, Dante told Troy about the situation with Lucy. While he vented, his brother sat and listened. He didn't judge nor did he offer a simple solution to his problems. It felt good to talk to someone who knew him inside and out. Troy encouraged him to act on his feelings for Lucy and to try to fix things between them.

Once they reached the Coffee Bean, Troy pulled him aside before they entered the café.

"Hey, man. I need to talk to you about something," his brother said. He looked a bit shaky. "I don't want to be insensitive considering what's going on with you and Lucy."

Troy had his full attention. "Go for it. You can tell me anything. Is everything all right? You look a little rattled." Dante hoped it didn't have anything to do with their mother. Ever since they'd lost their father, he'd worried about losing her as well. He couldn't imagine their family without her being the glue to hold them all together.

Troy's eyes went wide. "Yeah, I'm good. Better than good actually." He reached into his pocket and pulled out a velvet box. When he popped it open, a sparkling engagement ring winked back at him.

Troy wiped a hand across his forehead. "I'm proposing to Noelle. And I'm petrified in case you didn't already guess. Any suggestions?" Troy's hands were trembling as he showed off the dazzling ring.

Dante let out a low whistle. "Wow. That's some kind of bling you've got there. She's going to love it. You did a great job picking it out."

"Thanks. I know the proposal is an important step, but I just want to fast-forward to the moment I can make her my wife. If she says yes, that is."

Dante gripped his brother's shoulder. "You don't have a single thing to worry about, bro. The two of you are perfect together. Just make sure to mention Jimmy in the proposal.

Let her know you're not just proposing to her. You know they're a package deal."

Troy grinned. "That's a great idea, Dante. I'm sorry if my timing is off. I don't want to pour salt in any wounds."

"Don't ever apologize for happy news," Dante reassured him. "It actually gives me hope."

Troy exhaled a deep breath. "Thanks. That makes me feel better. Should I wait for Christmas Eve to make it more special?" Troy seemed to be waiting with bated breath for his answer.

Dante chuckled at his brother's nervousness. He'd never seen him like this, and it was proof that he was head over heels in love with his lady. "Only if you can wait that long. I think it's going to be memorable for Noelle whenever you pop the question. Trust your instincts."

"I will," he said with a nod. "Thanks. Your opinion means a lot."

Dante was happy at least one of them had found their other half. Troy deserved every ounce of happiness he'd earned for himself. Dante leaned in for a hug. It was nice to be in a good place with his brother so he could celebrate with him.

Just as they were about to walk into the café, Lucy walked out. Coming face-to-face with her made Dante feel as if his heart was going to jump out of his chest.

Lucy appeared shell-shocked at the sight of him too.

"Hey, Lucy," Dante said, hoping to ease the tension floating in the air.

"Hi, Dante. Troy," Lucy said with a nod.

Troy looked back and forth between them. "Why don't I go check in on the order? Merry Christmas, Lucy."

"Merry Christmas, Troy," Lucy said as Troy dashed into the coffeehouse as if his feet were on fire.

Once it was just the two of them, the awkwardness intensified. All Dante wanted to do was sweep his palm across her cheek and press a kiss against her temple. He had to stop himself from taking her in his arms and holding her next to his heart.

"You haven't responded to any of my messages." Dante kept his voice even, tamping down his frustration in the hopes of bridging the gap between them.

"I've been busy," Lucy said, her tone frosty. "This time of year is pretty hectic."

Dante steepled his hands in front of him. "Tess came to see me. She told me you're upset with me."

She sighed. "I shouldn't be surprised. Tess has big ears and an even bigger mouth," Lucy muttered. "I'm sorry. It's not her place to do that."

Dante took a step closer. "Lucy, it wasn't what you thought. Not even close. There's nothing between Missy and me other than a working relationship."

As Lucy shook her head, waves of dark hair fell around her shoulders. "I know what I saw, Dante." Her expression was stern while her features were slightly pinched.

"What you saw wasn't anything incriminating."

Lucy scoffed. "You didn't make me any promises, Dante, but it wasn't fair to make me think—" Lucy stopped short and bowed her head.

"Make you think what?" he asked softly. "Talk to me, Luce."

She raised her head and shrugged. "It doesn't matter anymore."

He ran a hand over his face and let out a frustrated sound. "You don't trust me, Lucy. That's what this is all about. And at this point, no matter what I do, I'm not sure that you ever will."

\* \* \*

For the last two days Lucy hadn't been able to focus on anything other than Dante's final words to her before they'd parted ways at the Coffee Bean. *You don't trust me, Lucy.* It played like a continuous loop in her head. She'd heard the resignation in Dante's voice. It mirrored her own feelings. How did a person bury the past so they could forge something new? She didn't know how to let go of all the things she'd been holding on to and believe in a future with Dante. Or even a present. At the root were her own insecurities and fears that the past would repeat itself. Maybe she simply didn't feel that a small-town librarian was enough for a famous movie star. Perhaps she wasn't being fair to him. She'd been wearing a coat of armor for almost nine years now, and it felt strange to relinquish it. Because if she did, bad things might happen.

"*Deck the halls with boughs of holly. Fa la la la la, la la la la.*" Lucy belted out her favorite holiday song in the hopes of lifting her mood and willing the Christmas spirit to come over her. She was sitting at the circulation desk at the library, counting down the hours until she could lock up the place and officially declare she was on Christmas vacation.

It was no surprise that the library was empty. The townsfolk of Mistletoe were no doubt doing their last-minute shopping, wrapping gifts, and making fruitcake and figgy pudding. Lucy snorted at the thought of figgy pudding. It was just as terrible as it sounded. Her great-aunt Myrtle used to make it for Thanksgiving and Christmas. She and Stella had gotten creative about making it disappear from their plates.

The library would be closed for five straight days, during which Lucy would be cooking, wrapping presents, lounging in her favorite reindeer pajamas, reading, and preparing to celebrate Christmas with the Marshall clan. The sound of the door opening followed by the clickety-clack of heels on the gleaming hardwood floors immediately drew Lucy's attention.

Who on earth would be wearing heels in December in Maine? Maybe it was Stella playing a prank on her to make Lucy laugh. Just then, she got her answer when Missy came into view wearing a ridiculously hot-pink coat with matching leggings. Her feet were encased in a pair of black stilettos that were completely incompatible with the wintry weather. Lucy knew her mouth was hanging open, and she had to force herself to close it.

"Hi, Lucy. I just wanted to return this book. It was a fascinating read." Missy slid the book across the counter, her long pink nails looking freshly manicured. Lucy picked up the thick book and read the title. Shakespeare's *Complete Sonnets and Poems*. Lucy had learned a long time ago not to be surprised by a patron's reading material. Although Missy was a bit froufrou, she clearly loved books with substance. This particular book was one of Lucy's own favorites.

Lucy forced herself to smile at Missy. It was hard not to think of the kiss she'd witnessed, but she had no right to take it out on her. "Thank you, Missy. I'm glad you were able to use the visitor's card. It comes in handy for out-of-towners."

"Me too. Now I can go home and recite sonnets to my husband," Missy said in a chirpy tone.

Lucy sputtered. Had she misheard her? "Husband?" she asked. "You're married?"

A sheepish expression appeared on Missy's face. "Yes, I'm married. Through some small miracle I've been able to keep it from the press." She wrinkled her nose. "We've been through some ups and downs, including a separation, but we're going to spend Christmas at this isolated cabin in Montana so we can hash out our problems. I'm really hopeful."

"What about Dante?" Lucy blurted out the question before she could rein herself in.

Missy knitted her brows together. "What about him?"

Protectiveness swept over her. Lucy cared about Dante, and she didn't want someone to jerk him around. It was a strange feeling to still want the best for him when her own heart wasn't whole. "Aren't the two of you together?" she asked.

Missy let out a hoot of laughter. "You've been reading too many gossip rags. We're friends. I'll be honest with you, Lucy. I tried to push for more on a few occasions, but he wasn't having it. He's a good guy. He set me straight in no uncertain terms."

*Friends.* Just like Dante had told her. A dizzying sensation caused her knees to wobble. After all her accusations against Dante, he'd been nothing more than friends with Missy. She'd misconstrued what she'd seen in the court-yard, and as a result, ruined things with Dante. Why hadn't she trusted him? He'd told her time and again how much he'd worked on being a better man over the years. And she'd seen the evidence of it in his words and deeds. Still, it hadn't been enough for her.

"Lucy, are you all right?" Missy asked, concern in her voice.

"I-I'm fine. Just a little hangry," she lied, knowing it was the furthest thing from the truth. She wasn't fine at all. She'd made the most foolish mistake of her life, and there was no coming back from it. Dante was out of her life because of her own actions. He was due to leave Mistletoe right after Christmas and there wouldn't be a third chance for them. She knew it deep down in her gut.

"Okay. That's good. I need to head out to the airport so I can meet up with my hubby. Montana, here I come!" Missy raised her arm in the air in a celebratory gesture.

"Bye, Missy. Have a safe trip home." She really did

wish Missy well. Everyone deserved a second chance to make things right with the person they loved. She wished she hadn't failed so miserably at her own. If she had only trusted Dante.

Missy turned back toward her and winked. "Good luck with Dante. As far as I'm concerned, he's a keeper." With a wave of her hand she clickety-clacked away from Lucy and sailed through the doors of the library. As soon as Missy was out of sight, Lucy sank down into a chair and let out a ragged sigh. Her limbs were trembling and her mouth felt as dry as a desert. Missy's unexpected visit to the library had been revealing and heartbreaking. Lucy still felt shaken by her own stupidity.

Even though she was trying her best to get in the holiday spirit, she couldn't ignore that this was shaping up to be the worst Christmas ever.

\* \* \*

Dante wasn't quite sure what to do with himself. He'd finished principal filming in Mistletoe and all the cast and crew were now scattered around the globe for the holidays. In a few weeks he would shoot additional scenes in Los Angeles, then focus on postproduction. He was looking forward to seeing the final product and making any adjustments before *Without You* was completed. He'd finally hit upon a title that spoke to him. Considering everything that had gone down between him and Lucy, it seemed fitting.

Lucy appeared to be avoiding him just as much as he'd

been dodging her. Their last face-to-face encounter had left them at an impasse. All he knew was that she'd hurt him in ways he hadn't imagined possible. He'd worked so hard to become a better person over the years, only to be second-guessed by Lucy. It had been crystal clear to him that she would never be able to have complete faith in him.

Nick had invited him over to eat dinner with him and Miles this evening. He was excited to finally spend some quality time with his godson and one of his closest friends. It would help lift the heavy weight off his chest. As he drove into Nick's circular driveway, Dante couldn't help but chuckle at the epic Christmas decorations in their front yard. A neon-green six-foot Grinch sat next to an inflatable Rudolph with a blinking red nose. A big-bellied Santa Claus was standing next to Mrs. Claus and a gaggle of elves. Flashing lights lit up their roof. It was the type of over-the-top decorations people drove past in their cars to see for themselves.

When Dante rang the bell, the chorus to "Blue Christmas" rang out, proving that Nick and Miles were totally rocking the holiday theme. They'd really gone all out this year.

As soon as he opened the door, Nick started in on him. His friend rubbed his eyes as if he couldn't believe what he was seeing. "What's going on? You look terrible, man," Nick said as he gave Dante the once-over. "I hate to tell you this, but most people wouldn't even recognize you as a world-famous movie star. You look like you haven't shaved in days. Or slept."

"Thanks, Nick. Nice to see you too," Dante drawled as he stepped over the threshold.

"Any time. Is that five-o'clock shadow for a movie role or something?" Nick asked, peering closely at his face and running his finger along his jawline.

"No, it's not. I'm just trying something new," he answered, swatting his hand away. He didn't want to admit he was just going through the motions these days. He'd been in a funk for days. He needed an infusion of holiday cheer.

Miles came running toward him at lightning speed, catapulting himself against Dante's chest. "Dante!" Miles cried out. "You're here. I kept asking Dad when you could come over."

"Well, I'm here, buddy," Dante said, wrapping the boy up in a tight bear hug. He lifted him off the ground, causing Miles to let out a squeal of excitement.

Once Miles was back on the ground, he tugged on Dante's hand. "Come see my Star Wars Lego world I built. It's the one you sent me last month."

"Cool. I can't wait to see it all set up," Dante said, buoyed by the boy's enthusiasm. "I had the feeling you'd like it."

"Like it," Nick said with a snort. "He's talked of nothing else for weeks."

Miles grinned, showcasing a gap-toothed smile as well as a resemblance to his mother. It was uncanny how much his godson resembled Kara. Despite the tragedy of his wife's death, Dante imagined that it was gratifying to Nick to have a miniature version of her in his house.

"Dinner will be ready soon, so when I call you, Miles, you need to wash up then head into the kitchen. Deal?" Nick asked his son.

"Deal," Miles said. "C'mon, Dante. Let's go."

Dante allowed himself to be pulled down the hall toward the playroom before he even had a chance to take off his coat. Miles happily showed him the ropes of playing Star Wars Legos. Dante figured he must be a big kid at heart since playing with his godson was the most fun he'd had in weeks. When Nick called them, Miles let out a groan before begrudgingly getting up and heading toward the kitchen. Dante trailed after him, washing his own hands in the sink right after Miles finished.

A full meal was laid out on the kitchen table. Roasted chicken. Potatoes. Baked bread. Salad. Nick had gone all out in fixing him a home-cooked meal. A warm feeling settled in his chest at being treated to such a spread.

"Take a seat, guys," Nick said. "Sit wherever you like."

"I'm impressed, Nick. You set a fine table," Dante said. "I didn't know you could cook."

"Daddy is a really great cook. So was my mom," Miles said, smiling as he placed a piece of chicken on his plate.

Dante saw Nick flinch at the mention of Kara. He was a man still dealing with his massive grief. Even though it was healthy for Miles to talk about his mother, Nick didn't seem as if he could handle it. Christmas must be an especially hard time for them, with a void in their lives the size of an ocean. He understood it. Even though it wasn't the same, there was a hole in his family's heart where his father used to be. Dante felt it every time he walked inside the family home.

"Your mom was awesome," Dante said. "The most popular girl in high school."

"Whoa," Miles said, turning to look at his dad for confirmation.

"She was," Nick said with a nod. "And the prettiest."

"Well, I figured that," Miles said, making a goofy face that made them both laugh.

Being with Miles and Nick was lightening his mood. Miles was a precocious kid who had an opinion on everything under the sun. They enjoyed a wonderful dinner with lots of commentary from Miles.

"If you're done eating, why don't you put your pajamas on? Then maybe we can play a few rounds of Scrabble," Nick suggested when his son's plate was empty.

Miles jumped up from his seat and raced down the hall. "I'll be back in a flash," he called. "Don't start dessert without me."

Nick and Dante chuckled. Miles had mentioned several times during dinner that he was saving space in his stomach for chocolate cake. It was one of the things he had a favorable opinion about.

When they heard Miles's door shut, Nick pulled out two bottles of beer from the fridge and slid one over to Dante. "I didn't want to ask in front of Miles, but what's going on with you and Lucy? No offense, but you seem a bit off-kilter."

Dante scoffed. "There is no Lucy and me. It crashed and burned, just like last time."

"I'm surprised to hear that," Nick said. "I thought this was your second chance to walk off into the sunset together."

Dante took a sip of his beer. "There you go again with your romantic happy endings. Sadly, my friend, life isn't like the movies." He leaned across the table. "Let me give you an example. In real life, a person gets accused of making out with his costar when in reality she was laying a kiss on him. A person did the right thing and handled it the best way he could, but it wasn't enough because he's deemed as not being trustworthy. You see, he's still being judged for what happened in the past. It's pretty hard to walk off into the sunset when you're completely at odds with the other person."

Nick gaped at him. "Sounds like a lot went down between the two of you."

"Yeah. You could say that. Merry Christmas. Bah humbug."

Nick held up his hands. "Okay, before you get all Grinchy, maybe the two of you can work through it. It's a misunderstanding. Just lay it all out for her."

He raised an eyebrow at Nick. "Not trusting someone is way bigger than a misunderstanding."

"That's true," he conceded. "All I'm saying is that I would give anything to have another chance with Kara. If you have a shot at fixing things, what are you doing moping around instead of getting your girl?"

Ouch. Nick wasn't playing fair by bringing up his wife. Nick and Kara had been one of those idyllic couples. He would bet they'd never even had a single fight.

"She doesn't want me. End of story. Period," he snapped.

Nick leaned in his direction. "So, answer me this. Do you love her?"

Dante hesitated for a moment before answering. If he responded to Nick truthfully, something would shift monumentally in his universe. The very idea of it was terrifying. Earth-shattering. But he was done running from it. It was the realest thing he'd ever known, and he needed to express it. "Yes, I love her. Truth is, I always have." Just putting it into words made him feel stronger and more centered.

A smile slowly came to life on Nick's face. "Have you told her?"

"No," Dante said in a low voice. "I didn't really have a chance before all hell broke loose."

"Then why are you sitting here with me instead of telling her how you feel?"

"I'm scared, man. What if she laughs in my face or just pushes me away?"

"Dante, this is Lucy we're talking about. She's not going to do either of those things if you look her straight in the eye and speak from your heart."

"She might," Dante said.

"If you think about it, Lucy has every reason to be cautious. I know you've been beaten up about it a million times, but you broke her spirit. You wounded her. I can't imagine trusting someone after that, but she tried her best from the sounds of it. Part of loving someone is lifting them up when they can't do it themselves. Try thinking of it that way, Dante. You have to show her what's possible for the two of you."

Lucy. Sweet, trusting Lucy. She was kind and loving, and despite everything he'd done to wound her, she'd forgiven him for the past. It was his turn to show her that he believed in them. He hadn't done a single thing in the past to fight for them. He'd let everything slip through his fingers. Nick was right. What kind of man would he be if he didn't reach for the brass ring with Lucy?

Everything he'd truly ever wanted was in Mistletoe. Home. Hearth. Family. Lucy.

Most of all, Lucy. He was going to step out of his comfort zone and lay it all on the line for Lucy. This time around, Dante was going to fight for his happily ever after.

# CHAPTER TWENTY-ONE

It was Christmas Eve, which had always been Lucy's favorite part of the holiday. Christmas morning was wonderful too, but the night before was always filled with so much anticipation. Every year Lucy's parents invited a few people over for a special celebration. It was a festive evening she looked forward to each holiday season. Despite feeling as if she might shatter into little pieces, Lucy was determined to put on a cheery face. She'd made plenty of treats—deviled eggs, garlic shrimp, and chocolate mint brownies, as well as her special peppermint eggnog. Lucy had a million Christmas songs on her playlist, so she planned to attach her phone to a speaker and let the good times roll.

"You look merry." Stella came up beside her and placed her arm around her waist.

"Do you like it?" she asked, twirling around to show off her emerald-green dress with the red-sequined belt. Getting decked out in her holiday finery had cheered Lucy up a bit. Just because her love life had come crashing down around her didn't mean she couldn't still get blinged out.

Stella gave her the once-over. "It's nice. Very glittery. Glinda the Good Witch has nothing on you."

"I'll take that as the highest of compliments. She's pretty epic."

"You're doing great, Lucy. I'm proud of you."

Lucy winked at her. "Right back atcha. Look at us. Founders of the Broken Hearts at Christmas Club."

"Nope," Stella said, vehemently shaking her head. "That's a club I don't want to belong to, never mind being one of its founders. We're survivors. This too shall pass, right?"

"Absolutely," Lucy agreed, even though she had serious doubts. What made her think she would ever get over Dante when she'd been in love with him for as long as she could remember? Perhaps she would walk through life with this dull ache as her constant companion.

She was going to be fine, she told herself. Better than fine. It was almost Christmas. She wouldn't feel this way forever. She might never fall out of love with Dante, but she knew that she could live without him. She'd done it once before. Now if she could only find a way to ease the pressure in her heart. It was a physical ache that just wouldn't let up. Maybe if she lived to be a hundred, the pain would go away.

Lucy focused on setting up the buffet table with food and drinks. She put on a festive apron to shield her outfit from getting any stains. If she just concentrated on the holidays, then maybe she could get Dante out of her mind. She inhaled the aroma of her mother's famous Swedish meatballs. After taking a quick look around her to make sure no one was watching, Lucy picked up a toothpick and jabbed at one of the meatballs. She quickly stuffed it in her mouth, letting out a groan of pleasure as it hit her taste buds. Perhaps this is what she needed to get herself over the hump—a steady diet of Swedish meatballs and peppermint eggnog.

"Lucy, you need to come outside right now. It's an emergency." Tess was tugging on her sleeve with urgency. Her eyes threatened to pop out of her head. Lucy bit back an exasperated sigh. In Tess's eyes, an emergency constituted running out of chocolate cupcakes with buttercream frosting or a cute dog being walked in the neighborhood.

"Sweetie, I'm a little busy at the moment," Lucy said as she placed her shrimp tray on the table and set out utensils.

"Please. It's really, really important," Tess pleaded. "It's an actual E-M-E-R-G-E-N-C-Y," she said, spelling out the word.

"On a scale of one to ten, with a ten being a raging fire at my house, what is this?" Lucy asked.

Tess bit her lip, appearing uncertain. She seemed to be really focusing on Lucy's question. "A ten! No, wait. A nine. It's a definite nine."

"I wouldn't be coming outside for anything less than a nine," Lucy told Tess.

Lucy didn't bother taking off her Santa's Little Helper

apron even though it made her think of Dante. There was a cute brown Santa emblazoned on it with an equally adorable female elf sitting on his lap. She didn't even know why she'd worn it. She was a total glutton for punishment. Honestly, she didn't need the apron for reminders of Dante. He was everywhere. In her heart and mind. There wasn't a place in town that didn't bring back recollections of him and what they'd once been to each other.

After grabbing her red parka, Lucy followed Tess outside to the front lawn. Lucy walked down the steps and came to a crashing halt when she spotted Dante standing a few feet away. She almost wanted to rub her eyes to make sure she wasn't seeing things. Was Dante really here? What was Tess playing at?

Dante was positioned under her family's tree, dressed in a black tuxedo. Her heart lurched wildly at the sight of him. Have mercy! Dante had no right to look this smoking hot, like a Black James Bond. Debonair. Classy. Move over, Idris Elba.

"Dante, what are you doing here?" she asked, unable to hide the shock in her voice.

What in the world was going on? He looked pretty swanky for Christmas Eve in Mistletoe. Was he trying to torture her by looking so delicious? Surely this couldn't be the emergency she'd been called outside to address. She looked around her, but Tess was nowhere to be found. She'd begged Lucy to come outside and now she'd disappeared in a puff of smoke.

"And why are you dressed up like you're going to the

Academy Awards?" She blurted out the question. He must be freezing with no coat or winter gear on.

He let loose with a chuckle. "I wanted to look nice...for you. As far as grand gestures go, this is mine. I'm here, Lucy, because I don't want to go another day without you." Suddenly, he looked a bit nervous, and he began shifting from one foot to the other and fiddling with the collar of his crisp white shirt.

His statement was so shocking and unexpected, it rendered Lucy speechless. She almost wanted to ask him to repeat it, if only so she could hear him utter the sweet words all over again.

"We lost so many years because of my stupidity," he continued. "I don't want to waste any more time. I don't want to lose us ever again. I've never felt for any other woman what I feel for you. I love you, Lucy Marshall. And if you feel even a small portion of what I feel, I'm going to fight to hold on to this. I know it might be hard to trust me, but I'm all in. I'm not that same guy who was too proud to admit he'd messed up. I've grown and matured a lot. I learned the hard way that pride isn't worth losing the love of your life. Or your family. I'm a better man these days, and I hope you've seen it with your own eyes. I hope you can move past your doubts and embrace love. Because I think you love me too."

The weight of Dante's declaration crashed over her. It was more magical and wonderful than she ever could have imagined. Her throat felt clogged with emotion. She wasn't sure if she could speak.

"Say something, Luce. I need to know how you feel." She could hear the uncertainty in his tone and it endeared him to her in so many ways. How could Dante not have seen the obvious? Of course she loved him. She always had.

Lucy moved toward him so that there was no distance between them. "I-I've always believed in the magic of Christmas, and this is way more than I ever dared to dream. I thought we'd lost each other all over again."

"You'll never lose me. Not if I have anything to say about it. I want to be with you for the long haul. Truthfully, I can't imagine a life without you in it. Being back here in Mistletoe with you makes me realize that this is where I want to be."

"I love you, Dante," Lucy said, her voice quivering. "To be honest, I can't remember a time when I didn't love you. Even when we were kids I adored you. I never imagined we would be able to find our way back to one another. I'm sorry for doubting you and for letting my fears push you away. I should have trusted you." This moment was everything she'd ever wanted. Her heart was overflowing with joy.

Dante swept his hand across her face. "It's okay, baby. I should have set Missy straight earlier instead of ignoring her behavior. I've made so many mistakes. Forgiveness is part of loving."

Lucy blinked back tears. "It is, Dante. And I'm sure we'll make plenty of mistakes in the future, but if we believe in each other and our love we'll never lose our way again."

"We won't. Not ever." He pointed toward the sky. "Look up, Lucy."

Lucy tilted her head upward. Dangling from the snow-covered tree were countless sprigs of mistletoe. She hadn't even noticed them when she'd first come outside. She'd been too busy staring at Dante in his impeccable attire. Lucy gasped. She couldn't remember ever seeing anything so beautiful. When she swung her gaze back to Dante, Lucy saw him through a haze of tears. He'd done all this for her! To make the woman he loved happy.

"It's been years since we kissed under the mistletoe, but I seem to recall you saying it was the most romantic kiss ever," Dante said. "I figured we could re-create it."

"I can't believe you remember that."

"I remember everything. It's all right here," he said, tapping a place near his heart. "I haven't worked out all the logistics, but I plan to relocate to Mistletoe and fly out to the West Coast when needed. I want to make a life with you right here."

"Can you do that without sacrificing your career?" Lucy asked. She was nervous to even ask the question and run the risk of ruining this beautiful moment.

The steely glint in his eyes hinted at his resolve. "Yes, I can. And I will. I don't have to live in Los Angeles to make movies. It might not be easy, but it can't be harder than a life without you, Luce."

He leaned down and placed his lips over hers. Tenderly. Sweetly. She met his kiss eagerly, secure in the knowledge that Dante loved her as much as she loved him. Thousands of miles wouldn't be separating them. Their love story was back on track. This was the best Christmas gift she would ever receive.

Above all else, the kiss was filled with hope. It hung in the air around them, crackling with intensity and ripe with promise. It signified their desire to be together and to put all the ghosts of the past firmly behind them.

As they broke apart, Lucy could swear she heard clapping and music playing. The grin on Dante's face as he looked behind her confirmed it. She turned around to see her entire family standing in the yard—Stella, her parents, and Tess. Nick was standing off to the side with Miles holding up a boom box blaring "Have Yourself a Merry Little Christmas." Nick flashed them a thumb's-up signal. Lucy shook her head, her loose curls swirling around her shoulders.

"You really thought of everything, didn't you?" she asked, looking up at him.

"I had to give it my best shot. Merry Christmas, Lucy," Dante said.

"Merry Christmas," Lucy said, basking in the knowledge that this Christmas was shaping up to be the best one of their lives.

# EPILOGUE

TWO MONTHS LATER

Lucy peered out of the window of the library as snow began to cascade from the sky in huge clumps of fat, gorgeous snowflakes. As a lifelong Mainer, Lucy could tell that this snow was the type to stick around. She bit her lip as a dozen different scenarios played out in her head. Dante's plane might be grounded. The airport could have shut down. He might be rerouted to another destination.

"He's not going to be able to make it through this storm," she said out loud, voicing her fears.

The snow hadn't yet begun to accumulate, but the local forecasters were now predicting that Maine was in line to get a direct hit from the Snowpocalypse. This was the one time in her entire life that Lucy had wished and prayed for no snow. Dante was scheduled to arrive in Mistletoe later this evening, and it wasn't looking promising. The airport in Bangor was rumored to be closing down in a few hours because of the inclement weather.

Tears sprung to her eyes at the thought of Dante's flight being canceled. She missed him so much, and it had been weeks and weeks since they'd seen each other. It was during moments like this that she felt the hardship of dating a big-time Hollywood actor-director. Their relationship was still going strong, and Lucy was more in love with him than ever. But she was tired of missing him and aching to be held in his arms. In the past two months Dante had been back to Mistletoe several times while she'd joined him twice on the West Coast. She'd used vacation time she'd accrued over the years to make those trips possible. Every visit had been eye-opening, showing Lucy so much about the world Dante inhabited. Finally, she felt like she was getting a glimpse of life outside of New England.

There was so much more to look forward to. So many adventures they had yet to experience. Being with Dante was thrilling and nurturing and more than she'd ever dared to dream.

A sudden knocking at the front door pulled her from her thoughts. Who on earth would want to visit the library with a storm looming? Hadn't they seen the CLOSED sign on the door? With a sigh of frustration, Lucy quickly walked toward the entrance, fully prepared to scold the patron on the other side of the door. She knew her current mood was tied up in Dante's absence, as well as the impending snowstorm.

*Just breathe*, she reminded herself as she pulled open the door. And smile. She had no right to take out her disappointment on anyone else. It was her mission to spread smiles, not unpleasantness.

When she saw who had knocked, all the blood in her body rushed to her head. The love of her life was standing right in front of her. "Dante!" she cried out, catapulting herself against his chest and throwing her arms around his neck.

"Lucy, I can't breathe," Dante said in a muffled voice.

"Oh, I'm sorry," she said as she let go and pulled him inside by the hem of his jacket. Once he was through the doorway, he shook the snow off his hair and coat as Lucy looked on with awe. It was such an amazing surprise to have him here by her side. Just when she'd felt as if all was lost, he'd surprised her by showing up.

"How are you standing here? I thought your plane wasn't arriving until tonight. I've been trying to reach you all day."

Dante grinned at her. "I have friends in high places. Chet lent me his private plane and his pilot. When I saw the forecast last night I moved heaven and earth to make this happen." He leaned down and placed a searing kiss on her lips. She breathed in the scent of him—a heady woodsy scent that increased the intensity of their embrace.

"Sorry about not keeping you in the loop. In the rush to get to the airport, I left my phone in the limo. I'll have my assistant FedEx it here tomorrow. I'm just stoked to be here with you, Luce. It looks like this storm is going to be bad."

"It doesn't matter now because you're here," Lucy said,

twirling around in a circle. "Let me lock up the library so we can get out of here. I have a fully stocked kitchen, so I can make a special dinner to celebrate. I bought all of your favorites."

"Wait a second," Dante said. "There's something I need to do first."

Before she could blink, Dante was on bended knee holding a bright red velvet box out in front of him. Lucy gasped and covered her mouth with her hands.

Dante looked up at her with raw emotion in his eyes. His hands were slightly trembling as he popped open the box. Lucy let out a squeal of excitement as the diamond ring winked back at her. It was almost blinding her with its sparkly beauty. She couldn't be sure, but it looked like a vintage setting. It was the perfect ring for her—an emerald-cut diamond in the middle surrounded by a row of smaller diamonds. It was elegant and classic. She would never have wanted something gigantic or flashy. It wouldn't have been in keeping with her job as head librarian.

"Lucy Marshall, I've been in love with you since we were in middle school. I was too scared to tell you until we were sixteen, but I want to say it to you for the rest of our lives. Will you walk through life with me? Will you be my best friend till the end of our days?"

"Yes. Yes. Yes," Lucy shouted as she jumped up and down. Dante managed to reach for her wildly flailing arm, then placed the ring on her finger.

"Please stand up so I can wrap my arms around you," she said, holding back an onslaught of tears. They were welling up in her eyes and she knew it was only a matter of time before the deluge started.

Dante got to his feet just as Lucy threw herself against him and wrapped her arms around his waist. Lucy didn't bother to wipe away the tears coursing down her face. These were rare tears for her. They'd been born out of sheer happiness.

"I can't believe we're getting married."

"Believe it, Lucy." He dipped his head down and pressed a kiss on her forehead. "You've already said yes, so no backtracking now."

"Where are we going to live full-time?" Lucy asked with a frown. "California or Maine?" Lucy wanted to make sure Dante hadn't changed his mind about a life in Mistletoe. Although she knew she would follow Dante to the ends of the earth, she didn't want to leave her beloved hometown. What would she do without her family, friends, and the library she adored? She didn't want Tess to grow up without her. And Stella was her best friend. And she needed to support her mother through her MS. Her goal of increasing funding for the library was a beautiful work in progress. It would be so hard to walk away from her position as head librarian.

"Like I told you on Christmas Eve, I want Mistletoe to be home base. Nothing has changed in that regard. Everything I've ever wanted in this world is right here," Dante said. "But I'm still going to keep my California house so we can spend time there as well, especially if I'm filming. I'm going to be more creative about the locations for my films. Now that *Without You* is a wrap, I'm going to make more films in this area. I don't want to be away from you, Luce."

"That sounds perfect. I don't want to be apart either," she said, going up on tippy-toes to press a kiss against his lips. She wrapped her arms around his neck, drawing him closer. As he moved his mouth over hers, intensifying the kiss, Lucy sighed. "This. A lifetime of this. Yes, please."

"We should get going before we get snowed in," Dante said in a teasing voice.

"I wouldn't mind getting snowed in with you," Lucy said. The thought of being snowbound in her cozy little house with Dante gave her a warm and fuzzy feeling. Just the two of them drinking hot cocoa by the fire and playing with Astro and Tess in the snow. It suddenly dawned on Lucy that she had no idea if Dante wanted kids to be a part of their future. She hoped they were in agreement.

"By the way, I've always wanted at least a few kids," Lucy said. "Not right away, of course. I want you all to myself for a while."

"We're on the same page then," he said, grazing his knuckles against her cheek. "I'm good with however many you want, even if it's a houseful. I love the idea of having little Lucys running around."

"Hmm. Weren't you the one who was nervous being around small children when I asked you to be Santa Claus?"

"Who me?" he asked. "That was ages ago. I'm ready, willing, and able to have babies with you Lucy. You just have to promise me one thing."

"Anything," she said as euphoria swept through her. She had never dreamed that she and Dante would be spending the rest of their lives together. She was engaged to be married to this amazing man. She looked down at her ring finger, basking in the dazzling symbol of their love.

She locked gazes with Dante. The love emanating from his eyes made her feel like the luckiest woman in the world. "Wherever this journey leads us, let's promise to stick it out together," Dante said, joining their hands. "You're the focus of my world. Not Hollywood. Not movie sets. Not anything but you."

"I promise, Dante. I'm with you, come what may," she whispered, pressing her lips against his in a celebratory kiss.

Don't miss the next book in the
Mistletoe, Maine series!

Coming Summer 2022

# ABOUT THE AUTHOR

**Belle Calhoune** grew up in a small town in Massachusetts as one of five children. Although both her parents worked in the medical field, Belle never considered science as the pathway to her future. Growing up across the street from a public library was a huge influence on her life. Married to her college sweetheart, she is raising two lovely daughters in Connecticut. A dog lover, she has one mini poodle named Copper and a black Lab, Beau.

She is a *Publishers Weekly* bestselling author as well as a member of RWA's Honor Roll. In 2019 her book *An Alaskan Christmas* was made into a movie (*Love, Alaska*) by Brain Power Studio and aired on UPtv. She is the author of more than forty novels and published by Harlequin Love Inspired and Grand Central Forever Publishing.

# Can't get enough of that small-town charm? Forever has you covered with these heartwarming contemporary romances!

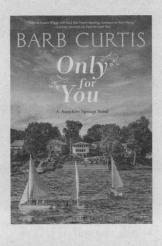

### *ONLY FOR YOU*
### by Barb Curtis

After Emily Holland's friend gets his heart broken on national TV, he proposes a plan to stop town gossip: a fake relationship with *her*. Emily has secretly wanted Tim Fraser for years, but pretending her feelings are only for show never factored into her fantasy. Still, her long-standing crush makes it impossible to say no. But with each date, the lines between pretend and reality blur, giving Tim and Emily a tantalizing taste of life outside the friend zone... Can they find the courage to give *real* love a real chance?

### *THE HOUSE ON SUNSHINE CORNER*
### by Phoebe Mills

Abby Engel has a great life. She's the owner of Sunshine Corner, the daycare she runs with her girlfriends; she has the most adoring grandmother (aka the Baby Whisperer); and she lives in a hidden gem of a town. All that's missing is love. Then her ex returns home to win back the one woman he's never been able to forget. But after breaking her heart years ago, can Carter convince Abby that he's her happily-ever-after?

*Find more great reads on Instagram with @ReadForever*

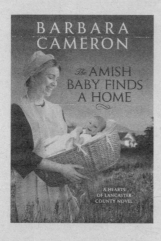

**THE AMISH BABY FINDS A HOME**
by Barbara Cameron

Amish woodworker Gideon Troyer is ready to share his full life with someone special. And his friendship with Hannah Stoltzfus, the lovely owner of a quilt shop, is growing into something deeper. But before Gideon can tell Hannah how he feels, she makes a discovery in his shop: a baby…one sharing an unmistakable Troyer family resemblance. As they care for the sweet abandoned *boppli* and search for his family, will they find they're ready for a *familye* of their own?

**NO ORDINARY CHRISTMAS**
by Belle Calhoune

Mistletoe, Maine, is buzzing, and not just because Christmas is near! Dante West, local cutie turned Hollywood hunk, is returning home to make his next movie. Everyone in town is excited except librarian Lucy Marshall, whose heart was broken when Dante took off for LA. But Dante makes an offer Lucy's struggling library can't refuse: a major donation in exchange for allowing them to film on site. Will this holiday season give their first love a second chance?

**THE INN ON SWEETBRIAR LANE**
**by Jeannie Chin**

June Wu is in over her head. Her family's inn is empty, and the surly stranger next door is driving away her last guests! But when ex-soldier Clay Hawthorne asks for June's help, she can't say no. The town leaders are trying to stop his bar from opening, and June thinks his new venture is just what Blue Cedar Falls needs to bring in more tourists. But can two total opposites really learn to meet each other in the middle? Includes a bonus story by Annie Rains!

**TO ALL THE DOGS I'VE LOVED BEFORE**
**by Lizzie Shane**

The last person librarian Elinor Rodriguez wants to see at her door is her first love, town sheriff Levi Jackson, but her mischievous rescue dog has other ideas. Without fail, Dory slips from the house whenever Elinor's back is turned—and it's up to Levi to bring her back. The quietly intense lawman broke Elinor's heart years ago, and she's determined to move on, no matter how much she misses him. But will this four-legged friend prove that a second chance is in store? Includes a bonus story by Hope Ramsay!

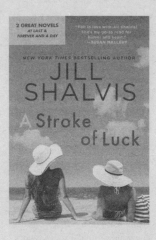

### A STROKE OF LUCK
### (2-IN-1 EDITION)
### by Jill Shalvis

Get swept off your feet with two Lucky Harbor novels! In *At Last*, a weekend hike for Amy Michaels accidentally gets her up close and personal with forest ranger Matt Bowers. Will Matt be able to convince Amy that they can build a future together? In *Forever and a Day*, single dad and ER doctor Josh Scott has no time for anything outside of his clinic and son—until the beautiful Grace Brooks arrives in town and becomes his new nanny. And in a town like Lucky Harbor, a lifetime of love can start with just one kiss.

### DREAM KEEPER
### by Kristen Ashley

Single mom Pepper Hannigan has sworn off romance because she refuses to put the heart of her daughter, Juno, at risk. Only Juno thinks her mom and August Hero are meant to be. Despite his name, the serious, stern commando is anything *but* a knight in shining armor. However, he can't deny how much he wants to take care of Pepper and her little girl. And when Juno's matchmaking brings danger close to home, August will need to save both Pepper and Juno to prove that happy endings aren't just for fairy tales.